THE PLACE SEBASTIAN BROUGHT ANGIE TO WAS NOT WHAT SHE'D BEEN EXPECTING.

Angie knew there were safe houses for demon hunters all over the world, places they could stay when working or between hunts. Places to heal if they got injured in a fight. Places to sleep safely after they'd exerted too much will banishing a demon.

But for some reason, Angie assumed these safe houses were…rooms in hotels or small apartments.

This house, this mansion… Was not.

The whole thing looked like a strange sort of castle plopped down into the middle of Manhattan.

"How is this subtle?" she asked as they stood on the sidewalk looking up at the five-story building.

"It's not meant to be. That's the point. Who would think demon hunters lived here?"

"But…how many of you stay here at any given point in time?"

"Since New York is a hub for us, it can be as many as ten. As few as one. The council have their own homes."

Angie looked from the mansion to Sebastian and said, "You chose, voluntarily, to stay at my tiny apartment all these months when you had *this* to live in?"

"This place is missing something very important," he said.

"What?"

"You."

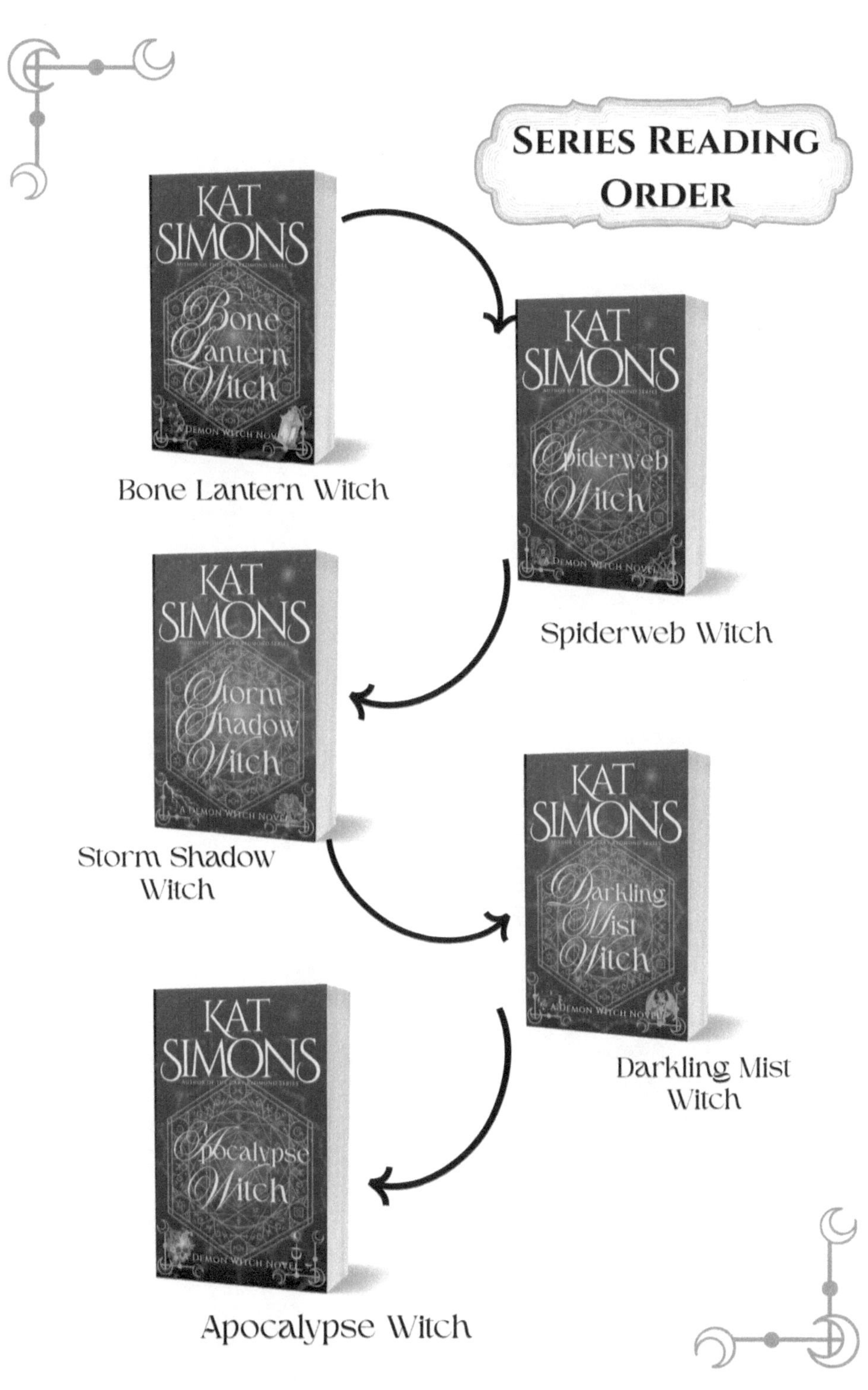

Bone Lantern Witch

Spiderweb Witch

Storm Shadow Witch

Darkling Mist Witch

Apocalypse Witch

DARKLING MIST WITCH

A DEMON WITCH NOVEL

KAT SIMONS

T&D PUBLISHING

Darkling Mist Witch

For my favorite hero and our heroes in training…

CHAPTER ONE

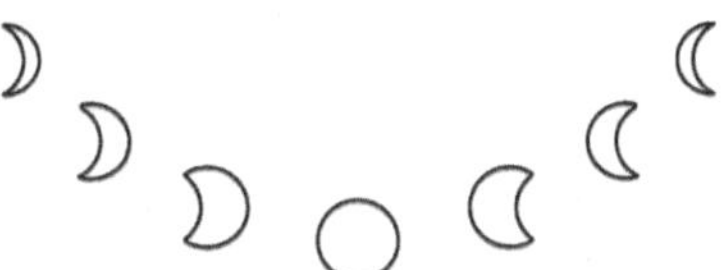

ngie Jordan had been back in New York City for a week, restlessly waiting for this moment. And she still wasn't sure she was ready for it. Yet the time felt overdue. This was something she should have done months ago.

It had taken New Mexico and the incident in the desert to really push the demon hunters to give in to her requests.

Now, all this knowledge might be too late.

She glanced at Sebastian as he stared up at the building in front of them. It was a nondescript office building in Midtown Manhattan, close to Times Square and relatively indistinguishable from all the other buildings around it. Floor after floor of steel and black smoked glass rising up into the bright afternoon sky, casting long shadows across the busy sidewalk.

Late spring warmth had taken hold of the day, which

meant the sunshine felt lovely and warm on her skin, but the shadows were still cool and a good contrast to the growing heat. After time back home in Albuquerque, the cool shadows felt particularly cold. Or maybe that was the ominous sense of dread filling her gut. Even the scent of a nearby food truck selling tacos couldn't overcome that dread, though the smell did make her stomach growl. She'd eaten before coming this time, not wanting to make the mistake of being hungry before facing this situation, but tacos were always a good idea as far as her stomach was concerned. Except just then, with the churn of anxiety and the weird mixture of anticipation and hesitance holding her here on the overly crowded sidewalks.

Fortunately, there was a bubble of space around her and Sebastian, a little haven of isolation despite the crowds of tourists and locals pushing past so thickly they moved like one entity. A bubble of peace Sebastian had willed into existence.

Demon hunters' wills were awesome things. And Sebastian was one of the best demon hunters working.

She'd only learned just how powerful he was in the desert, though. And what that meant to the demon hunters.

And that he was the real reason she had a powerful hunter who wanted her dead.

"You're ready?" he asked without looking at her.

"Past ready. And yet…"

He finally looked down at her. "And yet," he echoed with a nod, his soft English accent rolling the words to make them sound less ominous.

She was tempted to reach out and grab his hand, for the support and reassurance, but she was also afraid she'd read him on accident because her nerves were so jangled, so she kept her hands to herself. Being a touch psychic had its benefits—it was the reason she could do the work she did, giving psychic readings at Dana's Cauldron in the Village—but it had its drawbacks when she wasn't feeling as controlled as she might like.

The time in New Mexico, studying with her original and most beloved mentor, had definitely helped the control that had been slipping before the trip. She did have control of her magic now, all of it, even the magic she'd absorbed on accident in a demon realm.

It was just that that control felt more delicate than she liked.

"What if we find out there's nothing that will help?" she said, voicing her fears. Again.

This wasn't the first time she'd talked about this with Sebastian. They'd discussed the situation multiple times over the last two weeks, before they'd even returned from New Mexico. But this was the rubber-hits-the-road moment when she'd find out if her fears were founded. If the hunter who wanted her dead, Morty, had told her the truth in the desert.

She didn't feel like she was dying. She didn't feel like she was being overwhelmed by the demon magic she'd absorbed and worked into her own magic on accident.

But she no longer felt entirely like herself either.

More than the thought of dying, that scared the shit out of her.

"We'll find something," Sebastian assured. "According to Morty, you should be dead already. He was lying. We all knew it."

"But Jacob hasn't been in touch either and he wanted to find a solution."

"He won't have access to these records. It's taken *us* months to get access to the full histories of the demon witches. Jacob means well—"

She interrupted that sentiment with a snort. She didn't have a great opinion of that particularly demon hunter now either. Not since he shoved her into a demon realm.

Sebastian tilted his head in acknowledgment of the grace he shouldn't be giving Jacob and finished, "He wants you to live so you can be used as a tool against the demons."

She nodded. That was a much more accurate description of Jacob's goal in all this.

"But even he doesn't have the connections to get into these files. And if there are answers, they'll be here."

She let out a slow breath and looked up at the building again. She really hoped Sebastian was right.

Because the magic she'd intertwined with her own magic inside the demon realm had made itself at home in her web of power, and she couldn't see any way of removing it without disaster.

In her world, disasters meant death.

THE LOBBY OF THE OFFICE BUILDING WAS A HUGE OPEN SPACE with two story high ceilings and a lot of bland gray carpeting against black marble floors. A long reception desk against one wall allowed visitors through to the banks of elevators behind swipe card security entrances. No one got into the building who didn't belong or wasn't signed in.

There were visitor badges waiting for Angie and Sebastian at the desk. No pictures attached. And there were orders with the badges not to take pictures. That the security guards complied with that request meant someone in this building carried a lot of power.

And why not? The hunters would hardly store their most valuable records in a place that just anyone could get into past guards who couldn't follow directions.

She and Sebastian went to the elevator bank farthest from the desk after swiping through the security gates. The floors had to be punched into a panel at one end of the bank and then they were directed to a specific elevator to bring them where they were going. When they entered the fourteenth floor, the digital screen blinked a few times with an error warning. And then abruptly directed them to elevator seven.

No one else was waiting in front of elevator seven, though there were plenty of people waiting at the other six in the corridor. She and Sebastian didn't have to wait long either. Elevator seven opened ten seconds after they paused in front of it, as if it had been waiting for them.

No one else followed them inside.

When the doors slid closed, the low level noise of the lobby, all the various conversations and talking that had fallen into background white noise for her, cut off abruptly.

The silence felt heavy and ominous and didn't help the jangly nerves tightening her stomach.

She watched Sebastian in the shiny reflective silver of the elevator doors. He was dressed relatively casually, in dark wash jeans and a white button up shirt that looked sharp and clean against his dark brown skin. His goatee was neatly trimmed and his tightly cut black hair, with just a hint of gray at the temples, gleamed faintly under the elevator light. He looked gorgeous and strong and sometimes she forgot how much he could take her breath away. The urge to touch him, to take comfort in holding hands, made her restless, and she gripped the strap of her large purse where it lay across her chest tighter to stop herself. As she watched him, his hand flex into a fist and then relax as he also resisted the urge to reach out to her. He knew her well, and she'd warned him ahead of time touching might be bad. But not grabbing onto him and holding tight felt retched.

Instead of touch, she moved a little closer to him, standing close enough, she could practically feel his arm alongside hers, even if they weren't in direct contact. That helped. Both of them because his shoulders in his reflection relaxed.

When the doors slid open, Gabriella was waiting for them.

"I thought you'd stand on the sidewalk all day," the older woman said, her expression serious and a touch annoyed.

Angie wasn't sure why she was surprised the hunters had cameras at the street level to monitor who came in and out of the building. Of course they would. Still, realizing Gabriella had been watching her waffle and hesitate to come upstairs was embarrassing.

The fact that the hunter was showing her annoyance meant she wanted Angie to know about it, too. Demon hunters only revealed what they wanted to. And while Angie had never seen Gabriella in a demon fight, she was a member of the hunter council and not someone Angie had ever taken lightly.

She might even say she respected Gabriella on a certain level. If the hunter wasn't so insistent that Angie should join their ranks and be a demon hunter herself. Months of Gabriella's insistence, while Angie got no closer to being a proper demon hunter, hadn't seemed to diminish Gabriella's commitment to the idea, though.

She was an average looking woman, as most hunters were, a few inches shorter than Angie, even in her low black heels, wearing dark gray suit pants and a fitted blue dress shirt that would blend in well with any of the suits they'd passed in the lobby. She kept her dark hair, shot through with strands of steel gray, pulled back into a severe bun most of the time, leaving her sharp features sharper and her baring uncompromising.

That impression was only amplified by her narrowed dark eyes. "Are you dying yet?"

"Not that I've noticed," Angie said with matching bluntness. She actually appreciated Gabriella being blunt. They were well past dancing around information, trying to keep as much from the other as possible.

"Good. Follow me." Gabriella turned on her heels and

walked them down a long corridor that led away from the elevator bank.

Angie realized with a start that where the rest of the elevators should be, there were only light brown walls with a few nondescript paintings hanging on them. Either that was an illusion, the hunter was willing her not to see the other elevators, or the other building elevators just simply couldn't stop here.

Probably the latter.

"I think she meant that good," Sebastian leaned in to whisper to Angie.

"I did," Gabriella said, without missing a beat. "I don't want you dead, Angela. You should know that by now."

"Wouldn't want to take your feelings on the matter for granted," Angie said. "Especially after what happened in New Mexico."

Gabriella glanced back, her mouth flattened into a line. She sucked in a breath through her nostrils, then let it out on a huff. "Morty and Jacob have a great deal to answer for."

Angie couldn't agree more.

Gabriella led them through what seemed like an empty office space, though there were no desks or conference tables or even those open-plan dividers sectioning off work spaces. Even the thought of those made Angie shiver so she didn't dwell on the image—office work was anathema to her—but she did make note of the very obvious absence of actual office furnishings.

"Not even pretending here, huh?" she asked Gabriella.

"This space is the padding," Gabriella said. "The

gauntlet, if you will. Passing through here without an escort is…more dangerous than it seems on the surface."

That got Angie looking closer at her surroundings, this time opening her senses. And there, just at the edge of her peripheral vision, impossible to see if she tried to look directly at it, but there nonetheless, a series of sporadic blue lights, faint but clear. Magical spells.

"Traps," she murmured, nodding. Then frowned. "A witch set these."

Demon hunters didn't have magic or do magic most of the time. Their will and the way they wielded it could *look* like magic from the outside. But it wasn't technical magic.

The spell traps set around the open office space were actual magic, witch magic by the flavor and look of it. Which meant the hunters had to have hired the spells put into place.

"It's amazing what you can get done these days," Gabriella said. "People selling all kinds of services. And in this case, the price was very reasonable since a hunter had saved the witch in question from her own hubris." Gabriella glanced over her shoulder. "This was many years back. And she wasn't a demon witch."

"Figured," Angie said. Because, according to what little information the hunters would admit to her, there hadn't been another demon witch in centuries. And all the witches they had records on had turned toward evil, tried to unleash demons on the world, and had to be killed—or were killed by the demons they let loose. So Angie doubted the hunters would hire one to set traps protecting their most precious histories.

Gabriella walked through a door that led into an empty conference room. This time Angie felt the magic the minute she crossed the threshold. A sort of searching spell that tingled along her nerve endings. The moment she was through, the tingling stopped. She blinked and looked back at the doorway.

"A portal?" she asked.

"Of a sort," Gabriella confirmed.

So. Now they weren't technically in the building in the middle of Midtown anymore. Or at least not precisely. Angie wasn't sure *where* they were—or when for that matter. Magical portals were tricky that way—and it might not even be that far away from where they'd been just moments ago. They might have just moved to a different building in Midtown. But they were definitely now "somewhere else."

A level of security she had to admired.

"Always suspected you all used portals," she said to Gabriella's back as the hunter crossed the empty board room to another door.

"The fireplace in the council's meeting room?" Gabriella opened the door and stood to one side to let Angie and Sebastian through first. "Yes. There's a portal there."

"I knew it." Angie tried not to get too smug about having figured that out. But it did feel good to know the hunters hadn't gotten anything over on her.

She paused at the threshold, looking past Gabriella. The doorway opened onto a storage room, with row after row of metal shelves all stacked with boxes and crates. And beyond those shelves, Angie caught sight of what looked like a library, wooden shelves this time, all lined with books.

"Portal again? Or trap?" She glanced at Gabriella.

"No traps here. If you've gotten this far, you've been invited."

Angie respected Gabriella hadn't even blinked at her suspicions. "So portal then."

"Portal." Gabriella moved just a little in front of Angie, though, before Angie could step through the doorway. "Are you sure you want to do this?"

"Yes. There's information in there I need."

"And if it doesn't answer your questions?"

"Then I'll know where I have to forge answers for myself."

Gabriella dipped her head in acknowledgement. Then stepped to the side.

And Angie crossed through the doorway.

CHAPTER TWO

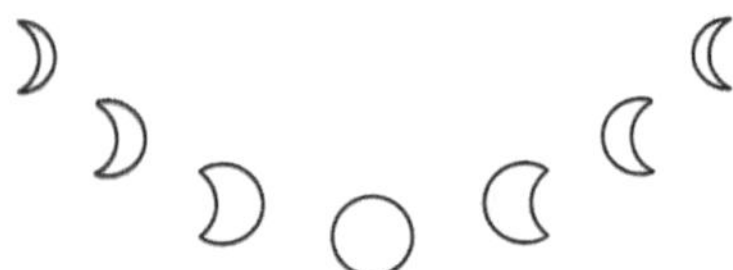

The portal doorway left a stinging sort of buzz along Angie's skin as she stepped though. Into what had looked like a storage room while still standing inside the conference room that may or may not have still been in Midtown Manhattan. Now that she stood on this side of the portal, the "storage room" looked more like the basement of a museum. Still a storage room. But one with an extensive collection of artifacts and art that could rival the greatest museums in the world.

The smell of the place even reminded Angie of a museum. That sort of clean ancient smell, the smell of old things filtered through modern air purifiers.

Rows and rows of wooden and metal shelves spread out to each side of her. The floor was red marble, polished so smoothly, Angie could see her reflection in it. The ceiling above was decorated with elaborate crown molding etched in gold and beautiful murals of scenes she couldn't quite make out from her vantage. She suspected the scenes would make more sense if she was standing in the middle of the huge room.

A series of crystal chandeliers lit the space as well as electric lamps scattered around the room. The walls were lined with more wooden shelves, all filled with books, some covered by glass, others open. The bookshelves went all the way to the ceiling, and a narrow, wrought iron balcony circled at about the midpoint on the shelves, providing access to the higher sections.

In between all the shelves and stacks on the main floor, there were also long wooden reading tables. Some of them piled with books or other artifacts. Some empty. There were only a handful of chairs around the tables, though. And none of the chair looked like comfortable reading seats —all hard, straight-backed wood without cushion or padding.

The space had looked large from the other side of the portal, but from this side, it looked enormous.

Sebastian stepped up beside her and let out a low whistle.

She glanced at him. He was scanning the giant room, his eyes wide. In this light, she barely saw the faint dot of red in the depths of brown.

"Is it what you thought it would be?" she asked. There were other records that most hunters could see, but this was the secret archive, and he'd never been here either.

"Bigger," he said. Then glanced back at Gabriella. "A lot more's been kept secret than I realized."

"There are some things it's best not many people know," Gabriella said.

When Angie glanced at her, she realized the door back to the conference room was gone. No door was there at all. Just more of the enormous room, spreading out behind Gabriella as far as it spread out in front of Angie and Sebastian.

"We've been keeping history for millennia," Gabriella added with a shrug. "Can't keep all of it in one place."

"That's not why the other hunters haven't seen this room," Angie said.

"No. It's not. This way. What you need is all in one section."

Angie and Sebastian fell into step behind Gabriella, both of them gawking at the room as they wove around shelves and tables.

"Is that…a Botticelli?" Angie asked, nodding to a wall fresco that had been removed from some wall somewhere and was now leaning up against a shelf, casually, like it wasn't particularly valuable.

"Always loved the way he drew women," Sebastian commented without confirming or denying if the fresco was actually a Botticelli.

"Has Aidan been here?" Angie asked. If she had been, she'd never told Sebastian.

"Three times," Gabriella said. "As far as I know."

"As far as you know?"

"I was not privy to all of Aidan's movements before I joined the council. And of course, I wouldn't have known anything about how often she'd visited this place before I became a demon hunter myself."

Angie blinked a few times, as Gabriella oh-so-casually upended her world with that last sentence.

Aidan was a legendary demon hunter, and Sebastian's mentor. She was the hunter who'd rescued Angie when Angie was only five and had accidentally unleashed a hoard of demons on her father's church parking lot because, at the time, Angie hadn't known that looking into the V of a tree trunk would breach the barrier between this realm and the demon realm. At least for her. Aiden had shown up, somehow returned the demons to their realm, and proceeded to ensure Angie's family understood what she was capable of and introduced Angie to the witch that would prove the most foundational magic mentor of Angie's life. The very mentor she'd just gone to Albuquerque to train with.

Like most other hunters, Aidan was pretty unremarkable looking. An ordinary woman moving through the world without drawing too much attention to herself. At least, that was how she presented herself, how she appeared every time Angie had seen her. And Angie had known Aidan was older than she looked because she hadn't appeared to age in all the years Angie had known her. Twenty-three years was a long time for a person to never show signs of aging. Hunters didn't have to show their age. They didn't even have to age at a normal human rate. They willed themselves to age slower. So most of them were much older than they looked. Even Sebastian, who had allowed some gray to thread through his dark black curls, didn't look his forty-three years.

So Aidan being older than she appeared wasn't a surprise. What was surprising was that, in the back of her mind, Angie had always assumed Aidan was in her fifties or sixties. Still young enough that the vague mid-thirties look she presented the world wasn't all that far off her real age.

Gabriella had just implied that Aidan was a lot older than that.

"Did you…know?" she murmured to Sebastian.

"Suspected," he said, knowing what Angie was asking without her having to say the words. "But never confirmed."

"So you don't know how old she is either?"

"Not that she's admitted. I've never asked." He flashed her a charming smile. "Bit of a cheeky question to ask a woman, though, innit?"

Angie rolled her eyes, snorting a laugh that surprised her in the midst of all this.

They ended up in a section of the room that wasn't too dissimilar to the rest of the place. There was a long wooden table in front of a wall of bookshelves and a few standing shelves in front of it. The area created a sort of room inside the room, with the standing bookshelves serving as a wall on two sides of the table, leaving only one side open to walk in.

There was glass covering the standing shelves, and Angie had to get closer to them to see what was behind the glass. What she'd assumed were ordinary books, turned out to be artifacts alongside books that didn't look like they should be outside the glass.

Not demon books, she thought. The dangerous ones, the ones the demon hunters took out of circulation when they found them and stored safely. She imagined those were collected in a different part of the room. She'd encountered some of those over the years. Nearly gotten rolled under by one that had a connection to a Molder demon last fall. They weren't the sort of books she wanted to come into contact with again, especially now that she had this demon magic now solidly threaded through her magic web.

But those weren't the books behind the glass in this section. The books here were magic books. Witches' books. Grimoires. If she turned her head and looked at them just right, she could even see their auras. Magic glistened with blue light around them. Some of that blue magic was dark dark blue. Darker than she'd ever encountered.

And some of it was demon witch red.

The artifacts with the books seemed to be an odd collection of household objects. Metal bowls. Marble mortar and pestles. Glass and pewter goblets. A few wooden spoons and bowls. A lot of cloth wrapped around things she couldn't see. The cloth itself seemed infused with magic, so she assumed that was a protective barrier of some kind to whatever the material covered. There were a few pieces of jewelry, too. Necklaces and amulets. Some rings. And one whole case filled with athames, the small knives witches often used during ceremonial magic. Usually to cut herbs or to cut magical lines. Sometimes used as extensions of a witch's power finger.

In certain blood magic, an athame could be used as a real knife.

Angie didn't deal in blood magic at all, had avoided it as

much as possible in her life. There were times when drops of blood were necessary to spells. And she'd encountered witches who used blood magic, both for ill and for good, depending on the witch. But it wasn't a type of magic she came to naturally.

Given her demon witch skills, that was probably for the best. Mixing demon and blood had always felt like a bad idea.

She paused at the cabinet of athames and considered some of them. A lot of very simple, small daggers. Ordinary silver blades. One or two with beautiful crystal hilts. Another few with the hilt wrapped in leather. There was one quite elaborate dagger with symbols etched on the short thick blade and copper wire wound tightly around the hilt. That entire dagger glowed in a light blue color that was almost purple. Most of the other daggers were without that glow of magic, looking perfectly harmless.

Given they were set behind glass, which Angie suspected had blocks for magic on it, she knew that harmless appearance was deceptive.

"The histories aren't just written records," Gabriella said, coming up next to Angie to consider the athames, not looking directly at Angie. "The histories are kept in the belongings of those who came before as well."

"That's why there are artifacts here and not just books."

Gabriella nodded, finally glanced at her. "What you want is all here. Everything we have on the demon witches. Everything we've been able to find anyway. We know there are things out in the world that we haven't been able to retrieve."

"Older records?"

"And even some more recent, relatively speaking. That notorious witch who was killed by her coven? Her cottage was subsumed under a larger mansion built up around it, similarly to the way Sarah Winchester built extensions constantly onto the Winchester house in California. This house has been under constant construction for the last few centuries. There are still relics there, but the ancestors of that witch don't allow access to the mansion."

"No one's tried to break in and just steal the stuff?" Angie asked, somewhat cynically. Technically, the demon hunters were the good guys. But there was a lot of gray in this world, and that gray found its way into hunter morals just as fast as it did the morals of other people. Sometimes it was hard to tell the good guys from the bad guys.

"No one has…been able to break in. I won't say there haven't been attempts."

Angie snorted. Of course.

"At any rate, what we do have is all here. Very few have had access to this information. And if Morty and Jacob hadn't nearly killed you and Sebastian, if you hadn't managed to survive a demon realm and get out alive, I'm not sure I could have talked the council into letting you see this now."

"Is Morty still on the council?" No one had said he'd been relieved of that position. Or removed himself.

"He is. Though he's lost a lot of the power he'd built up. His…opinions are more suspect now."

"*Now?*" Angie shook her head. "He's been advocating for my death for months, maybe years, and it's only *now* you all decided to be suspicious of his opinions?"

"His was a pragmatic opinion, not considered particularly sinister."

Angie almost choked on that comment. Except, standing here surrounded by all the records of people like her, knowing what she did know about the hunters' encounters with demon witches over the years, she supposed she shouldn't have been surprised. Especially given how pragmatic hunters could be. Almost to a fault. And killing someone who could unleash a hoard of demons directly onto this realm would seem to make sense from a certain perspective.

If you weren't that someone they were talking about killing.

Angie had no intention of releasing a hoard of demons onto this world. Not if she could help it. Not if *she* had any say in the matter.

But she couldn't entirely blame the hunters for not trusting her opinion on what she would or wouldn't do when what she *could* do was so dangerous.

Learning just recently that only Sebastian and Aidan were strong enough to send back freed demons of a certain power level had only made the position of some of the other hunters more understandable.

Again, so long as you weren't the one they wanted to kill.

Angie decided to let that argument go. Whether Morty kept his position on the demon hunter council or not wasn't her decision. She'd like for it to not be her problem either. She wanted to convince the council—Gabriella in particular—that she wasn't suited to being a demon hunter, which Gabriella insisted she was born for, and that she wasn't a danger, which Morty insisted she was. If she could just convince them of these two facts, they could all leave her alone and she could go back to just being a witch.

A witch with a demon hunter boyfriend she had no intention of giving up ever again, the way she'd once tried to in order to get out of the demon hunter world. But still. Just a witch.

Unfortunately, she couldn't do any of that convincing at the moment. Because thanks to her time in a demon realm, she was both more dangerous and more useful to the hunters now.

In ways no one could have predicted.

She looked at the collection of artifacts and books around her. "Where do I start?"

"Here." Gabrialle went to one of the shelves lining the wall and plucked a leatherbound book off a middle shelf. "This will get you started. It's the complete history of everything we know, in broad strokes. We can move from this into the specifics once you're done."

Angie looked at the size and thickness of the book Gabriella set down on the wooden table in the center of the cubby. A table that had exactly one, very uncomfortable looking chair around it.

"This is going to take a while," she muttered.

"That's why I fed you before we came," Sebastian said, coming up behind her. "And I brought snacks."

Smart man.

CHAPTER THREE

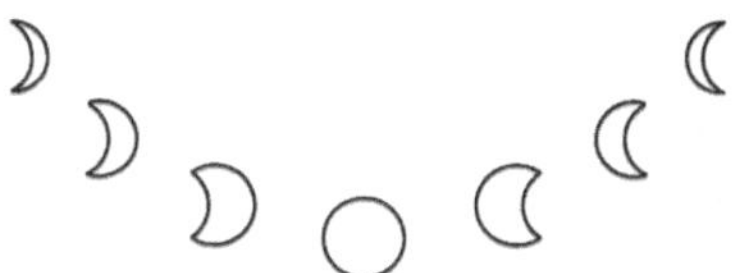

The reading was fascinating. Horrifying. Enlightening.

And incomplete.

Angie knew the records wouldn't be complete. Of course they weren't. No history ever was. And despite their best efforts, demon hunters weren't omnipresent. They couldn't know and keep everything. Gabriella had even said there were artifacts and information they knew existed but they couldn't get at that stuff for reasons.

The missing information was frustrating. But the stuff that was in those records…

Angie had a whole new appreciation for both Gabriella *and* Morty's logic for dealing with someone like her.

Demon witches had not had the most auspicious histories.

Gabriella had not lied about all the encounters the demon hunters had had with demon witches over the centuries. None of them ended well. For anyone, but least of all for the witch herself—and going through the records confirmed all the demon witches appeared to be women. Hard to say if this was accurate or not when tracing back so far, and it was possible some of the witches being referred to as her were not, in fact, hers, but the records maintained by the hunters pointed in that direction.

"Nothing but death and destruction as far as the eye can see," she muttered as she flipped through yet another book, this one on a particularly bad encounter with a witch in the fifth century c.e. who wanted to overthrow the Byzantine Empire. The witch had unleashed so many demons on a small village not far from modern day Istanbul that the town had literally been buried in blood and bodies and had to be burned afterward. The hunters had nearly lost that fight. And the witch had been one of the bodies, destroyed by the demons she'd unleashed.

"I tried to warn you," Gabriella said.

"Don't be smug."

"You can stop at any time if it's too much."

"I haven't found what I need yet."

"I'm not sure there's anything that can help you." This Gabriella said more quietly. "I've never heard of anyone going into a demon realm and surviving. Nonetheless coming out with…more than they went in with."

"That was a very delicate way of putting it."

"What I'm trying to say is that what has happened to you, what you've survived, what you can do now… If it's ever happened in the history of demon witches, it's a footnote about a witch who died quickly."

"I'm not dead yet."

"True. And I have to say, this irritates the hell out of Morty."

Angie chuckled at that. "I'm delighted to hear it."

"But he was right in saying you probably should be. Humans can't…handle the kind of magic you now have in your body."

"Then why can I?"

"Got me," Gabriella said with a shrug. "Maybe it's to do with some combination of your other powers? Everyone is unique."

"But…?" Angie had heard the hanging "but" as surely as if Gabriella had said it.

"But…I'm afraid Morty is right and there's no way for you to survive this."

That, coming from the blunt Gabriella, was a blow Angie hadn't been prepared for. She leaned back against the straight, hard chairback and stared across the table at Gabriella. The hunter was leaning a hip on the table, her arms crossed, her gaze steady. But her eyes softened as she held Angie's gaze.

"I'm very sorry," she said quietly.

"I'm not dying," Angie said. "I would know I was dying if I was dying."

"How?"

"I'm psychic. I'd know."

"Have you ever gotten psychic readings on yourself?"

Angie flattened her mouth, annoyed that Gabriella had pointed out the obvious flaw in Angie's logic. Angie couldn't see her own aura, couldn't touch her hand and see her future or her past, couldn't stare into a bowl of water and receive visions of her own future. The closest she'd come was getting flashes of possibilities during spell work, but even that was usually just her subconscious trying to work out what her conscious brain couldn't grasp. Her touch psychic skills were reserved for reading *other* people and other things.

Still… "I would feel it if I were dying. I feel fine. A little tired sometimes, but I've also been doing a lot of magic work to get my control back. I'm supposed to be tired after all that."

She refused to admit the magic work actually hadn't been making her tired. In fact, she felt electrified after working magic, especially when she carefully nudged up against the red threads of demon magic in her web of power. What left her exhausted were the times when she didn't access that web for a long period of time. That was new, and not something she was prepared to discuss with Gabriella, though she had talked about that with her teacher, Esmerelda, and with Sebastian.

"If the magic overwhelms you," Gabriella said, "you might not know until too late."

"It's not overwhelming me, though. It's actually remained perfectly contained."

Unlike her own demon witch magic, which had, not too long ago, started to bleed into her witch magic and screw up her control, the threads of demon magic she'd brought out of the demon realm remained as their own, distinct part of her magic, not mixing with anything else. The new magic had even succeeded, where other things hadn't, at realigning her demon witch magic back into its own thread. Her powers were more balanced now than they'd been since discovering the vision of a spiderweb that was her way of visualizing her magic.

She wasn't prepared to say or accept that perhaps she was made to hold this kind of power. The very thought left her panicky and ready to run. But her body didn't seem terribly bothered by it all.

"We can hope," Gabriella said. "Perhaps this really won't kill you. And maybe it's just that no other demon witch has survived long enough in a demon realm to return with whatever magic they accumulated there."

"I had help." Sebastian had been there with her. But he hadn't been the only one.

Carmen, a witch whose vigilante efforts seemed to cause more trouble than they solved, had also been there. Angie had thought of Carmen as an enemy once. She was responsible for Angie breaking open her demon witch magic and learning to use it in ways that she hadn't even suspected were possible. Carmen had also nearly gotten Sebastian killed. Angie did not like Carmen. She didn't trust her. And she was certain the woman would stab her in the back as soon as look at her.

But she didn't really think of Carmen as the enemy anymore either. Not an ally for sure. But not an enemy. Their time in the demon realm had…shifted things.

Gabriella sighed and glanced around the shelves surrounding their nook, her gaze settling on Sebastian. He was behind Angie, studying some of the shelves lining the walls, occasionally bringing a new book to add to the stack of things Angie was reading. He hadn't commented during the entire conversation, and now Angie was very curious what he was thinking.

"We can't afford to lose either of you," Gabriella said. "Not if we want to keep the demons at bay. The last century has seen too many compromises. Too much gone wrong. Not enough hunters. And not enough hunters who are strong enough to do what needs doing. We *need* both of you. Which is the entire reason you've been allowed here. Because, outside of Morty, and maybe Karen, the rest of the council wants you to live."

"Gee, thanks?"

"You can kill demons now," Gabriella said bluntly.

This wasn't a topic Angie liked to talk about and so had refused to really face since she'd killed a Molder demon. Humans couldn't kill demons. They could summon them, they could will them back to their realm, they could fight them, they could be possessed and die by them. But they couldn't kill them.

Only a demon could kill another demon.

Yet, Angie had killed not one, but two demons. One a very powerful Molder demon.

That, more than her potential impending death, was the thing that had brought her here. If word got out what she could do, there'd be a target on her back so glaring and bright, even normal humans might see it.

And worse, that target would put Sebastian in danger. A thought she really couldn't tolerate.

"I'm not going to go around killing demons. You know that, right?"

"I'm not asking you to right now," Gabriella said. "I'm saying it is a valuable skill and if necessary… Well, I will ask you to. But only if necessary."

"None of this is helping," Sebastian said, his first comment for hours. He handed Angie a protein bar he pulled from somewhere, which she took gratefully. Then said, "Angie can't have been the only one this has happened to. Somewhere in here, we'll find the answers. And if not here, somewhere else. Someone has to know how this was done and how it can be reversed."

"Reversed?" Gabriella straightened away from the table. "Why reversed?"

"To save her life."

"She just said she's not dying."

"And you just said I probably was and just don't know it," Angie pointed out.

"I'm not talking about the demon magic killing her," Sebastian said. "I'm talking about the demons that will come after her once they realize she can kill them. The longer she stays this way, the better chance word of her condition spreads to demons who will come after her for it. I won't allow that."

Angie blinked up at him, her heart pounding hard. This

was the crux of the problem and they both knew it. Hearing it said aloud to Gabriella made it all so much more real and worse.

She watched him reach for her and then check the gesture, letting his hand fall back to his side. Angie turned her focus inward long enough to ensure her touch psychic skills were locked down—she'd been keeping them that way with all the books she'd been touching, but she didn't want to take chances something had slipped while she was distracted—and then she reached out for Sebastian's hand. He gripped her instantly, his fingers wrapping tight around her palm. And she felt the tremor that shivered through him.

He let out a long breath through his nose, then handed her another book with his free hand. "Try this one," he said quietly to her. "This witch apparently knew more about the demon realms than some of the others. She sketched out the different realms. Had some thoughts on the various places that I haven't seen before."

Angie took the book, not loosening her grip on his hand, and began flipping through it with her free hand, ignoring the slight headshake Gabriella gave them.

SEVERAL HOURS LATER, THE CLOSEST ANGIE COULD FIND TO any of the answers she needed came in one of the more innocuous looking books that Sebastian handed her. Simple brown cardboard backing, no leather or elaborate symbols. A handwritten accounting of a demon witch from an outsider's perspective, but not one of the demon hunters. The book was a diary of a woman who'd been in love with a demon witch, and had gone through the witch's rise and descent with her.

The diarist talked about her lover taking "journeys" through the demon realms, though it was hard to tell from the writing—which was a bit flowery and also quite vague in places—whether these were real journeys or metaphorical. The witch told the diarist about the different realms, the different layers of demon worlds. Revealed the existence of one that was a place for demon gods, a place even some demons couldn't go and where the gods reigned with brutality and pain.

Brutality and pain were a common refrain in demon realms. The god realm was something Angie personally hadn't encountered before, but when she'd asked, after a brief glance at each other, Sebastian and Gabriella had confirmed such a thing existed. That demons from that realm never came to this one because they didn't need to. And that was a good thing because demon gods were so deadly, typical demon hunter ways of fighting demons might not even work.

"Fortunately," Gabriella said, "we can't get to that realm and accessing our realm from the god realm is impossible. There is no direct route. So the gods aren't summoned here either. Not that they'd answer. But better they aren't temped to."

"Yeah it is." Angie blew out a breath. "So knowledge of the demon god realm is pretty common, then? That's how this witch would have known about it?"

Another look exchanged between Sebastian and Gabriella.

"It's been common knowledge among demon hunters for a couple of centuries," Sebastian said. "But not as far back as this diary goes." He held Gabriella's gaze as he spoke and the other hunter's expression closed up, so it was impossible to read, though there was a little bunched line between her brows.

"So…" Angie glanced up at Sebastian. "So how did the diarist know about the god realm? How did this witch?"

"Good questions," Gabriella said. "We've never known. A guess? Some lesser demon told her?"

"The diarist records her lover as saying she'd *seen* the god realm. Is she talking vision?"

If no one could get to the demon god realm, then a vision of some kind made as much sense as a lesser demon telling them about it. Especially for a witch. The diarist—who never gave her own name or her witch lover's name—did imply more than once her witch had psychic powers to go with her ability to access demon realms, but they didn't have the same vocabulary as modern times, so it was hard to be certain.

That link between a witch having some sort of psychic skill as well as the demon witch power wasn't something Angie had seen a lot of in these records so far, but she'd suspected for a few months now that, with her own magic, there was some sort of link there.

Reading about another witch who was both psychic and a demon witch was interesting, even if it was a little hard to decipher.

"Possible," Gabriella said, her gaze dancing away. "A vision would explain her knowledge."

Angie narrowed her gaze. "You don't suspect this witch actually *went* to the god realm? Do you? You just said that was impossible."

"As I said, we've never really known. The diarist's words can be interpreted in several ways. Most hunters lean toward a logical explanation. Lesser demon, a vision, a now destroyed record of some kind. Going to a god realm herself isn't logical. Everything we know about it confirms it's inaccessible from here."

"But some of you worry she did go there?"

Sebastian raised his eyebrows at Gabriella, also a question. There weren't many hunters who would know about the diarist and her demon witch lover, or else this book would be kept in the more generally accessible history records. But there were some who knew about it. And Gabriella had been very specific in saying "most hunters" instead of hunters or all hunters.

"There might have been a hunter or two over the years who argued in favor of the witch having really gone to the god realm, but most dismiss those arguments. A human would never survive it. And it's simply not accessible."

"Even for a demon witch?"

Angie didn't pick and choose which realm she opened. She suspected she opened portals onto the same realm most of the time, but she didn't control it. She looked between the natural V created in a tree trunk and there was a demon realm beyond. The realm she'd been trapped in, twice, had seemed like the same place, with belching volcanos and ground like black glass cutting at her bare skin.

And the chittering demons. The realm she opened always seemed to have the chittering demons.

She'd never opened one of the frozen realms, where it would be like opening a window onto temperatures nearly as cold as space, and anything in front of the portal would freeze instantly. She'd always assumed that was luck. But… maybe her magic was picking a specific realm on purpose?

Could a demon witch *control* which realm she breached?

Could she open a portal into the god realm?

She'd never considered controlling the process. But then, she'd never known it was possible to open a breach without a tree, yet here she was able to do just that now. If she could open a breach wherever she wanted now, maybe she could also access *whatever* realm she wanted to as well.

Angie leaned back in her seat, frowning down at the diary, her fingers resting gently on the open page. She had her psychic skills locked down so she wouldn't read anything from all these books. But she wondered, with this one…

The last time she'd opened to a book about demons, she'd almost been bowled under by a Molder demon. She was not inclined to repeat that experience.

But this wasn't a demon book. This was a book by a human who'd loved a demon witch. No demons should have had access to this, and demon energy shouldn't be lingering in the pages.

Unlike spells and potions and the other kinds of magic Angie worked, both her psychic power and her demon witch magic happened automatically unless she put effort into controlling them. She had to *work* to make a spell happen.

With both her psychic ability and her demon witch skill, the magic worked without any effort at all. All the *work* went into preventing the skill from randomly happening.

That's why Angie suspected a link between the two. And now she had the diary of a woman close to a witch who may have had that same combination of powers.

What would she find if she opened to the book and let her psychic senses take in more direct images from the diarist? It was possible there wouldn't be much there from the original source. The book had passed through other hands. And it was possible she'd get readings from all those other people and not be able to pick out the original diarist's energy. That happened with books that had multiple owners.

Was it worth the risk?

Safely here inside a protected demon hunter archive? Yes, Angie thought, yes it seemed like it might well be worth the risk.

"I'm going to open to the book and see if I can read anything from the diarist," she told Sebastian. Only fair to warn him. Especially if something went wrong.

"You sure that's a good idea? It's been through a lot of hands."

"Worth a try. There's a lot here, but there's a lot implied and not spelled out. I'd like to see if I can see if the witch actually *went* to demon realms or just learned of them through taking with a summoned demon. Any information a demon passed on to her is obviously suspect, especially filtered through the words of her lover. But if she actually *went* to the demon realms and came back, if she was able to *pick* which realms she went to, if she actually *saw* these places with her own eyes, and learned something. If she returned…" She let the thought trail off, but she and Sebastian both knew the rest of that sentence. Even Gabriella did.

If this other witch returned, did she bring any of the magic back with her? And if she had, had she survived or had it killed her?

"I need to try," she finished. "I need to see if there's more to learn here."

Sebastian let out a long breath, then nodded. "I'm here if you need me. I'll pull you out if you get into trouble."

She smiled, reached up to him and pulled him down for a gentle kiss, a touch to settle her before she opened to her psychic senses. He smelled reassuringly of that spicy soap he loved, that she loved too, and his warm breath against her cheek made her sigh. She opened her eyes and met his, so close the red was in the depths of the deep brown was impossible to miss. He cupped her cheek, his thumb rubbing against her cheekbone. And then he released her and straightened away, no longer touching her, moving just far enough away to give her space without going so far he couldn't pull her out of any psychic trouble she might get into.

Goddess, she loved him so much.

When she glanced away, she noticed Gabriella giving them a hooded look that Angie couldn't read. She didn't try. Whether Gabriella disapproved or approved of her relationship with Sebastian hardly mattered. Angie had lost him once. She wasn't going to lose him again. Even to her own stupid decisions.

She took in a deep, settling breath, let her eyes fall half closed as she stared at the book, opened her senses. She held her hand above the book for a long moment, ensuring she was prepared.

Then carefully settled her hand on the open page, closing her eyes fully.

As the images rushed in.

CHAPTER FOUR

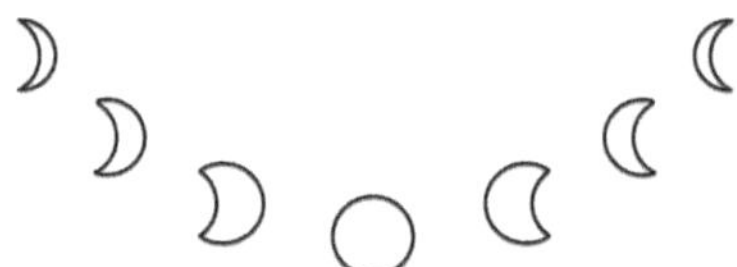

At first, all Angie saw was fire. Flicker flames inside a hearth. Nothing sinister. In fact, there was a comfort to the view, a feeling of peace and contentment. That sense of peace faded, though, as the flames brightened and grew, transformed.

Into a woman.

The impression of the woman was a little fuzzy at the edges, an indication the person who'd had this view had had very strong feelings for her, positive feelings. Which meant what Angie was seeing was the woman filtered through love. Through that love, the woman was a magnificent beauty, in a fierce and sharp way. Straight dark hair, dark eyes, pale tan skin with freckles over her nose, and full pink lips. She appeared tall and very curvy through the gaze of her lover. Dressed in a shift and overdress, with embroidery around the edges of the overdress. Angie couldn't place the historical period of the clothing, but she assumed it was contemporary to the diarist and her demon witch.

The image shifted once again. Fire rose up behind the witch, flames and blackness and beyond that… volcanos belching sulfur-scented smoke and lava into a red sky.

A demon realm.

Flickering images of other things. A loaf of bread and cheese. A bed. A woven blanket. A walk in the woods. A small village well. The everyday things from the life of the diarist imbedded inside the book as much as the demon witch.

In the part of her mind that wasn't carefully observing the images, Angie was surprised she wasn't picking up any of the other people who'd handled this book. But she was certain all these images came from the diarist. Her…essence, her mark on the book was so strong it was impossible to miss or mistake. And it dominated everything about the book. No one else who'd handled it must have been able to leave a strong enough impression to overcome the diarist's psychic signature.

That, in and of itself, was fascinating for Angie. But the roll of images she picked up took most of her focus.

From the everyday series of impressions, the images moved into something darker. A night filled with foreboding… The sky overhead was dotted with stars, but Angie didn't recognize the configuration or location. While she was an amateur astronomer, she wasn't good enough at her hobby to pick out a location on the planet based on the star constellations. And since this sky had existed centuries ago, she was even less likely to pick out the location.

The night hung above a forested area. Filled with trees, many of which had a natural V in them.

Angie realized suddenly she'd never encountered the sort of trees she needed to open a demon realm inside one of her visions. A realization she probably should have had before. When the images, presumably the view of the diarist, turned to one of those trees, Angie found herself bracing, attempting to avert her gaze so she didn't look through the V and see the demon realm beyond.

Faintly, sounding very far away, she heard Sebastian's quiet, "Ang?"

"I'm okay," she muttered, hoping she spoke the words aloud. Too much of her was inside the vision now.

Still avoiding looking directly into the V of trees as much as she could, out of habit as much as fear of what might happen inside the vision, Angie watched through the diarist's eyes as the other demon witch opened a portal breach between the V in a tree, staring into the tree's natural shape between the trunk. The diarist shouldn't have been able to see into the breach, only a demon witch—and the demons— could. But Angie still saw the demon realm beyond, and again wondered if that was because she was a demon witch and could, or because something was different about the diarist.

She hoped, in the part of her brain not subsumed inside the vision, that it was the latter, but if it was the former, it meant she might open a breach inside the vision on accident.

Which seemed impossible. She wasn't in a forest, she was in a library in Manhattan, several centuries after this event had taken place. She couldn't affect history, couldn't change what had been. And the vision was just that, a thing that had been. It wasn't really happening right now.

The realm beyond the V in the tree was that familiar landscape of black rock and rivers of lava, red sky overhead. The realm Angie had always thought of as "the demon realm." It was the place of her two worst moments, both stuck inside that realm. Once all alone and with no way to get out. Once with two other people who could have died. Though by that time, she'd discovered she did have a way out.

She no longer needed a tree.

As if the thought changed the vision, Angie watched the demon witch turn away from the tree and her own breach… which should have closed it. But it appeared to remain open, even through the eyes of the diarist. A thing that was terrifying in that split second…

Before *that* terror seemed quaint. Because the witch opened *another* breach. In another tree. Holding both open at the same time.

And then, to Angie's amazement, the witch opened a third. This one without needing the tree.

She opened a breach between this world and a demon realm in the open air. A swirling circle of space that looked into a lava spewing land of darkness and shadow. Beyond that breach, the world was so dark, the sky overhead black, that only the thick lines of red lava illuminated and defined the landscape. If not for those lines of glowing red, all beyond that breach would be impenetrable darkness.

Angie wanted to blink, to look away. To believe what she was seeing was impossible. Holding open a breach without looking at it. Holding *three* open at once. All three into different realms.

Impossible.

And yet, inside the demon realm, when she and Sebastian and Carmen had been trapped, Angie had held open a breach without looking at it. She'd looked away on accident, to fend off a demon and rescue Carmen, and when she'd looked back, afraid she'd closed the portal on accident, the tear between realities was still open.

Her gaze hadn't closed the breach, on the demon side or when she'd stepped through into the human realm again. She'd had to make an effort to close it from this side after she and the others had returned home.

She knew holding a breach without her gaze locked onto it was possible. She'd just been ignoring that fact for the last two weeks. Choosing to worry about other things.

Now the reality of that ability played out before her in the vision. Only not with just a single portal. With three. To three different realms.

The three portals were set in a triangle shape, too, Angie realized. The diarist saw all this from outside the triangle, but the witch stood at its center, surrounded by the portals she'd opened. And lines of blue magic glowed in the space between those breaches, tracing the shape of the triangle.

Forming a protective barrier. Not a circle, though.

All containment spaces Angie had ever worked in had been circles. Circles were the containment barriers used to summon demons into this realm, the things that kept them confined and linked to their own realms, kept them from crossing into this one. Summoning circles were always circles. Angie drew circles of protection around herself when working magic, or trying to defend against magic. All the magic Angie knew worked around circles.

Always circles.

Hell, even her spiderweb of powers was a vaguely circular shape with the threads spinning in a circle around her while the shaping threads speared out from her at the center of the image.

But circles weren't the only power shapes. Obviously. Pentagrams carried great power in certain practices, including hers. Others used cube, though that one had never been a shape that held much space in Angie's practice. The V in a tree was a power shape for a demon witch.

And what was a triangle but a closed V.

The realization left Angie breathless. Astonished that she'd never considered that before, never thought about triangles inside her magical work. Never realized a V shape was just an open triangle.

Shapes meant things in magic. She knew that. Her blind spot to the significance of triangles for a demon witch felt almost…deliberate in hindsight. A piece of knowledge her subconscious had hidden from her.

But she was seeing the truth of it now clearly, watching the other witch's magic rise, form a barrier in the spaces between her portals. The portals formed the vertices of the triangle. And when the diarist approached the edge of blue magic that made up the sides of the shape, she seemed unable to pass through. Remaining outside the protective barrier while her lover was inside.

Inside a space open to three different demon realms.

Angie couldn't be certain if the panic constricting her chest, making her breathe harder, was her own or the diarist. But the panic still clutched at her throat. She watched the witch move from the center of the triangle and step up close to one of the realms. The witch looked back at her.

"I'll be back in mere moments, love," she murmured. "Don't panic."

"Don't do this again," a voice traveled across the open space to the witch. Angie knew it was the voice of the diarist, yet felt like she'd spoken the words herself. "It's too dangerous."

"The answers are here," the witch said. "This is the only place I can find what I need."

"You've searched for months. Enough. Be done with this. It will kill you."

"Then I shall die in efforts of a good cause."

"How can any of this be good?"

"Trust me, love. Trust me."

With those words the witch stepped through the breach she'd opened without a tree, the portal into the realm so dark only lines of lava broke apart the sheet of blackness.

Angie reached out at the same time as the diarist, an

attempt to stop the witch. It was too late. And they couldn't reach through the lines of magic.

Moments ticked by in the vision.

And then everything changed again. Another night. Another forest. This time the fire came from torches. Torches illuminating faces in eerie, sinister orange light. The two women were surrounded on all sides. The torches, the faces closing in. Angie felt tears on her cheeks as she clung to the witch, felt the pain in her chest as panic nearly brought her to her knees. Her lover held her up, wrapped her arms tight around her to keep her from collapsing.

Against her ear, whispered, "Don't worry, love. Trust me. I will never let them have us."

A portal opened. The heat and scent of sulfur washing across her cheeks, drying the tears.

"We can't. We'll die there just as surely."

"Trust me," the witch murmured again.

A moment later, a screeching sound. And a winged demon swooped out of the breach.

Screams. Shouts. Cursing. Panic thick in the air. Dropped torches. More screaming. Fire. Pain. Searing heat.

The witch tugged her. And they stepped inside the dark realm. The portal closed.

Leaving a freed demon tearing through the men that had come for them.

Leaving them trapped inside the demon's realm.

CHAPTER FIVE

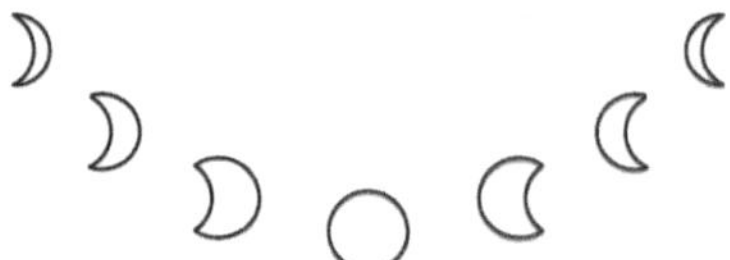

Angie jerked out of the vision so abruptly, her fingers stung, as if she'd ripped her hand away from a frozen pole. She almost expected to see skin left behind on the open pages of the book. Panic and fear clutched so tightly around her throat she couldn't breathe for a few seconds, and when she finally sucked in a breath, it was jerky and harsh, gasping. Choking.

The scent of sulfur and blood followed her out of the vision, hanging in the air around her. Bright light inside the archive did nothing to dispel the darkness in her mind's eyes. The torches and fire. The demon. The portal closing.

Trapping her again in that black, bleeding landscape of death and demons.

No. Not her. She was here in the records room. Not trapped centuries earlier in a demon realm.

She wanted to close her eyes, to breathe and settle, but

she was afraid closing her eyes would open her to the vision again, even if she wasn't touching the book, so she kept her eyes opened, focused on the dark, polished wood of the desk, the hard, straight-backed chair under her, the feel of her feet on the polished marble floor. The individual whorls in the wood. The book-lined shelves in her peripheral vision.

The scent of Sebastian's soap close. Close enough she could almost feel the warmth from his skin, but him still carefully not touching her.

Knowing he was worried, she forced out a few words, "I'm fine. Will be in a minute. Just…give me a minute."

She sensed more than saw his nod.

Her awareness of her surroundings slowly returning, she remembered Gabriella was there somewhere too. Watching this all play out.

When she could breathe steadier, she allowed herself to look up from the whorls in the woodgrain on the table to take in the rest of the huge room, the shelves of books, the bright overhead light, the nook with demon witch histories. Gabriella stood a few feet away, watching her warily, frowning. She had a hand on the table, like she'd been leaning on it.

Angie blinked a few times, the afterimage of the vision still clear in her mind's eyes, the stench of sulfur only slowly leaving her nose. The sounds of the men screaming as the demon tore into them still echoed through her head.

But she felt *here* now. Not in that distant time, with those distant women. She felt in her own moment, in her own time.

With only a residual of the panic and fear inside the vision still lingering in her gut.

Another deep breath, in through her nose, out slowly through her mouth.

Then she looked at Sebastian. The red in his eyes was more pronounced. The crease between his brows marring the smooth line of his forehead. His jaw was tight. His dark brown skin a little pale. And his hand rested on the table near her, but not touching her. He hovered over her where she sat, like he was trying to protect her from the vision with his own body.

That made her smile. "I'm fine," she assured him again. "Tough vision. But I'm fine. And I want to read the end of this book when I can risk touching it again."

Had the diarist and witch ever left the demon realm again? She hadn't read to the end of the diary before opening herself to that vision. She had no idea where it ended. And no idea if she'd witnessed the women's last moments or not.

"What did you see?" Gabriella asked.

Angie didn't turn to look at her again, keeping her gaze on Sebastian instead so she could assure him she was fine while also reassuring herself, remaining grounded in this moment instead of tumbling back into the vision world.

"She loosed a demon onto the men chasing after her and her lover," Angie murmured up at Sebastian. "The witch purposefully let a demon out into this realm to tear them apart. And then stepped into a demon realm with her lover and closed the portal."

Sebastian blinked slowly as he took this in.

"That was the last thing I saw before coming out," she said. "I'm not sure what happened after. I saw her go into a demon realm earlier, too. On purpose."

Angie fisted her hands in her lap to keep them from shaking as she told the two hunters about the vision and the different things she'd seen. Not long ago, she'd have kept most of this from Gabriella and waited to tell Sebastian. But while she still didn't entirely trust Gabriella, she did accept that the woman was, for the most part, her ally and Angie needed her help. She wouldn't be in this room, reading these books, studying these histories, if it weren't for Gabriella.

When she'd told them everything, she turned to Gabriella finally, and said, "Do you know how this diary ends? Do you know what the last entry is?"

Obviously, the witch had gone in and come back out again, at least once. Maybe more than that. But Angie had pulled out of the vision before being sure what had happened to the two women, because watching the portal close while she was seeing through the diarist's eyes had felt like being trapped in a demon realm herself all over again. Watching the demon tear into the men who'd been after the two women was bad enough. Watching that portal close, knowing where the women stood as it did, had activated her own lizard brain, her own panicked terror.

There were moments in that vision where she'd felt more *there*, more in that time and place, than an outside observer just watching what had happened in a past time. Moments when she'd felt so connected to the diarist, it was hard to tell where the line between them was, and that had made stepping into the demon realm with them even worse.

But now, with the lights in the huge archive pouring over her, with Gabriella and Sebastian nearby and the modern weight of her oversized purse at her feet next to the chair, with all the touchstones of her own reality to hand, she regretted pulling out of the vision that early. Regretted not seeing more of what happened with the women.

Not enough to touch the book again with her psychic senses open, though.

"The last entry in that particular diary," Gabriella said, "as far as I remember, details out a typical day, and then mentions something about the witch having to do another working that night. She refers to some medicine the witch found that isn't working anymore and she needed to find something else."

"Medicine? For what?" Angie had only been about halfway through the diary. There hadn't been mention of either the witch or diarist being sick. Maybe the medicine was for someone else? The diarist wasn't a witch, but she had been a midwife—though she hadn't used that word for her work—so maybe the medicine was for one of the pregnant women they looked after or one of the babies they helped birth?

Or maybe the demon witch had absorbed demon magic like Angie had and the "medicine" referred to some way she was attempting to keep that magic from killing her.

That last was the reason they were here, but if it was that

last, Gabriella had lied when telling Angie she wouldn't find answers here.

Or she'd known the diarist hadn't actually recorded the answers and so they were lost to time.

"Which is it?" she asked Gabriella, knowing she didn't need to clarify her thoughts for the hunter to know what she was asking.

"She never says," Gabriella confirmed. "By context, it seems the medicine is for the witch. Though even that can be interpreted in many ways. There's nothing in the diary, written down, to say what the medicine is for or to specifically say it's for the witch."

"You assumed she was killed though, by demons or others. You told me all the demon witches you had histories for were killed." Usually killed by hunters or demons but only after unleashing death and destruction. Gabriella had never mentioned a witch going into the demon realms and dying.

Though, Gabriella had been keeping a lot of information from Angie all these months, even when she'd been giving her some things. They'd both known that.

"We've always assumed, after the diarist's last entry, that the two women were killed. But… This witch wasn't included in the witches I told you about. Because we don't know her name or how her time ended. We only know her through her partner, through what's recorded here, and we have no other record of her to corroborate this. The witch isn't recorded in any other hunter histories. If the hunters encountered her, they failed to note it, which is…unlikely."

"You're saying this witch stayed under your radar. That the hunters never went after her."

"It seems she was one they never knew about. I told you we didn't have the names or complete records for all of the demon witches throughout history. And that we were certain some came and went without us ever needing to stop them."

Yes, Gabriella had told her that. But this wasn't a witch who ignored her demon witch magic and never dabbled in that realm. She'd gone *into* demon realms. At least twice, probably more based on what the diarist had said. And at least once she'd freed a demon who'd gone on to kill many people. That this demon witch had somehow avoided detection by the demon hunters was…impressive.

"Until just now, with your vision," Gabriella said, "I had no idea… We had no idea that she did any of the things you saw. The triangle of portals, opening into multiple realms… I've heard of that only once. The seventeenth century witch who had to be killed by her coven. She opened more than one portal during that battle."

"Simultaneously, like this witch?"

Gabriella gave a brief, jerky nod.

"Into more than one realm?"

Another jerky nod.

"And you kept that part of the story to yourself because?"

"What good would you knowing that was possible do? It was enough for you to know she'd been killed for unleashing a plague." Gabriella's eyes narrowed. "Do you *want* to open breaches into multiple realms at once and risk the consequences?"

She did not. "That information was still important."

Unfortunately, she couldn't actually argue with Gabriella keeping it to herself. She understood exactly why she had. And, for Angie at least, the knowledge at the time wouldn't have made any difference to anything that had come after.

She wasn't sure the knowledge was all that useful to her now. Except that knowing it could be done made her want to ensure she never did it.

"There's nothing in here that says outright what the 'medicine' was," Angie said, switching back to their earlier topic because arguing with Gabriella for withholding information was a losing battle. "But after my vision, and after knowing what happened to me, is it possible you missed details that might have revealed the 'medicine'?"

Gabriella shrugged, but her gaze danced away. "It's possible," she said reluctantly. "After your…incident in New Mexico, I reread some of the books and histories here. That diary wasn't one of them. I haven't read it for a while. And without your vision, I'm not sure I would have looked to it as a possible source of information. You saw more in those visions than the diarist ever dared write down. We had no idea this witch opened multiple portals. No idea she went into demon realms."

"If this was missed," Angie said slowly, turning in her seat to see more of the books and histories still lining the shelves, "that means there could definitely be more in here. More that isn't…written, but I might be able to see."

Gabriella's eyebrows rose. She ran a hand over the top of

her hair, needlessly smoothing her bun back into place. Then, slowly, nodded.

"It hadn't occurred to me how much more you might see or find in these books using your psychic ability. I'm certain it didn't occur to Morty either, or he wouldn't have agreed to allowing you in here. In hindsight, that was…stupid of us. We all know what you're capable of."

"I don't even know what I'm capable of anymore," Angie said with a huff.

"Fair enough. We all know you're a touch psychic. There's a reason the council members never offered to shake hands with you."

She'd assumed as much.

"So forgetting that you might use that skill to see more in these books than is written was shortsighted and stupid of us."

"Told you you should have let me in here sooner."

"Actually, had any of us put the facts together, you probably would have been denied access again. That you can know more from our histories than we do… The council wouldn't have tolerated that. The only reason they finally agreed to let you in here was because—" She cut herself off abruptly, flattening her mouth.

But Angie heard the end of the sentence clearly. "Because everyone assumes I'm going to die soon."

"Some of us don't want you to. But…yes. Even those on the council who want you to succeed are afraid Morty is more right than wrong about your inevitable end."

Angie nodded. This wasn't new information.

Because her nerves were still raw from the vision, but her head was spinning, she stood to pace the nook, careful not to touch anything as she settled. She'd locked down her touch psychic ability the minute she'd pulled out of the vision, but that didn't always guarantee something wouldn't get past while she was this sensitive after a vision.

As she passed him, Sebastian held out a wrapped protein bar for her. "You need food."

She smiled faintly as she took the bar, careful not to brush her fingers against his. "Thanks."

The chocolate protein bar went down easier than she would have suspected, given how unnerved the vision had left her. And when she passed Sebastian again on her pacing circuit, he wordlessly handed her a bottle of water he'd pulled out of her purse.

When she'd finished the water, and the protein bar had taken the edge off hunger she hadn't noticed until her first bite, she faced Gabriella again.

"I want to take the diary with me. I want to study it more. This witch went into and out of demon realms multiple times. On her own. Survived multiple times. And there's mention of medicine. I may well find something in here that was missed. But I'm not going to be able to touch it again for hours. It's the closest we've come to possible answers. I need to study it more."

"That's not part of the arrangement," Gabriella said, though she sounded regretful. "None of these books leave here. None of these objects leave here. Nothing that is here leaves here. It's too dangerous. All of these things are here on purpose. No one will agree to you taking that book out." Gabriella raised a hand when Angie opened her mouth to argue. "But, I can use this as an excuse to let you return. They'll want assurances you don't use your psychic ability on anything but the books relevant to your quest to stay alive."

"I can do that. I don't want to know or see most of the secrets in here. I just want to find out if I'm really dying, and if I am, how to stop it."

"Then I can get you more time. Will that suffice?"

"It'll have to." She needed more time with that diary.

"Do you want to continue with other texts now? Or save them for the next visit. We've been here for…a while."

Angie's stomach growled, despite the protein bar and full bottle of water she'd just finished. She winced. "My stomach apparently wants me to know it's been a while, too." Sebastian's soft smile made her roll her eyes. Honestly, sometimes her bodies constant food requirements were embarrassing.

"Are you sure you can get us back here, though?" Angie asked, reluctant to leave now that they were there. If they didn't let her back, she'd be losing access to possible answers. She'd rather stay and camp here than risk not being allowed back.

"I'll ensure they do. Given what you've seen today… Answers we'd assumed weren't here might well be. And some of those answers, some of what you find, could help us in our fights going forward." Gabriella shrugged. "I'll make them understand the importance of allowing you back."

"Morty will object to a second visit."

"Maybe. Maybe not. He still thinks you're dying and all of this is pointless."

Possibly. But Angie had her doubts. Morty had *said* he believed she was dying and so there was no point in trying to kill her anymore. But he'd also been lying. She just wasn't sure what he'd been lying about yet.

"You need to rest," Sebastian said quietly to Angie. "You won't be able to see what you need to see here if you're too warn out. You'll just miss things."

He was right. She knew he was right.

"Fine. We'll leave for now. But I want back in tomorrow. Can that be arranged?" A good night sleep and plenty of food and she'd be ready to face these demons, as well as her own, again.

"I'll see what I can do."

She'd have to trust Gabriella and hope for the best.

Angie still found leaving all this information and the possibility of real answers behind difficult, and hesitated as they walked away from the nook of demon witch books. Somewhere in there she knew she'd find what she needed. She was more certain of that now.

But it was a little like a needle in a haystack.

And she only had so much time to find that needle before everything collapsed.

CHAPTER SIX

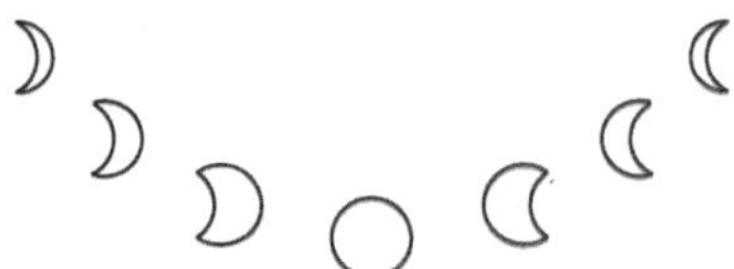

Thanks to the protein bar and bottle of water, Angie didn't need to dip into the first restaurant or fast-food place they passed, so they took their time, wandering down Broadway as it angle across the streets, heading toward Harold Square and a pizza place that Angie and Sebastian both liked. A couple of slices and a mental rest were in order.

While it had felt like they were in the records room for hours, most of a day at least, not much time had actually passed. Three hours at most. It was early enough in the evening to still get them caught in the pedestrian traffic at the end of a work day, and the car traffic was so thick she was glad she didn't bother driving in the city. She'd sold her car right after driving across country to move here.

She didn't like to think about that trip much, though.

She'd left Sebastian to move here. To try and escape the demon hunter world.

Fat lot of good that had done her. She'd broken both their hearts for, in the end, no reason. And she still resented, and regretted, that.

But she had him in her life again. That's what mattered.

She was still working on ensuring her raw psychic senses were contained, so they didn't hold hands as they maneuvered through the crowds. But he stuck close to her, despite all the people. And a few times, their path opened up enough, she knew he'd exerted a small amount of will to get people to move aside and leave them some space. Still, it took effort not to bounce off other people. And she wasn't entirely successful.

The first two times were fine. No accidental readings of strangers. But the third and fourth time she unfortunately picked up some details she'd have rather not. Well, one was innocuous enough. Just a tourist and their worries. She got similar during work hours when she was doing readings for her clients. But the second was someone who was an asshole thinking asshole thoughts that, if she allowed herself to focus on them, would send her into a spiral of being pissed off at humanity.

She was *way* too emotionally strung out for that kind of anger. So she pushed the brief vision aside and worked a little harder to avoid bumping into anyone.

Despite both hers and Sebastian's efforts, though, the sidewalks along Broadway between Times Square and Harold Square were jammed. They were crossing one of the wider streets, nearly to a more open near Macy's when yet another man bumped into her. Not a small man either. Someone a few inches taller than her, and wide enough to knock her a step sideways. She started to scowl.

Then the images rushed into her, rolling through her so fast she didn't have time to shut down her psychic senses. The whole thing was so fast, slamming into her so hard, she lost her breath. Froze in the middle of the crosswalk as the images poured in.

Death. Blood. Anger. Amusement. Sadistic pleasure. Screams. Satisfaction.

So much blood.

Angie wrenched her mind away from the horrid vision so hard, she stumbled. Sebastian caught her and then released her quickly enough she didn't accidentally read him as well.

"Ang?" he asked, standing next to her close enough to ensure the other pedestrians moved around her.

Which was good because she couldn't move. She stared at the man who was now standing on the sidewalk. Looking at her. Smiling.

His eyes flared red.

And then he turned into the crowds and disappeared.

Without thinking, Angie lurched forward to follow him. Pushing through the crowd while simultaneously trying not to touch anyone.

"Ang," Sebastian, more urgently now. "What is it?"

"A demon," she said. "A freed demon."

Sebastian stopped her by moving into her path. She came

up short of touching him and scowled. "What are you doing? He's getting away."

"A freed demon just happened to brush against you in a crowd, revealing himself to you while managing to hide himself from me, and you're going to chase after him without preparing or considering *why* he did that?"

Angie blinked hard at Sebastian as the stupidity of what she'd been doing hit her. What did she think she was going to do if she caught the demon anyway? All that blood and anguish he'd allowed her to see, he wasn't on his way to doing something this very minute. He was showing her who he was. Allowing her to know *what* he was. He wasn't on his way to kill anyone.

And he was free. A freed demon walking past a hunter without the hunter recognizing him. Able to walk through the human world unnoticed. In a city with more than one hunter in residence. Yet none of them had been called to deal with a newly freed demon.

That meant he'd been free for some time.

Slowly, slowly the implications sank in. Not a recently freed demon that the hunters had to go after and stop. Sebastian hadn't been called to the hunt. If this was a demon who'd been free for a while, that meant he was one of the ones who'd made…an arrangement with the hunters. Come to a sort of truce and understanding.

The very sort of arrangements some of the hunters, including Jacob, resented. Apparently, in the last century, because humans with the will to be hunters were becoming more and more rare, the number of hunters growing smaller and smaller, the hunters had had to make more of these arrangements with freed demons to save hunter lives. In exchange for not causing too much mayhem or releasing other demons on the human realm, the freed demons were left to their own devices.

When the demon wasn't particularly strong, and ripping into this realm had drained them even more, and they were just here to live quiet lives where they didn't have to worry about other demons, the demon was granted sanctuary and never caused any trouble again.

When the demon was very strong, and even ripping into this world still left them powerful enough to cause absolute mayhem, including the deaths of more hunters than could be spared, the granting of sanctuary was done out of self-preservation. A truce for both sides to end the fighting. And some of those powerful demons did fall into the sort of lives that didn't cause much trouble. They accumulated wealth and enjoyed the luxuries of this realm without doing anything too serious and destructive.

Others…were not so innocuous.

She'd brushed up against one of the more dangerous ones. She didn't know him, of course. She just knew, from that brief vision, that flash of knowledge he'd allowed her, that he was not living here quietly. And the way he'd been accumulating wealth and power involved the sort of crimes the hunters shouldn't have been tolerating.

Either this freed demon kept his crimes quiet enough they didn't draw the hunters' attention, he filtered most of the crime through human accomplices so he could claim a level of ignorance, or he did enough of both to remain under the radar.

Or he was so powerful, the hunters were tactically ignoring him to save their own lives.

That wasn't a very demon hunter thing to do, though. So Angie suspected the demon filtered his death and destruction through human minions.

But the visions she'd picked up from the man were so grotesque and horrible, so…demonic, she was shaking. Whether her own already sensitive nerves had made this vision worse, or it was just a vision that bad, she wasn't sure. She suspected the latter.

"I wasn't thinking," she said to Sebastian. "Sorry. The… What he showed me, what I picked up in that touch was horrible. I… I wasn't thinking."

Sebastian nodded, then eased her to the side of the sidewalk without actually touching her, willing them a bubble of space where no people got too close as Angie got herself together.

"Who the hell was that?" she asked, searching the crowd.

The man had completely disappeared. If he'd expected her to follow and keep up with him, he obviously hadn't wanted to make that too easy. Or maybe he hadn't expected her to follow. Could never be certain with demons. The bastards engaged in levels of complex machinations that usually made her head hurt.

"And why did he want me to know he was a demon?" She met Sebastian's gaze again.

"Good questions. Which I don't have answers to." He

followed the direction she'd been looking, taking in the thick crowds. "Whatever he wanted, he knew what he was doing. Who he was approaching."

"How did he even find us on a crowded random street in New York?"

"Another good question."

"Good questions do us no good without answers," she snapped, irritated and raw and shaken. She felt bad about snapping the instant the words left her mouth. "Sorry. I didn't mean to take my annoyance and fear out on you." Because she was afraid now. Very afraid.

She was trying to uncover a way to stop the demon magic she'd absorbed from killing her, harboring the knowledge that she could *kill* a demon now, and worried that somehow that information had gotten out to other demons. The last thing she needed was a demon stalking her and complicating things.

Putting a target on her back.

A target, she had to accept, might already be there thanks to what had happened in New Mexico.

"Let's get somewhere safe," Sebastian said. "With food. And I'll contact Gabriella. She'll have records of all the freed demons in this part of the country. You remember what his human form looked like?"

"And I can tell you what his demon form looks like. He didn't hide that from me in the vision."

"Good. That'll help. But we need to get you somewhere safe and private first."

He eased her to the edge of the road, put up a hand, and a

taxi pulled up three seconds later. She pressed her lips together, biting back a smile. Only a demon hunter with a will strong enough to fend off demons could will an available New York City taxi to the curb that quickly.

"Be sure your psychic senses are locked down," he murmured as he opened the back door. "This thing will be full of psychic residue."

She'd been trying to do just that and having a hell of a time controlling the skill thanks to her time in the archive. If she hadn't been having trouble already, a taxi wouldn't be an issue. But her normal control over the psychic talent was already wobbly. And now made even more wobbly thanks to that freed demon.

She sucked in a deep, city-scented breath, and climbed into the car, attempting to keep her hands in her lap and her mind blank and her senses, all her senses, shut down.

CHAPTER SEVEN

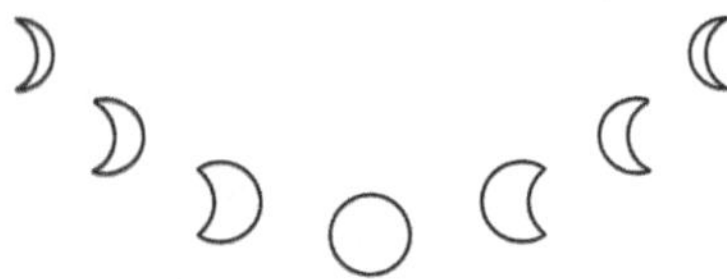

The focus it took to keep from reading anything inside the taxi took all Angie's concentration, so she let Sebastian deal with directing the driver and paying him. She only even noticed where they were going when she climbed carefully back out of the taxi and realized Sebastian had brought them back to her apartment building in the Village.

Upstairs, in her own apartment, she was finally able to take a breath, finally able to relax her concentration and focus. And the release of all the tension and concentration left her exhausted. She sank onto the couch in her living room with a groan, dropping her heavy purse next to the coffee table, and then curling up on the thick cushions as exhaustion swept through her.

She heard Sebastian in the kitchen, heard water, and the click of the electric kettle turning on, a cabinet door opening and closing. She focused on the domestic sounds of him moving around the kitchen, making them tea. Let her body and mind fall into a sort of meditative state, focused entirely on the present moment, the small sounds and feelings, the way the couch felt beneath her cheek, the familiar smell of her home—incense and candle wax under a stronger scent of tea and the soft, subtle smell of the flowers blooming on the cactus she had decorating her blocked off fireplace hearth.

By the time Sebastian joined her with two steaming cups of tea, the scent of Earl Gray wafting around her, she was able to sit up and breathe easy again.

"Well that was a lot of sucky all at once," she said.

"Drink your tea. I'll call Gabriella."

She let her mind continue to drift, only half listening to Sebastian's side of the conversation, as she sipped the rich tea and let its warmth sooth her jangled nerves.

When Sebastian disconnected and set his cellphone aside, she turned to him, her mug still cradled in her hands.

He sighed. "There are two possibilities," he said, "but the most likely is a freed demon that goes by the human name Will Fredericks and is linked with some very bad men. Including our old friend Sokolov."

"Shit."

Gregory Sokolov was a mob boss who was enthrall to a freed demon who absolutely hated Carmen and wanted her dead. Something to do with the Molder demon Carmen had once been enthrall to. Or at least Carmen had played as if she were enthrall to the demon. Angie still wasn't entirely sure that wasn't an act. With Carmen, it was impossible to tell what was real and what was part of some scheme. She seemed to have layers upon layers of deceptions and machinations, and Angie was never sure which was a truth and which was a part of the plan. Carmen wasn't even her real name. Just the name she went by with Angie and Sebastian.

Carmen had used Sokolov in her plan to force Angie to learn to open portals without trees. The plan had involved Sokolov nearly getting his head ripped off by a demon, so needless to say, the mobster hated Carmen on multiple levels now. And if the freed demon who'd purposefully shown himself to Angie earlier was the one Sokolov served, then he was a very bad, very dangerous demon.

Not that they weren't all bad and dangerous. But one who did evil through mobsters and still managed to *not* violate the terms of his hunter-granted sanctuary here was both extremely clever and probably also extremely powerful.

None of this was good news.

"Why the hell did he track me down and purposefully show himself to me?" she asked, setting her now empty mug aside.

"You want another?" Sebastian asked, nodding to the cup.

She waved that away. "I need food more, but…" She stilled him with a hand before he could get up. "First, did Gabriella say *why* this Will Fredericks—which is a weirdly boring name for a demon, by the way—has decided to reveal himself to me?"

"She doesn't know. But I have a suspicion."

"Sokolov? He's…trying to repay us for saving him or

something?" The mobster had tried to make a deal with them as repayment and Sebastian had been very clear and very specific about there being no deals made between them—because Sebastian had known about Sokolov's links with a demon and knew what any of those deals would mean.

"Or he's still after Carmen. Or they've learned about your newest ability."

"How the hell could they know about that? It's only been two weeks."

But she'd been afraid news might have traveled through the demon world. Afraid somehow word had spread. She'd been worried since New Mexico that there was a target on her back. And if this demon had tracked her down for that reason, her worst fears were true.

"We won't know for sure until he finds us again," Sebastian said. "Don't panic yet. This likely has to do with Sokolov thinking he owes us for his life."

"They could have tracked us down months ago if this was that," she said. "The timing, now, is too coincidental."

Sebastian's mouth tightened, but he didn't attempt to convince her otherwise.

"Shit," she said again. "Now what?"

"Now? You eat."

He rose to go to her landline, which had the number of her favorite delivery places programed into it, just as, from inside the depths of her purse, her cellphone buzzed with an incoming text.

She dug out the cell, worried it might be her mother—who'd been texting with her regularly since New Mexico to make sure everything was okay. Her mother didn't know all the details, but she knew something had happened. And while she didn't push Angie for answers, answers they both knew Angie couldn't give for her parents' safety—the less they knew the better—she did know things were…dangerous for Angie now.

And Angie worried about her parents more since Morty had threatened them as a way of pushing Angie to lose control of her demon witch powers in a messed-up plan to prove to everyone, but most especially Sebastian, that she was too dangerous to leave alive. Morty claimed he was no longer after her family because she was as good as dead now anyway, with the magic she'd absorbed, but Angie didn't trust Morty even a little bit. So she and her mother had been checking in regularly as a way to reassure each other everything was fine.

But when she opened her phone, the message wasn't from her mother.

"Shit." That seemed to be her go-to word this evening.

"What now?" Sebastian set the phone back into the cradle without dialing.

"It's Carmen."

Speak of the devil.

Carmen: *Hey, chica, you still alive?*

Angie snarled at that message before returning: *Fuck off.*

C: *Good. We have a problem.*

A: *Your problems are not my problems.*

C: *This one is. Meet me at that diner you love. Ten minutes.*

"She wants us to meet her," Angie told Sebastian, showing him the texts.

He lifted his brows, but his mouth turned down in a frown. "Don't trust her."

"Of course not. But this can't be a coincidence. Sokolov's demon boss revealing himself to me and Carmen texts less than an hour later?"

"Definitely not a coincidence."

"She's asking to meet in a public place," Angie said.

"And it has food. Which you need anyway."

And it was her favorite diner. And they probably did need to know what Carmen considered a problem for both of them.

A: *Fine. You're buying our dinner. And I'm starving.*

Carmen didn't reply to that, but Angie didn't care. She was already dropping her phone back into her purse as she and Sebastian headed for the door. Her stomach growled in objection to not getting fed yet, but she reassured her body she'd feed it soon.

And Carmen had better hope the food came quick. Angie was not in the mood for bullshit on an empty stomach.

CHAPTER EIGHT

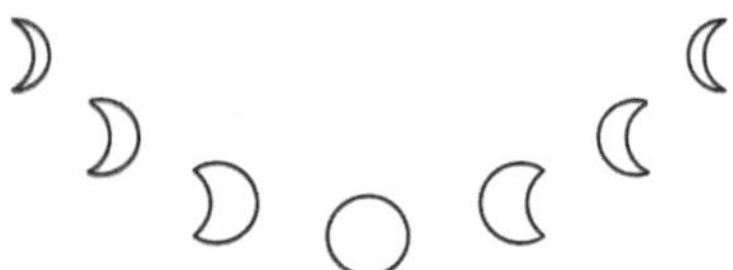

The diner was crowded since it was dinner time for the early eaters, but Carmen had managed to land one of the few booths at the back of the long, narrow restaurant, beyond the long counter with its individual, round swivel seats for customers, and a series of smaller tables and two person booths that lined the wall. The rear of the restaurant opened up a little wider, allowing more space to move, and there were stairs that led up to a second level, with more seating, but that section had been closed off for the last two months for renovation, so the main floor of the diner was even more crowded than usual.

The booth Carmen had finagled was set against the wall near the staircase. Carmen sat on the side that faced the front door. Which meant Angie and Sebastian had to sit across from her with their backs to the door as well as the rest of the restaurant, facing the closed off staircase. That position would make Sebastian a bit twitchy. He liked to be able to see everything going on around them.

Angie slid in first, letting Sebastian stay on the outer part of the bench where he could get up and out fast, knowing he'd be more comfortable that way. She held Carmen's gaze, and didn't snarl at her smirk, but only because she was so hungry now she couldn't be bothered.

"You look feral," Carmen commented. "When did you last eat?"

"Long enough ago that I'm both starving and low on patience. Why are we here?"

"I ordered you a burger and fries already." Carmen smiled at Sebastian. "You too, big guy. Hope that'll work?"

Sebastian grunted.

Carmen turned her smug gaze back on Angie, but the smugness dropped away after a beat. "You remember Sokolov."

"Fuck." Angie didn't even need to hear more. Of *course* this was all linked.

"Word is, his master has decided to take more of an interest in you."

"Why?" Although Angie could already guess.

"New Mexico."

Angie cursed again. "We better stop talking until after I eat or I'm going to break something."

Her anger churned along with the acid in her empty stomach and that made a volatile cocktail. She had control over her anger and the way it made her magic rise again. She'd gone to New Mexico because her anger was calling her magic without any effort on Angie's part, and she'd worried her lack of control was dangerous—for her, lack of control was always dangerous. The work she'd done there with her teacher, Esmerelda, had restored her control. But that didn't mean she wasn't more dangerous when angry. And hungry and angry increased that danger exponentially.

The burgers Carmen had ordered them all arrived within minutes of Angie and Sebastian sitting down, which proved Carmen might be a lot of not good things, but one thing she was was smart. The burger was cooked exactly as Angie liked, the pretzel bun and melted cheese on the meat savory perfection, and the French fries were salted just right. Angie scarfed down half her burger and most of her fries before she felt settled enough to speak. She was still pissed off, but at least it wasn't worsened by hunger.

"Tell me the rest," she said, motioning to Carmen with a French fry.

"I don't know how he found out," Carmen started. "I've kept my mouth shut. But Jacob and Morty might not have been so discrete."

"You think Morty would have sicced a freed demon on me?"

"He still wants you dead. And you're not yet. Maybe."

It was possible, she supposed. Morty had proved semi-patient with waiting on her to get killed but not indefinitely patient. The problem with Morty being behind this new twist was that he wanted to ensure Sebastian stayed alive and working with the hunters. A lot of Morty's trouble with her stemmed not just from her potential to unleash a demon plague—on accident or on purpose—but the fact that her relationship with Sebastian meant he was more loyal to her than the hunters. And the hunters *needed* Sebastian to continue fighting with them. He and Aidan were the only two hunters who could will certain powerful freed demons back to their realm. Most other hunters could barely handle lower-level freed demons these days. In fact, very few of them still could. It was a problem.

A problem different hunters had different solutions for.

"Jacob doesn't want me dead," she said. "He isn't likely to go telling demons about me."

Jacob wanted her alive and working with the hunters now that he'd seen what she could do. He'd wanted her as far from the hunters as possible before New Mexico, because he thought she weakened them, made things too easy and they weren't developing their wills enough. He'd changed his mind when he saw her kill a demon.

"Unless he wants you to kill Sokolov's boss," Carmen said. "You know how he is about freed demons. Maybe he's setting this one up, rather than trying to get you killed."

Angie sighed and closed her eyes briefly, shaking her head. "Possible," she acknowledged. "Where do you come into all this?"

"Sokolov's boss has wanted me dead for a long time, because of my...relationship to the Molder demon. They were enemies."

"Are there any non-enemies among demons?"

"Alliance form. Just like with humans. And they break apart just like with humans. These two had different ideas of how they wanted to rule this realm. Sokolov's boss wants to keep doing what he's doing. He finds it satisfying and rewarding."

Angie snarled. She'd seen just enough in that brief flash to know what a demon found satisfying and rewarding and it was gross and evil on so many levels it made her head hurt.

Carmen shrugged. "He is a demon."

"Your Molder wanted to unleash his realm on this one. I assume Sokolov's boss didn't approve."

"It would have wrecked the empire he's built. Changed the dynamic with humans. Upended all his decades of work. Of course he didn't approve. I even heard them argue about it once, when the Molder was riding my former associate."

Angie had almost forgotten about that guy. He'd been working with Carmen when they'd first met, and he let the Molder demon ride around in his head, seeing this realm and even being able to interact with it a little through his host, without actually being in this realm. It wasn't like a proper possession, where the demon took over its host in order to enter this realm without losing power. The demon was just a sort of psychic piggy-backer. Here without being *here*. The Molder had used Carmen's associate that way a few times.

After the bone lantern incident, that guy had been taken into custody for various frauds and thefts and was currently serving time in a human prison. All arranged by the hunters. The hunters had not been able to ensure the same thing happened with Carmen. But Angie realized, and Carmen confirmed later, that there were—or had been—at least one powerful hunter who'd been protecting her. Carmen kept skating away from justice thanks to that protection. She didn't have that protection anymore though, according to Carmen. Which made her current predicament even more deadly.

"They aren't the only demons with different…plans for this realm, of course," Carmen continued. "They all have some sort of plan, and that plan usually involves them being the rulers of the realm or some shit. Sometimes they fight over who gets to do what. My former demon associate and Sokolov's boss hated each other, and by extension, hated the humans working with and for the other one. Which means Sokolov's boss hates me."

"And after what you did to Sokolov, I imagine the grudge is worse."

Carmen shrugged. "Sokolov might hate me more. His boss would have been inconvenienced by his death but not enough to want me any more dead than he already did. The problem now is that Sokolov's boss knows I helped you. And will absolutely keep you away from him. He wants you enthrall to him. That requires I die."

Angie stared at Carmen for a long time, trying to believe, or even understand, what she had just said. Carmen wasn't her friend. They weren't close. And Carmen had done some monumentally horrible things to Angie and Sebastian. Angie wanted Carmen in jail and no longer working with demons for her revenge plots. Angie thought Carmen's brand of vigilante justice was dangerous and got innocent people killed.

They were *not* friends.

The idea that Carmen would help her and try to keep her from being killed by demon enemies didn't match up with Angie's *idea* of Carmen. There had to be an ulterior motive—which could just be as simple as, like Jacob, Carmen wanted to use Angie's newfound demon killing skills for her own machinations. Angie couldn't trust Carmen as far as she could throw her. So there *had* to be an ulterior motive for Carmen here.

"I will not be enthralled to a demon," Angie said. "So Sokolov's boss is barking up the wrong tree. So to speak."

"Tell him that," Carmen said.

"If he tries to get anywhere near her, the terms of his sanctuary will be canceled and all bets will be off," Sebastian said.

That surprised Angie enough, she turned to face him. "How so? I thought he could get away with all that evil through loopholes and stuff. Using humans to do the dirty work."

"He can. He does. But coming after you isn't the same. Even if he sends his humans to do it."

"Why?"

Sebastian met her gaze, the faint red in the depths of his eyes easy to confuse for a trick of the light in the bright diner. "Because, technically, you're still a demon hunter."

"Even if I suck at the job as it's supposed to be done?"

"Even if," he said with a slight smile. "And part of the terms of sanctuary are that the demons do not go after or interfere with the hunters in any way. Going after you, trying to use or kill or enthrall you, all of that is interfering with a demon hunter, and means the demon violates his sanctuary terms. Deals off. He can be sent back to the demon realms."

"But can he? I mean that literally. Can he? The hunters wouldn't have made a deal with him if he wasn't powerful enough to have been killing hunters before being given sanctuary, right?"

That was the whole reason Jacob feared her weakening the hunters and now wanted her to work with them. The compromises the hunters had had to make with certain powerful demons over the years didn't sit well with him.

"I can send him back," Sebastian said, with so much confidence, Angie believed him. "If Aidan joins me, there won't be a question."

"And if I open a portal?"

"Even less complicated."

"Which is why he's after Sebastian," Carmen said.

"Wait, what?"

"He will come for Sebastian. Kill him first. You'll be weak in your grief and easier to enthrall. He wins."

"And you're just a bonus kill?" But Angie's heartbeat had started to thump so hard she was nearly dizzy with it. The thought of Sebastian being killed left her breathless, terrified in a way that nothing but a threat to her family could replicate. A panic rushed through her blood, and she wanted to spin up a protection circle around Sebastian this very moment, keep him in a bubble of protection where no one could get to him. Especially this demon.

He was capable. He was a really strong demon hunter. His will had bested some of the strongest demons. He'd survived inside a demon realm and kept Carmen alive while doing it. He'd had her back while she got them out of the demon realm. He'd been working as a demon hunter for longer than he'd admit to her. And he was still alive.

He wasn't as vulnerable as her more ordinary family who didn't know much about or deal with demons on a regular basis.

And all that knowledge did nothing to prevent her from wanting to wrap him up in protective magic and keep him safe forever.

She let the panic building under her skin ease out with slow, deep breaths, but the rush of adrenaline had her hands shaking. She fisted them in her lap so Carmen wouldn't see.

"I'm an old grudge," Carmen said. "In the way, since I'm on your side."

"That sounds wrong."

"It's true, chica, even if you don't want to believe it."

"I believe you want to use me," Angie said.

"Which is why I'm on your side."

Angie rolled her eyes. But what did she expect from Carmen. Actually, Angie did like Carmen's blunt honesty when it came to her motivations. At least some of her motivations.

"But getting to either of us, enthralling you, won't work

if your demon hunter boyfriend gets in the way. He'll attempt to kill Sebastian. Then he'll come for you."

"No," Sebastian said.

That was it. That simple. Just a no.

"No to what?" Carmen asked.

"All of it. No to him killing me. No to him enthralling Angie. No to all of it."

"Including killing me?" Carmen asked with a brow raise.

"If I wanted you dead, you would have stayed in the demon realm," he said.

Carmen gave him that with a head tilt. "Fair enough. You might also want to warn Aidan. She's the only other hunter with a hope of sending him back. He'll want her dead too so she can't get in the way of him enthralling our demon witch."

"I am not *your* demon witch."

Carmen just smiled.

"Thank you for filling us in," Angie said after a moment, reluctantly, but sincerely. Carmen hadn't had to warn them. "What will you do?"

"I'll be around, and careful. But I might call on you if things get dicey. We have a mutually beneficial reason to stop this guy."

Angie let out a long breath. She was very reluctant to trust Carmen enough to work on the same side of anything as her, and yet, as Sebastian said, they didn't want Carmen dead. They wanted her to have consequences for her actions. Angie also couldn't trust that Carmen had told them everything. She'd told them what she needed to to ensure they did what she wanted them to do.

What did she want them to do?

"We can't go after this demon until he's somehow broken sanctuary, can we?" she asked Sebastian, just to be certain.

"No. He's protected until he violates the deal he made."

"Demon deals," she huffed. "What are the chances he's found a loophole in that deal?"

"Excellent," Carmen said. "He's a vicious, dangerous, deadly asshole. But he's smart as all hell. One of the smartest demons I've ever encountered."

"Then why the hell did you get on his bad side by using one of his men in that plot to force me to open portals without trees?"

"Sokolov is a bad person. If Sebastian hadn't had a strong enough will to keep that demon from killing him, and he'd had his head ripped off, the world wouldn't miss him. Neither would I. Besides, I was already on the demon's shit list because of my former associate. Killing Sokolov wouldn't have made that worse. What's making him come for me now is you."

Angie hated that on so many levels, but she was more upset that all this had brought Sebastian to the demon's attention.

"You haven't been using his human name," Angie said. She hadn't either. Demon names had power. But they rarely gave out their real names. The demon hunters were the same, rarely using the names they were born with, certainly not sharing them. But, as far as she'd been able to tell, using a freed demon's adopted "human" name didn't have that same sort of power. She'd just been following Carmen's lead without thinking about it, and it had only just occurred to her what they were doing.

"Habit," Carmen said. "I learned his real name, his demon name, while I was working with the Molder. I don't want to slip and say that on accident. It's how I think of him, rather than as Will Fredericks, so I don't use either."

That was fair enough. With demons, safer was always better. Not that Carmen did that nearly as often as she should with demons.

"So what now? We can't go after him unless he breaks the rules of his deal with the hunters. But if he comes after me or Sebastian, that is him breaking the rules, so we can defend ourselves *and* send him back. Right?"

Sebastian grunted an affirmative.

"So…we wait?"

"Or you ignore hunter rules and take him out before he gets to you," Carmen said. She held Angie's gaze. "You can kill him now."

She murmured this quietly, even though there was little need. From the start, they all knew Sebastian was willing other diners not to overhear them or they wouldn't have been able to talk so freely.

"I'm not sure how many times I have to tell you I'm not a murderer for you to believe me, but I'm not a murderer, and I'm not going to just go kill someone because it would make my life easier. They come after me or mine, I will defend myself and the people I love. That is a different animal than hunting someone down to murder them."

This was not the first time Carmen had suggested she go

after a threat and kill them before they could kill her. And maybe in Carmen's world that made sense. Even to the pragmatic-to-a-fault demon hunters, that might make sense. Morty had definitely been walking that line.

But it went against everything Angie believed in. Her witch's soul believed in balance, and that what you put out into the world would come back to you. She didn't do real magic curses for that very reason. She might do a spell that involved people getting what they put out into the world, but those spells only turned negative if the person in question was doing negative things.

In Angie's world, hunting someone down to murder them, even if it eliminated a threat, was evil. She had enough people thinking she was evil because of the demon witch powers. She wasn't about to add actual murderer to their list of reasons to view her as dangerous.

"One day," Carmen said, "you'll have to accept that sometimes getting your hands dirty and doing what's necessary is the only option for justice."

"No," Angie said. And left it at that.

"Fine," Carmen said with a shrug, "but don't say I didn't warn you."

"Why is it that every time you warn me about something, that something blows up in my face?"

"Can't blame me for Morty. He hates what you are without my help."

"Sokolov and his boss I can blame you for. I wouldn't be on their radar without you."

"You also wouldn't have escaped that demon realm

without me pushing you to learn you could open portals without trees."

"You'd have been dead there too." She scowled. "And we wouldn't have been in that demon realm without me opening a portal without a tree."

"Then Jacob's demon would have just killed us all. Accept it, chica. I'm your patron saint. I'm the one ensuring you survive."

"No," Angie said again. Because while Carmen was right on some level, a lot of Angie's current predicament could be traced to things Carmen did. Not all. Morty and Jacob had a lot to answer for. So did the entire demon hunter council. But Carmen's part wasn't loaded with good intentions.

Angie paused as something occurred to her, not for the first time. "You've seen the histories the hunters keep, haven't you? The ones that use the term demon witch. Is that where you learned portals without trees were possible?"

That information had been in the big overview book of the history of demon witches, the first thing she'd read that day. Information that Morty and Gabriella had had well before Angie knew it was possible. And information Carmen had had.

Carmen ignored the question. "Sokolov's boss is patient and vicious. But now that he's decided he wants you, he'll come for Sebastian soon. Don't let your guards down. And if you have to kill him, don't hesitate. The world is better off without him. Even the demon realms are better off without him."

Angie didn't even have to know more about the demon

than that brief vision to know this was one thing she and Carmen could agree on. The world would be better off without this particular demon moving through it.

But Angie didn't want to be forced into doing what Carmen suggested. Mostly because she was afraid.

Afraid that if she killed another demon, she risked becoming a monster herself.

CHAPTER NINE

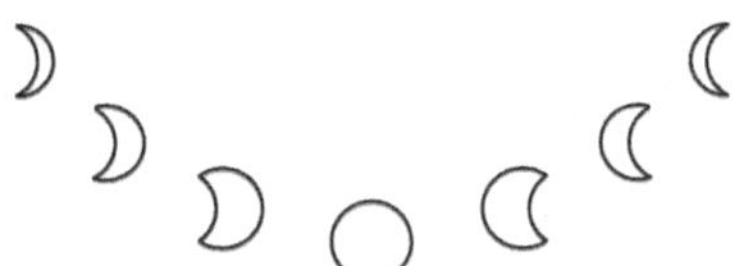

At work the next afternoon, Angie found it hard to focus her complete attention on her clients. She'd only done a couple of readings since returning, for some regulars, and only two full shifts. And she'd been distracted those days too, but for different reasons. Then, she'd been anxious about getting to see the hidden histories on demon witches that the hunters kept. Now, she couldn't stop thinking about the newest demonic threat, a threat that put Sebastian in danger. Again.

Not that Sebastian wasn't always in danger from demons. It was his job. But this felt too personal. Not the ordinary demon trouble.

She forced herself to focus on the young woman who'd walked in off the street for a reading, and who was having trouble at college. Angie usually liked working with people like this, seekers who just wanted some clarity when it came to a decision they'd essentially already made. Being able to lead them to accept that decision always felt very satisfying, when she could see the decision was the right one for them. But the effort to keep her focus on her client took a toll and she was exhausted by the end of the reading.

She watched the grateful, relieved woman leave through the velvet, stars and moon covered drape that covered the door into the reading room Angie had been assigned that day. She usually loved this room. The energy in it felt good to her and she seemed to do her best work in here. The large round wooden table in the center, the ever-present scent of incense, even when she wasn't burning anything, the dim lighting that let her concentrate. Most of the time, she didn't use cards or the scrying bowls or crystal balls that some of the other psychics might use when working with clients. But there was a lovely copper scrying bowl in this room that she had used before and sometimes did like to pull out as a prop for readings.

Mostly, she just liked this space, and she liked the soft murmur of the other people working on the third floor of Dana's Cauldron, her colleagues and friends. She felt more at home here than she did in most other places. And if she could, she'd have left the demon world far behind to just be a witch and live this life.

Unfortunately, the demon world refused to give her up.

She wasn't due another client for a half hour, and no walk-ins needed her, so she headed to the second floor of the shop for a tea, an herby blend that the owners had started mixing up as an exclusive to the shop. A combination of cardamom and green tea and lemon that Angie really loved. Then she went down to the main floor of the shop to visit with Laura and make sure all was well.

The threats looming meant she was restless. But sometimes her restlessness meant something bad was about to happen.

Sometimes, it just meant she needed a snack.

Laura Fuentes was an older witch who'd been working at Dana's for decades, probably since the owners had opened the place. She kept her thick, steel gray hair pulled back in a braid most days, and today was sporting a shirt that looked like a tie-dyed poet shirt in bright reds and pinks and greens. The colors suited her pale brown complexion. Her leather choker with the shark's tooth hanging from it was framed by the loose shirt collar. The choker was gift from her friends when she came out as trans in the seventies. The shark's tooth came from a cheap jewelry shop around the corner from Dana's, but Laura liked to tell people who asked that she got it as a gift from a shark she was communing with in the Pacific Ocean. More than a few of the tourists believed that story.

Laura was also a superb aura reader, and often used that skill when she was working the retail floor and cash register. Sometimes to ensure the customers and clients were safe for the staff, sometimes just out of habit because she could be nosey. Before New Mexico, Laura had been helping Angie work on her skills at aura reading. Angie still wasn't up to Laura's talent, but she was much better than she'd been before they started working together.

And as soon as she settled her current demon-related trouble, she wanted to get back to those lessons. Working with Laura on witchy skills kept Angie grounded and reminded her she was a witch, first and foremost. That assurance that she was really, in her bones, a witch and not a demon hunter—or, her worst fear, somehow becoming as monstrous as the demons—kept her from losing her focus. Now that she had control over her magic again, she intended on doing more witchy things, too. Beyond just her day job and training with Laura. If she survived this latest threat, she wanted to concentrate on being *more* a witch than anything else.

She hoped she'd get a chance to do that.

The main floor of the store, the retail part with tables and shelves of all things pagan and witchy, was busy that afternoon. As the weather warmed up, more people went for walks, and more locals as well as tourists dropped in to scan the shelves. The scent of incense and wax from a handful of lit candles blended with the slight chlorine smell from a small waterfall display near the register. The glass cabinet under the register was filled with crystals and some of the more specialized and expensive tarot decks. The lighting was up this afternoon as it was bright and sunny outside, and that meant some of the wear and tear on the wooden shelves and well-loved older tables could be seen. But it all just added to the overall ambiance.

Angie loved this place. It was her home away from home. And even filled with tourists, half of whom had just come to gawk at the "witches," Dana's always felt like a sanctuary to her.

So when she spotted Gregory Sokolov stepping through the main door, the little bell overhead ringing merrily, she snarled.

"Isn't that that mob guy?" Laura asked under her breath, her attention also zeroed in on Sokolov.

"That's him."

"What's he doing here again? Thought that…situation was handled."

"It was. Something new has come up."

They had a few moments to observe Sokolov before he noticed Angie, and in those few minutes, he seemed extremely uncomfortable. Edgy. His gaze dancing around, a scowl wrinkling his brow, his hands running up and down the lapels of his dark, immaculate suit. The last time he'd been here, he'd looked around casually, curious but not necessarily dismissive. Maybe a little bored? But he'd been comfortable enough.

This time he looked like he wanted to bolt for the door before doing whatever it was he came here to do.

Which meant he was here intending harm.

The owners of Dana's Cauldron kept the place encircled and bespelled. They couldn't cut it off from the outside world obviously, because it had to welcome in strangers off the street. But they had arranged a circle that made people who wished ill toward the inhabitants of the store, or the store itself, edgy and uncomfortable when they walked inside. The circle ensured people who were dangerous left fast, before they could cause any harm. It was one of the reasons Angie felt safe here. Why she loved the place so much.

A demon or demon minion could walk inside Dana's. A witch or wizard will ill intent could walk in. Hell, any bad guy really, including ordinary human threats, could walk in. They might even manage to stay for a few minutes. But if they intended harm, they left fast. The spell left them so uncomfortable, so nervous and jittery and threatened, they turned and exited within minutes. And before they left, there were any number of witches on staff ready to defend the place if needs be.

In the two and a half years Angie had worked here, the circle had never failed to do its job. The witches had never had to do more than wait out an intruder and keep an eye on them until they left. No one had ever been hurt inside Dana's. No one had had to even feel uncomfortable for very long.

Sokolov hadn't meant harm the last time he'd been here. He was looking for Angie to repay her for what she'd done to help his brother-in-law. Until Carmen had kidnapped and used him in one of her plots, Angie thought that would be the extent of her dealings with the gangster. And even after that, since she and Sebastian had saved Sokolov's life, she'd assumed any dealings with him after would be...cordial at least.

But he was sweating and fidgeting and his gaze kept jumping back to the door. Which meant he was a danger to someone in here. Maybe her. Maybe the entire place. There was no telling. A danger she'd brought here.

One she intended on getting rid of before he caused trouble for anyone else.

"I'll get him out of here. We can talk on the street," she told Laura. "I won't go far."

"Step back inside if things get dicey." Laura motioned to the counter under the register. "After that minion with the demon riding him managed to remain in the store so long, the owners have been working on a backup to the circle. They installed it while you were gone. If needs be, I can press this button and trigger a spell that will shut the place up tight. No one allowed inside. No one can get out either, but so long as we keep the customers distracted, no one inside will notice they can't leave. It'll last long enough to keep us safe from most threats and we can turn it off again when the threat leaves."

Angie smiled and let out a long sigh. "I love this place and all of you so much."

"We've got your back. Stay near the door. I'll watch from here. If his aura changes, I'll flash the lights over the door. That'll be your signal to come back inside."

"Got it." She gave Laura a quick hug, then made her way through the display tables and cabinets to reach Sokolov.

The minute she started toward him, he spotted her. His expression changed, a welcoming smile lifting his mouth, the creases along his brow smoothing. He was a distinguished looking older man, blond hair and light blue eyes. A sharp, hard jaw. He wore his power and position the way he wore that perfectly tailored suit, easily and like he was owed it all. A man who was used to getting his way in all things.

Not someone to cross.

The smile of greeting dropped even before she reached him though as the spell on the place went back to work making him edgy and feeling the need to leave.

"Angela Jordan," he greeted when she got close enough he didn't have to speak loudly. "It's a pleasure to see you again. Long time."

"I assumed the last time was the last time, Gregory Sokolov," she said. "I'm afraid I can't return the sentiment that this is a pleasure. Shall we step outside to speak. More privacy."

He looked so relieved at her suggestion, he let her insult go without comment.

They moved back out onto the narrow, crowded Village sidewalk. She stayed closed to the door, tucked back against the large window with the display of an Indian goddess and various crystals and incense and soft patterned material draped to show off the merchandise. This time of the afternoon, the side of the road where Dana's was located was in shade, which left it cooler and, for Angie, more comfortable than if they'd been standing in full sun.

She watched the pedestrians passing, the cars inch down the narrow one-way street, ensuring Sokolov hadn't brought and stationed any of his associates nearby. She even tried to scan for the auras of any dangerous people. In such a crush of individuals, her efforts weren't very successful. But she was pretty sure this conversation was just between her and Sokolov. For now.

"What brings you here?" Angie asked. "I thought our business was finished months ago."

"I thought you might like to know that my niece is doing much better thanks to the witch healer's information. The doctors have found out what the problem was, and she's been receiving the appropriate treatment for the last six months. She's nearly recovered. She will be able to live a long time. Thanks to you."

"I'm glad to hear she's well."

Sokolov's brother-in-law had a child that, when they'd met, was seriously ill. Carmen had used that information to talk the brother-in-law into summoning a demon to help cure his child. It was a test for Angie and Sebastian. And it was one of the many things that Carmen had done that ensured Angie couldn't actually like the woman. The way she used people's deepest vulnerabilities in her plots, without any thought to the harm she did those people, just pissed Angie off.

"Between that and your help with the other witch, I am in your debt."

"No. No debts between us. No deals." She'd learned from Sebastian to ensure that was made very clear.

Sokolov smiled faintly, his narrow lips pulled tight with the expression. "You assume I'll form some sort of demon deal with you?"

"Your boss purposefully brushed up against me yesterday. Let me know who he was. What he was."

Sokolov titled his head in a shrug of acknowledgement. "You are a fascination to him."

"You told him what happened. In that office building. With Carmen."

"Of course. And I told him what you could do. He's been…interested in you since. But something has changed in that interest in the last few weeks. I think you have developed new skills, no? Something that makes you even more interesting."

"Nothing I'm going to discuss. With you or your boss. I'm not interested in whatever it is he's selling. He can turn his interest to someone else."

"He can be interested in more than one thing at once. Carmen for instance. He's been very interested in her for some time. He would like to…deal finally with that interest."

"That's between him and Carmen."

Though Angie had a sinking feeling she'd get pulled into helping Carmen with that situation whether she liked it or not. Carmen's methods appalled her. But she didn't wish death by demon on even her worst enemies. Carmen might be courting that kind of death, but if Angie could prevent it, she would.

She wouldn't be happy about getting sucked into another of Carmen's plots and troubles, but she'd keep the woman alive if she could.

"You are right," Sokolov said. "That is not why I'm here. I'm here to convey my boss's wish for a meeting."

"No." Angie had to fight the knee-jerk reaction to be polite in her refusal. But any weakness would be played on. And even social niceties could be considered weaknesses when dealing with a demon. Or in this case, a demon's minion.

"No…what?"

"I do not wish to have a meeting with your boss. I will not be meeting with your boss."

"You seem to assume this is an invitation you can refuse. It is not. My boss wishes to meet with you. Therefore, you will meet with him."

"No. Invitation or not, I'm not at your boss's beck and call. I will not be meeting with him."

"Voluntarily or involuntarily are of little difference to him."

"He attempts to bring me involuntarily, he'll regret it."

Sokolov's mouth lifted in another of those soft smiles. "I suspect that's exactly why he wishes to speak with you." He glanced back at the shop window just as the light overhead flickered. "We'll be going to him now. You should go get your bag and let your employer know you need the rest of the day off."

Angie made a show of working her jaw, of keeping in a snarl. Made a show of being reluctant and wanting to argue and showing all the stubborn refusals rising to the surface at that order. She wouldn't consider herself much of an actress, not like Carmen, but she felt every one of the emotions she was showing Sokolov. Every single one. Which meant showing him her resistance to his order was easy.

"No," she said again. Just to ensure Sokolov bought her act.

"It will be easier on you if we do this…cordially,"

Sokolov said, all hints of smiles dropping away. His expression hardened and his eyes took on that dead, dangerous look she'd seen when he'd looked at Carmen all those months ago. This was the dangerous, deadly gangster who did not take no for an answer. "Your boyfriend saved my life that day. Kept the witch's demon from killing me. I would hate to repay that effort by killing him. But that would not stop me. Or my boss."

Angie snarled and took a step toward Sokolov before she even thought about what she was doing. She felt her magic rising under her skin, and fisted her hands to control the sparks dancing along her fingertips. She shut down the rise in power fast, and controlled the anger with two deep breaths.

But that automatic reaction had revealed too much. Nothing Sokolov hadn't already known, or suspected. Still, she cursed in her head when she realized she'd played right into his hands.

The light overhead flickered again.

Angie stepped back from Sokolov, pulling in a long, deep breath. "Wait here. I'll be right back." She snarled at him and turned into the shop.

The minute she was through the door, she felt the spell come up. Felt the shield lock the place down. Everyone inside was now completely sealed off and protected from everything outside. Including Sokolov.

She turned back to look at him through the display windows. He was scanning the street and seemed unaware of the change for a beat, two. And then he snarled and looked back at the store. He went for the door handle and jerked his hand away, shaking it hard, like he'd gotten an electrical shock.

He met her gaze through the window. Shook his head.

She held his gaze without reacting at all. No headshakes, no smiles, no sign of emotion he might use against her.

Because she made an effort to look, she saw his aura flare and change. It happened too fast for her to pick out the colors and interpret them. She just wasn't good enough yet. But the change was obvious to her.

Another moment passed, him holding her gaze. Then he mouthed, "I'll be back." And turned down the street, heading away from Dana's.

Laura came up behind Angie, watching Sokolov disappear into the crowd with her. "We'll announce a sale on tea and pastries upstairs, keep everyone occupied for a half hour to make sure he's gone."

"Thanks." Angie gave Laura a shoulder hug. "Thanks for all this."

"We've got your back," Laura repeated. "But you might want to call Sebastian."

"Yeah. Yeah, I think I'd better."

Because there was definitely a demon after him now.

CHAPTER TEN

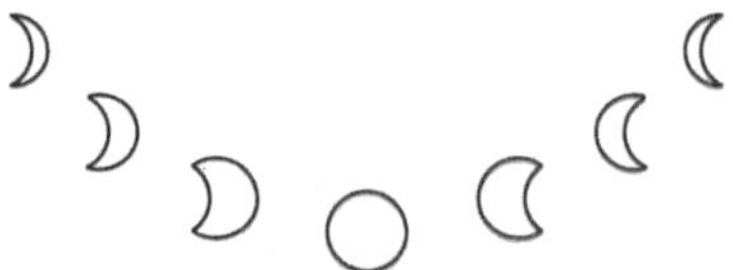

Sebastian was waiting outside Dana's the minute they released the lockdown and opened the place back up to the public.

Angie walked right into his arms, more than relieved he was okay. The scent of his soap surrounded her, reassuring and settling. The threats against him were going to make leaving him alone impossible. How where they supposed to get any work done?

He pulled back and brushed her hair back from her face, cupping her cheeks. "You're okay?"

"Fine. More worried about you. I had backup." She nodded to Laura who was currently behind the register helping a customer who'd realized they were late for something and had to leave immediately.

Laura hadn't mentioned it, but apparently, there was a little light time-confusion spell mixed in with the spell that locked the place down, so that the ordinary humans trapped inside didn't realize how much time passed while they were locked inside.

That spell collapsed when the lockdown spell was shut off, so now a few people were realizing they'd spent entirely too much time browsing. That was, ironically, good for business. People remembered the stores and cafes where they lost track of time and just enjoyed themselves, remembered those places fondly, and returned frequently. Like bookstores and libraries, shops that made them forget time were precious.

"I've never been so relieved you work in a shop full of witches and run by witches," Sebastian said, leaning his forehead against hers. "Tell me everything."

She took him upstairs to the small café so they could get tea—the tea here met his snobby tea standards—and sat in a corner. The seating area, so recently hopping with people, slowly emptied until there were only two humans sitting at the other tables, reading and sipping their drinks. Sebastian used a little bit of will to ensure their conversation was quiet and Angie told him about the conversation with Sokolov.

"Confirms what Carmen said. They'll come after you to get to me." Angie sipped her cardamon and citrus blend, but had to wrap her hands tight around the porcelain mug to keep them from visibly trembling. The adrenaline rush of fear as she'd waited for Sebastian to get here was ebbing now, leaving her shakier and more rattled than the standoff with Sokolov had.

Sebastian stared down into his cup for a long moment,

before saying, "I wasn't going to tell you this, because the last few months have been a lot, and you've a lot on your mind, but…"

She paused with the cup halfway to her mouth. "But?"

"Sokolov's people have been attempting to follow me. For months. Not doing anything about it, just trying to trace my comings and goings. They fail the minute I leave your apartment, of course. But they know where you live, so…"

"So, they know where you are when you're there." She tightened her hold on her mug, focused her rising anger and fear on warming the water without boiling it. The effort to channel the rising magic into a spell that didn't go too far, that had to be carefully controlled, gave her the time and focus necessary to redirect the sharp and instant rise in her magic from the terror of what could have happened at any point in the last six months.

While she'd been too distracted worrying about herself.

"Fuck," she muttered when she'd finished with the spell and her tea was warmer than it had been the moment before. "Fuck."

"Given the…change in their goals," Sebastian said slowly, "it might be good if we didn't stay in your apartment for a few days."

"I'll still have to come into work, though." She didn't ask where they'd stay. He'd had someplace to live before they'd gotten back together. He'd never told her where, but she'd assumed that was because it was one of the many properties demon hunters owned to give their hunters places to stay around the world when they were between hunts.

"And you're not willing to take more time off."

He wasn't asking a question, she noticed. He knew her too well. "I've already gotten so much leeway from the owners. I can't ask them to do more."

"Even with the threat that could endanger their customers?"

Angie let loose another series of cusses, knowing it would be safer for everyone at Dana's if she weren't here. But also… "What if Sokolov and his boss try to use this place, these people, to draw me out. The way they want to use you? If I'm not here, that doesn't keep them from attempting to take hostages or threaten the lives of the staff. Dana's can't remain in a state of lockdown. It's a business. It has to remain open for people coming in and out."

Sebastian nodded. "Then we come in for your shifts, I come with you, and we ensure everyone here is safe."

"When I'm not on shift?"

Sebastian's turn to curse into his tea. "I hate dealing with gangsters. As bad as demons."

"And in this case, we're dealing with both." Angie sighed, looking off into the middle distance and shaking her head. "I would never do what Carmen suggested, but sometimes her 'strike first' thinking really is tempting. Cut to the chase and just get the confrontation over with. No waiting around. No risking other people's lives."

"Confront this demon, and you might have to kill him. Are you prepared to do that?"

"If they attack us? Yes. But I don't want to go into a situation with the plan to assassinate the demon, or Sokolov or anyone else." She softened her voice, dropping to an unnecessary whisper to say, "I don't want to be like Carmen, and I don't want to become what she wants me to be. What Jacob would like me to be. I want to be a witch, reading palms in my lovely witch store. I want you. I want a quiet life. I do not want to become a demon assassin. Any more than I've ever wanted to release a demon hoard on the world."

"One day, we'll find a way for you to have that quiet life." He sighed. "I just don't know how to get you there yet."

She wasn't sure either. But her longing for peace had only gotten stronger over this last year. She'd accepted that she'd need to do some demon work to convince the hunters to leave her alone. But things had gotten so much more complicated. Especially since New Mexico.

"Some good news," Sebastian said. "Gabriella says we can return to the records room tomorrow. Morty isn't raising objections anymore. The council agreed to allowing you access easily this time."

"That's suspicious as all hell."

"It is. But in the meantime, we'll be able to do more reading. We still haven't found a way to deal with…"

With the fact that she might die from the magic she'd absorbed in the demon realm. Yeah, she didn't much want to say that part out loud again either.

"So far, it isn't interfering in my work, or my psychic readings. It doesn't seem to affect my witch magic." Except that she got tired when she wasn't using her magic. But she kept hoping that had a more mundane cause, like mental exhaustion from everything that had happened in the last month. "And I really don't feel like I'm dying."

"It still can't be good," Sebastian said. "You're still human and that magic is not."

"But what if…what if there's no way to remove it. Esmerelda didn't think it was going to be possible. What if I'm stuck this way? Then what?"

His jaw worked and he glanced away. They hadn't faced up to that possible reality yet. They'd both been holding onto the idea that they could just get rid of the magic. But what if they couldn't? What if she was stuck this way? What if it didn't kill her, but it did permanently change her?

"Then," Sebastian said, after a moment, "we go forward and deal with that. If it isn't going to kill you, we have time to adjust."

"So long as the demons who, apparently, now know what I can do don't keep trying to kill or use me?"

"That was always a risk. Even when it was just your demon witch powers. There's a reason the hunters attempt to ensure everyone—including demons—think people like you are a myth. Until you, that was relatively easy. Demon witches are rare. Ensuring the stories are turned into tales that could easily be fiction is easier when there isn't a new demon witch popping up every few years."

She snorted a reluctant laugh. "Demons are long-lived. Some of them will remember the last witches."

"Not if they never dealt with them." He shrugged. "That's

not really our problem right now. Right now, we have to deal with Sokolov and his demon boss."

"Without getting anyone killed."

"And without turning you into a killer."

"Fuck," she said again and drank the rest of her tea.

"Exactly," Sebastian said, as he finished his.

HE STAYED IN DANA'S FOR THE REST OF HER SHIFT, AND walked with her home after. Reluctantly, because she loved her apartment, and because she did have wards and protections set up here to keep her and Sebastian safe, she agreed to go somewhere else. For his sake more than her own. If Sokolov knew he could find Sebastian there, he'd come there looking for him while Angie was at work. That was dangerous to everyone in the building, not just Sebastian. Better that the demon and his minions lose track of her and Sebastian all together. At least when they weren't at her place of work.

After some debate, she'd arranged a phone call with the two witches who owned Dana's. They only came into the store a few times a month, and weren't due in for a few weeks, so Angie had to have the conversation over the phone. Though she didn't want to endanger them by revealing too much, and there were things she *couldn't* tell them about the hunters and hunter council, letting them know that a potential Russian gangster and his demon boss might be a threat to the store wasn't something she had to keep secret.

And her fear of being fired to rid them of the person

bringing all this trouble to their store wasn't enough of a reason to keep the danger to herself.

The owners assured her she wasn't being fired, and they'd increase security, warning all the magical and non-magical staff alike what to look out for. They'd even run some drills in the next few days so everyone was prepared.

To her surprise, Dana—the store's namesake—had assured her this wasn't the first time something like this had happened over the last forty years of them being in business. They'd ensure everyone was safe.

And Angie had never loved an employer or a work place more than she did after that conversation.

She packed up a small rolling suitcase, the one she'd used on her trip to New Mexico, which was still sitting half unpacked in the corner of her bedroom, and added a few of her witchy paraphernalia for good measure. She ensured her cactus garden in the sealed off fireplace was watered and could last for several weeks without tending. Then she tossed some of the good tea she kept here for Sebastian into her purse because she couldn't be sure what a demon hunter apartment or house might have on hand.

He smiled softly at that gesture, an expression which still made her stomach dance after all these years.

When she was ready, he called a taxi and Angie locked her apartment up tight, including a magical ward on the door that would *nudge* her if someone tried to get inside. On the sidewalk outside her building, she glanced up at the window of her apartment and sighed. She hoped this wasn't a permanent move. She loved that apartment. But it was safer to be somewhere the demon and his minions would have a harder time finding Sebastian.

"Ready?" Sebastian asked as the taxi pulled up to the curb.

To keep him safe? "Yeah, I'm ready."

CHAPTER ELEVEN

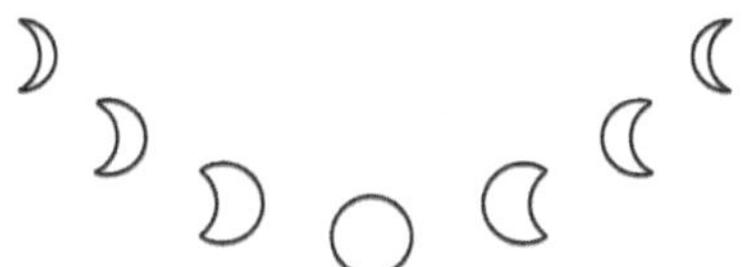

The place Sebastian brought her to was not what she'd been expecting. Angie knew there were safe houses for demon hunters all over the world, places they could stay when working or between hunts. Places to heal if they got injured in a fight. Places to sleep safely after they'd exerted too much will banishing a demon.

But for some reason, Angie assumed these safe houses were…rooms in hotels or small apartments. In places where a house would be less conspicuous, then a small house that blended into its surroundings, or was, conversely, in the middle of nowhere so no one saw it. She assumed that wherever the demon hunters stayed, it would be subtle and blend in and not look like something that would draw attention. That the buildings would be like the hunters themselves. Innocuous looking on the outside. So ordinary they went mostly unnoticed.

Now, she knew, because of Sebastian, that some of that ordinariness was their will at work, allowing them to blend in even if they were, like Sebastian, not ordinary looking. Angie still wasn't entirely sure if Aidan was as average looking as she appeared to be or if that was a disguise. Sebastian could make himself look innocuous and blend in when he wanted to. But that was a kind of camouflage.

Still, whether they were naturally average looking or put on an average look when they needed to blend in, demon hunters *blended in* to their surroundings.

This house, this mansion… Did not.

The mansion was on the Upper West Side, and she supposed it did fit in with the other surrounding Brownstones and luxury apartment buildings lining Central Park a few blocks away. But it was still a mansion all on its own. And not a subtle mansion at that.

The stone steps leading up to the heavy wooden front doors were bracketed by gargoyles, like a weird sort of honor guard. The façade of the building was thick sandstone bricks that looked pink in the streetlight, but were likely redder in sunlight. The windows were arched, and many of them had stained-glass with… She narrowed her eyes. Yeah, one of them was a religious scene the likes of which might be found in a Christian church. But another was a lovely patterned mosaic similar to what might be found in a Muslim Mosque. She noted an image of the Buddha in another of the scattered stained-glass windows. And yet another looked like a pretty starburst pattern.

The windows that weren't stained-glass were reinforced with cross hatched lines of steel. Some of the windows barely wide enough to be arrow slits. And all of them were surrounded by intricately carved white stone. There were two towers visible at the top of the mansion with crenelated borders, and a coat-of-arms hung above the double doors that led into the mansion, though she couldn't see the details in the design. The front doors themselves were huge, arched, heavy wood with thick bands of steel across them, and doorknobs the size of her head.

The whole thing looked like a strange sort of castle plopped down into the middle of Manhattan.

"How is this subtle?" she asked as they stood on the sidewalk looking up at the five-story building.

"It's not meant to be. That's the point. Who would think demon hunters lived here?"

"But…how many of you stay here at any given point in time?"

"Since New York is a hub for us, it can be as many as ten. As few as one. The council have their own homes."

Angie looked from the mansion to Sebastian and said, "You chose, voluntarily, to stay at my tiny apartment all these months when you had *this* to live in?"

"This place is missing something very important."

"What?"

"You."

He said it so matter-of-factly, she melted. "Ridiculous man," she muttered.

He chuckled. "Would you like to see the equally outrageous interior?"

"Of course. Does the rest of it look like a castle?"

"Some rooms. Others look like they'd fit right into a speakeasy. Some are very modern, like the kitchen. Others are… Well, you'll have to see."

"Do *any* of them look like ordinary rooms?"

"One or two of the bedrooms are relatively plain. But most of the place has character."

"Looking forward to it."

He chuckled again and set a hand to her lower back to guide her into the house.

They didn't enter through the huge double doors up the stairs, though. Instead, they walked down a narrower set of stone steps to the basement level. Those stairs weren't bracketed by gargoyles but were instead lined with planters filled with ivy. Ivy also climbed along the bricks at the basement level, giving this space a wilder look that appealed to Angie.

"Knew you'd like this entrance," Sebastian said, smiling at her when she pulled in a deep breath of the earthy scented greenery all around them.

"More cottage, less castle. Yeah, this I like."

The door was relatively ordinary compared to the one up the stairs. This one was just a single wooden door with a couple of locks and an outer gated door for added protection. Sebastian pulled out a set of keys from his pants pocket that were so large she wasn't sure those could have fit in his pocket without some magical help. He flipped through the large number of keys on the ring until he came to one and used it to open both the outer gate and two of the locks on the door. He used a second and third for the last two locks, and then led her inside.

"If I leave, can I get back in?"

She did still have work. Which was significantly farther away now. Her commute when she was in her own apartment was a ten-minute walk, fifteen minutes if she went to the bodega for a snack or sandwich before or after work. This commute involved a subway, a subway transfer, and a ten-minute walk to the nearest subway station.

"I'll have a set of keys for you by tomorrow. Gabriella is getting them ready."

"When did you contact Gabriella?"

"While you were packing. Even though you're a technical demon hunter, you haven't…been at this long enough to get your own keys for all the safe houses. Past time for that really."

"But I'm a sucky demon hunter because I can't feel when I need to go to a fight, so why bother with all the official stuff like keys?"

"More like you have made clear you'll quit the instant they let you, so giving you keys seemed pointless."

"Even to Gabriella?"

"Even to Gabriella."

"Smart woman."

They entered into a utilitarian section of the house. With a laundry room, boiler room, and a huge pantry stocked with a lot of shelf-stable food stuffs. There was a stairway at the back of the long central corridor, and an elevator next to that. Angie always considered elevators in private homes weird. Except this one had at least six stories. She lived on the fifth floor of an apartment building and would have hated it to be a walkup without an elevator. Especially when carrying groceries. She supposed if you lived in a place with the same number of floors as an apartment building, having an elevator made sense. Especially if there were staff having to move around all those floors to do things like clean.

She wondered about cleaning staff here, or did the hunters just clean up after themselves when they stayed. Given this place looked a bit like a castle, she thought they might have people come in occasionally to clean. Though, with hunters it was hard to say. They did like their privacy.

Up the stairs to the main floor, the house spread out more, and was just as eclectic as Sebastian had warned her. Some of the floors were polished hard wood, others marble, some carpeted in soft shag. There were rugs scattered around in places, most of them fitting weirdly into the section of floor. Some of the rooms had fireplaces. Others huge bay windows. The windows at the back of the mansion revealed a not insignificant backyard made up of manicured planting boxes and stone pathways and even a trellis near the stone wall at the back that had more ivy climbing on it. She did like all the ivy.

The rest of the house was…a lot.

"Warned you," Sebastian said.

"Are any other hunters here right now?"

"No. It'll just be us. Unless someone comes into town, and if they do, that'll mean…something."

She didn't have to ask. It would mean they were on a hunt and a demon was about to break loose, or they'd just finished a hunt and a demon had almost broken loose.

After thoroughly exploring the huge house, Angie and Sebastian picked a bedroom on the third floor that was essentially a small suite with its own sitting room and bathroom. Like a miniature apartment inside the larger building. That space made Angie feel less like an intruder in someone else's home.

And the bed in the bedroom was huge, and tall, and looked like a cloud.

"I could sleep there for days," she said.

Sebastian came up behind her and wrapped his arms around her waist, pulling her back against his chest. "Just sleep?"

She chuckled, then groaned when his hands slid up her ribcage and he nuzzled the skin along her neck, just under her ear. He knew exactly what that particular spot did to her.

Heartbeat starting to pick up speed, her breathing deepening, she said, "Okay, maybe other things, too. And then sleep."

She turned in his arms, prepared to take advantage of those other things, when his cellphone rang. He dropped his forehead against hers and groaned. She couldn't agree more.

She eased back so he could pull his phone out of his back pocket and answer. She wandered around the bedroom suite while he spoke to give him some privacy. She'd left her small suitcase in the sitting room so brought it into the bedroom. Then brought his backpack in too. By the time she'd dropped her huge purse on the floor next to the bed, he'd finished with his call.

"Naps and other things are going to have to wait," he said with another sigh.

"What's happened?"

"That was Gabriella."

"Again?" He'd already let her know they were staying at the house. What else could this be about?

"We're being given an earlier window to view the histories."

"Now?" Angie hadn't even eaten yet. She wouldn't be in any kind of shape to go through the books, *touch* those records, without food. "Guess I'm eating protein bars for dinner."

"No." Sebastian picked her purse up off the floor and settled the strap over her head so it rested across her chest again, adjusting the purse at her hip so it hung comfortably. She smiled at his care. "We're going to eat first," he said. "Then we'll go back to the archive. That was why the discussion took so long."

"Have you told her about Sokolov and his boss and *why* we needed to stay here yet?" He might have during their earlier conversation, but since Angie hadn't noticed that phone call because she'd been packing, she had assumed it was too short for him to fill in all the details.

"I told her I'd explain when we had more privacy. I'll tell her in the records room."

That was fair enough. And safer. Discussing things in person, in the very real privacy of the records room, would ensure no one associated with Sokolov or his boss, or even Carmen, would overhear.

"Should we warn Carmen? About Sokolov coming to see me at work?" Angie asked as they headed back out of the massive mansion.

"Text her. But I suspect she's already on top of all this."

That Angie hadn't thought to text Carmen earlier in the day made her feel just a tiny tiny bit bad. But since she still blamed Carmen for putting her on Sokolov's radar, maybe not that bad. As Sebastian said, the other witch probably already knew Sokolov had visited Angie's work.

She sent the text, then followed Sebastian back out into the New York night. This part of town had the good streetlights that didn't bother people living in the area, but were still bright enough to keep the sidewalks from being too shadowed. The treelined street, with illuminated windows in the surrounding Brownstones, felt cozy and several degrees of wealth above where she lived.

"Where to?" she asked.

"Restaurant two blocks away. Then the records room." He frowned as he looked up the street. That wasn't his "need to hunt" frown, but it wasn't an innocuous frown either.

"What's wrong?" Not that much was actually right.

"Something's nagging at me. Can't put my finger on it. It'll come to me."

"The way they moved up the time we could access to the records room?"

"Maybe. Not sure. Not a hunt, though. Just… I'm not sure."

"You'll figure it out. We both just need food."

"You always need food," he said, draping an arm over her shoulders.

He knew her so well.

CHAPTER TWELVE

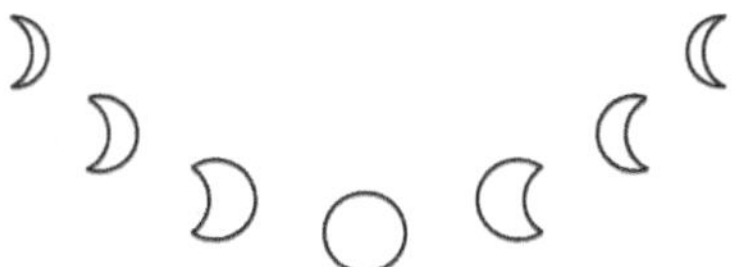

The session at the archive this time didn't have the added bonus of an exhausting vision experience because Angie kept herself closed off from the books this time. She still wanted to open to more visions from some of those histories, but she needed to get through as much reading as she could first and that wouldn't happen if she allowed another vision. Not if the last time was any indicator. Every opportunity to see these secret histories felt like it might be her only chance. That she'd gotten a second chance so quickly wasn't something she intended on taking for granted.

By the time she'd made her way through at least thirty more books, including reading the last passages of the diary from her last visit, she was so exhausted her eyes were closing as she tried to read, and she nearly bounced her head off the table three times before Sebastian made her stop.

She still hadn't found the answer to keeping the demon magic she'd absorbed from killing her, but she'd learned an awful lot more about what the demon hunters knew of her kind. And she'd learned there was a witch keeping this history, too. From witch records and information. That was something no one she'd ever discussed this with had known. Or at least they hadn't told her. She'd have to look up this historian witch soon.

After some sleep. And more food. And *if* they managed to survive the threat from Sokolov and his boss.

Sebastian had told Gabriella everything, quietly, in a different part of the archive, while Angie read. Angie assumed they moved away so she could have quiet to concentrate, but she also wondered if there weren't some things Sebastian wanted to discuss with Gabriella that neither of them wanted her to hear. Despite her official position as "demon hunter," most of the hunters, including Gabriella, still treated her like she was outside the fold. Not *quite* a hunter entitled to all that that implied.

She couldn't really blame them for that. She *wasn't* a demon hunter. She wasn't ever going to be one. And maybe now, finally, Gabriella was starting to realize that.

That wouldn't stop them from keeping her in the fold so she could use the powers she did have against demons. Especially this newest one.

"So," Sebastian said as they hit the sidewalk again. "No direct answers, just as Gabriella warned."

"Not yet, no," Angie said reluctantly. "But some things we should talk about. I did find a few interesting things that…aren't answers, but are interesting." She yawned and glanced around.

At this time of night—not as late as it should be given how long they were in the records room, but late enough to be after all the Broadway shows had let out and the offices closed—the sidewalks were significantly less crowded than the last time they'd been here. A few taxis motored past on Seventh as they walked toward a subway entrance, and after Angie stumbled in her exhaustion, Sebastian raised his hand and a taxi pulled up immediately to the curb.

"I can manage a subway ride," she muttered as she slid into the taxi.

"You're falling asleep on your feet. Taxi will be faster."

Since she drifted off to sleep as they drove uptown, snapping awake when they stopped outside the castle looking mansion, she had to acknowledge the wisdom of Sebastian's choice.

"Sleep first and then we can talk?" he asked as he let them into the castle-mansion at the ivy-covered basement level again.

"Probably best. Lot to discuss. But I'm too tired to think straight." Between her regular job, the confrontation with Sokolov, the move here, and the hours of reading, she was ready to drop.

As they entered the house, though, noise from somewhere on the next floor had both Sebastian and Angie freezing in place.

She frowned at him. "Another hunter?"

"Gabriella should have known and warned me," he said, quietly.

Almost without thought, he edged Angie behind him, and Angie simultaneously started murmuring a shield spell. Her exhaustion dropped away with the rush of adrenaline surging into her blood. Her heart pounded hard as they crept up the stairs, following the sounds of cabinets opening and closing and things tinking against countertops in the kitchen.

That didn't sound like someone who wasn't supposed to be here. It could well be another hunter. But as Sebastian said, if there'd been a fight, Gabriella would have known. And if there was about to be a hunt, Sebastian would feel that. If this was just a hunter passing through, they should have let Gabriella know.

But who else could it be?

The images Sokolov's boss had allowed her to see went through Angie's head, without her permission, showing her horrors and things she did not want to think about. Didn't even want to face in her nightmares. She blinked hard and forced those images away. This was hardly a demon. How the hell would a demon get into a demon hunter sanctuary?

More cabinets opening and closing. Sebastian stopped abruptly, straightening as he scowled at the kitchen. Then he let out a surprised breath and hurried forward.

Angie rushed to keep up with him. They were through the kitchen door before she even had a chance to ask him what was happening.

The ordinary looking woman standing in the middle of

the kitchen making tea glanced up at them and smiled. "Hey, you two. Long time no see."

Angie understood Sebastian's surprised gasp now. "Aidan?"

THEY SETTLED INTO A LIVING ROOM THAT ANGIE COULD ONLY call...grand. There were lots of dark woods and a few bookshelves, mostly filled with nicknacks rather than books, and a huge stone fireplace bracketed by more gargoyles. The chairs in front of the fireplace were also huge, well-cushioned high-back chairs that had enough room for Angie to curl her legs up under her. The chairs made her feel a little bit like a kid sitting in adult-sized furniture. But she was too comfortable to wonder at the weird proportions.

The mug of tea she cradled in her hands filled her immediate area with the strong citrusy scent of Earl Gray, but the soothing scent did nothing to mitigate her confusion. At least her exhaustion had dropped to a low ache in the back of her eyes and not an impending collapse. Adrenaline had a way of waking her up.

Sebastian had settled onto a thick cushioned ottoman instead of into one of the chairs. His mug of tea was on the small round table that sat between the ottomans, mostly ignored even though it was the good tea. Aidan reclined comfortably in one of the other high-backed seats, most of her attention on the fire happily crackling in the fireplace. The room was lit only by that fire, which felt cozy but had the weird effect of highlighting the faint red in the two hunters' eyes.

Angie studied Aidan. It had been a few years since she'd last seen the legendary hunter, but nothing about her had changed in that time. Nothing about Aidan ever seemed to change. She'd looked just this way when she'd rescued Angie in that church parking lot twenty-three years ago. At least, that's how Angie remembered her. It was possible she looked older now and Angie had just been so young when they'd first met—and so traumatized—she'd blurred past and present memories. But she didn't think so.

Aidan just simply never changed.

She was a medium sized woman, height and weight average and nothing that stood out too much. Not as tall as Angie, but maybe a little taller than average. She wasn't thin or fat, just…average. She had soft brown hair currently back in a braid, nothing particularly remarkable. Average features that made her neither particularly pretty nor particularly *not* pretty. Her brown eyes and pale skin weren't remarkable. Nothing about her stood out. Even her casual jeans and ordinary blue t-shirt without any pithy sayings or logos on it. She was about as ordinary as a woman could get. So easy to overlook.

In fact, when she wanted to, Aidan could disappear.

But that was a hunter trick. She willed people to look past her, to not see her. And she did it better than any other hunter Angie had ever seen, except for maybe Sebastian.

Sebastian leaned forward, resting his forearms on his

knees, watching his mentor for a quiet few minutes, before finally saying, "You were in France."

"And now I'm here." Aidan smiled faintly and turned to look at them instead of the fire. "Lot's happened while I was out of the country." She settled her gaze on Angie. "You doing okay?"

"I'm still alive. Apparently, that's unexpected and a good sign."

Aidan chuckled. "They have no idea how hard you will be to kill," she murmured, but almost like she was talking to herself. "Glad you're bucking the odds. Did you learn anything from the histories that the rest of us wouldn't have noticed?"

"A few things. Not much when it comes to my… condition. But some things I didn't know where possible for a demon witch."

"Multiple portal openings at once?"

Angie scowled. "How did you know that part? I only got it because of a vision. The diarist hadn't mentioned that detail in her writing."

Aidan didn't bother answering. "There have been a few demon witches over the centuries to go into and out of the demon realms."

And that would have been news to Angie just a few weeks ago.

"Despite what Morty implied—"

"Said outright," Sebastian cut in.

"Despite what Morty said," Aidan corrected, "we don't know much about what happened to them inside the demon realms. Or much about what they brought out. That most of those witches didn't live very long might have nothing to do with their forays into the demon worlds. The fact that they came back out is telling. But we don't know if they brought anything back out with them. The way you did."

"I think the diarist's witch did," Angie said. "I… This isn't something that was clear in the vision, just a sense I got from the diarist herself when I was inside her head in the vision. But I got the impression they were looking for something that was important to the witch's life. The diarist does say the witch is looking for medicine, but doesn't write who the medicine is for. I'm convinced that medicine was for the witch."

Sebastian cut her a look, but didn't comment.

She answered his unspoken question. "The essence of that feeling only made sense a bit later, when it all replayed in my head. It happens that way sometimes. Things that I pick up in a vision only get clear after there's some distance between me and the vision."

He nodded. "They were looking for a cure, but for some ordinary illness, like cancer…?"

"Or for what's happened to me? I don't know for sure. I couldn't tell. I just know that they were looking for something inside the realms the witch went into. And that while the diarist was terrified of what was happening, the witch herself was not. At least not that she revealed to her lover." Angie paused and frowned a little. "And…honestly, I'm not even sure if the witch was looking for a 'cure' for herself or the diarist, now I think about it. The medicine was important to the witch's life, but saving her love would have qualified. The diarist was scared for the witch going into the demon realms, but I'm not sure I would have picked up if she worried about her own health at all."

And that was an interesting realization. Angie knew she'd go to the ends of the world to save Sebastian. He'd reached into a demon realm he couldn't even see to rescue her once. The thought that the witch was looking for something to cure the love of her life rather than herself wasn't an unrealistic option.

"The diarist never mentions being ill," Aidan pointed out.

"She doesn't directly say her witch is ill either," Angie said. "There was a lot she didn't write down that came through in the vision."

And given the end of that vision, with the torches and the men after them, Angie understood why the diarist had left so much out. The fact that she'd included enough for her diary to be held in secret by the demon hunters was amazing.

Aidan pulled in a deep breath, let it out slowly. "Now that you've seen what the hunters have, at least most of it, I think it's obvious that…we don't know as much as we pretend to about demon witches. Our records document the bad stuff, the situations when witches lost control and loosed demons, the times when witches did something dramatic and died. But we have no records of the quiet witches who died of old age. Why would we? They weren't on anyone's radar."

"And you think there were demon witches like that? The others don't." She was thinking specifically of Morty.

Aidan was right, though. The witches who died

dramatically were the witches they knew of. And they didn't know everything about everything. Even their most secret records, the ones Angie had hoped would give her the information she needed to survive, had lots of holes and vague implications that weren't actually fact.

"Your vision is the closest we've gotten to *knowing* for sure that some demon witches travel into and out of the demon realms. We've suspected for a long time, of course. The witch whose coven had to kill her? She had maps of different realms. They've been locked up in her ancestor's home for the last couple of centuries, but they exist. A lot of things exist that aren't in the hunter's records, is what I'm saying."

"You're telling me not to lose hope for survival."

Aidan shrugged. "That. But also, to remember that the hunters don't know as much as they pretend to. The council are especially keen on making it seem they know everything. They do not."

Sebastian snorted, a derisive sound that made Angie smile faintly. The council really were a pain in the ass.

"You're not here just to tell me the council aren't as omniscient as they want me to believe, though," Angie said. "Why are you here, Aidan? Why now?"

"Besides to check on you and Sebastian..." Her gaze flicked back to the fire. "Rumors and innuendo," she whispered. Then, louder, "I know Sokolov's demon has decided to take an interest in you and that Sebastian is under threat because of that." She met Sebastian's gaze. "I also know how far you two will go to protect the other.

And I decided you needed a more neutral party for backup."

Aidan was still holding Sebastian's gaze as she spoke. The faint red in her eyes flared, though that could have been the fire spitting and settling as a log broke. Sebastian held his mentor's gaze in return. And it was very obvious there was more passing between them than just what Aidan had said aloud.

Angie watched that silent exchange for a long moment before finally asking outright, "What aren't you saying?"

Aidan flashed her a faint smile. "How long were you planning on hiding here from Sokolov's demon?"

"As long as we need to," Sebastian said.

"It won't be long," Aidan said. "He's coming for you sooner than that. He's sporadically patient, in a demon sort of way, but he's not as patient as he thinks he is. He wants Angie. He has plans for Angie. And he's not prepared to let any other demons get to her first."

"I'm not working for *any* demons," Angie said flatly.

"Of course not. Doesn't mean they won't come for you."

The hunter stared at Angie for a long moment and the look made Angie want to fidget, even though she wasn't sure why. The look sort of reminded her of the way her own mother looked at her sometimes. A combination of concern and contemplation. Like she was trying to work something about Angie out.

"The work with Esmerelda went well?" Aidan asked, changing the subject again.

"It did. I'm back in control of my magic."

"All of it." Aidan nodded.

She wasn't asking, and Angie wasn't sure whether to take that as a compliment or to be disturbed by Aidan's assuredness. Because, sometimes, Angie wasn't as certain about her control. Mostly with the new demon magic just lurking in the middle of her web of powers.

"You're about to fall asleep," Aidan said. "We can talk more in the morning. No demons are calling tonight."

Again, said with such assurance Angie had no choice but to believe her.

She went up to bed still a little worried about Aidan showing up out of nowhere. After the last few months, having her here, now, felt…ominous.

Reassuring—nothing like having a legendary demon hunter to guard your back.

But still…ominous.

CHAPTER THIRTEEN

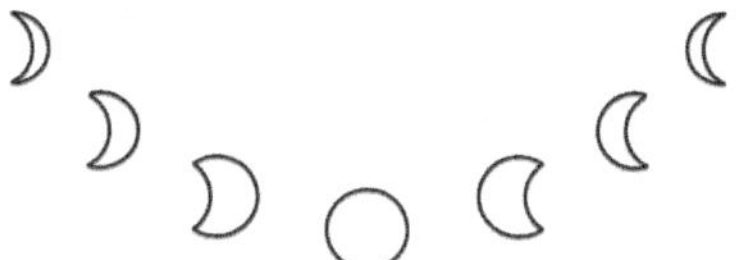

Sebastian came to bed after Angie had already fallen asleep. She woke knowing he'd stayed up late talking to Aidan. And she was extremely proud of her restraint in waiting for him to wake up on his own and finish his first cup of tea around the breakfast table in the kitchen before she started to grill him on that conversation.

"Spill," she said, sitting down across from him with her plate full of scrambled eggs and toast, a cup of coffee already steaming beside the plate. "Why is Aidan really here? What's going on that she didn't want to tell me while I was sleepy?"

Sebastian spun his mug, his second cup of tea that morning, between his hands and stared down at the table. "She's concerned."

"I figured. Or she wouldn't be here. About me?" She stared at Sebastian hard for a moment. "Or you?"

He met her gaze. "Me."

"That's what I thought." She shoveled in a forkful of eggs to settle her grumbling stomach, then said, "Out with it. Everything she said."

Sebastian remained silent for a long moment, staring down at his mug, a pensive look on his face that she'd rarely seen. She'd seen him worried, she'd seen him serious, she'd seen him seriously concerned. This was…different. There was a hesitance. A reluctance. Even when he didn't want to talk to her about something, he rarely looked so uncomfortable.

So out of his depth.

This almost made her stop eating. But when she did pause, he frowned a question at her, and since she didn't want to add to his worries, she went back to eating.

Finally, he leaned back from the table and took a deep breath. "My mother was very sick when I was a kid."

Angie blinked. Almost stopped eating again. Sebastian didn't talk about the time before he became a demon hunter. Not even with her. There'd been some vague hints. And most of the demon hunters of her acquaintance never talked about *how* they became hunters, but the hints were usually enough. Often someone trusted betrayed them. And even though a hunter showed up to save them, the future hunter had to use their own will to fend off a demon before help arrived.

She'd gotten vague hints that family had been involved in Sebastian becoming a hunter. And that he'd been young. But that was it. She was certain, given that Aidan had become his mentor, that Aidan was the hunter who'd showed up to help him. But neither of them discussed that or even admitted to whether Angie was right in her guess or not.

Even after all the years together, Sebastian had remained tightlipped about his past, and Angie had loved him enough and respected him enough to give him that privacy. To not push for what he didn't want to share.

The fact that now, after all this time, he even mentioned his mother, left her strangely panicky. Like what they were facing was so momentous, he had to tell her his history. But…they'd been trapped in a demon realm together and weren't sure they'd survive that. If that wasn't the time to discuss this, what was so much worse now that he had to tell her in this moment? So much worse that Aidan was here.

She did set her fork aside, but made a show of drinking her coffee so he didn't get derailed by encouraging her to keep eating. Her stomach was tight, but she hid her worry and encouraged him to keep going with a silent nod.

"My mother was sick," he repeated. "And no one knew what the illness was, but whatever it was, it was killing her. Slowly." His jaw worked a little before he continued. "Painfully. There didn't seem to be anything the doctors could do."

"I'm very sorry," Angie murmured, despite her determination to keep quiet. She couldn't help it. Her heart hurt for the child who'd been watching his mother die.

He gave her sympathy a brief nod, but then his gaze turned inward. "My father loved her so very much. He was desperate for a cure. Desperate to do something to save her. Anything at all."

Shit. Angie had heard, and seen, stories like this before. As recently as Sokolov's brother-in-law, Ivan Meknikov. Someone's desperation to save a loved one's life sends them down the horrible path of summoning a demon for help. To be fair, Ivan had been encouraged down that path by Carmen—as a warped sort of test for Angie and Sebastian—but Ivan had only tried it because he'd been desperate to save his daughter's life.

"What happened?" Angie asked quietly.

"The demon wanted a life for the cure," he said, his voice dull, matter-of-fact. "And my father was prepared to give his life in exchange for his wife. My mother didn't want that. They argued over it actually."

He wrapped his hands around his mug again, leaning forward to rest his forearms on the table. Sebastian was rarely restless. Most hunters had so much control over their bodies, they only fidgeted if they wanted to, to pretend at restlessness or indecisiveness. Watch Sebastian fidget with his mug and move around in his seat now was as disconcerting as his story was heartbreaking.

"My father attempted to negotiate with the demon he'd summoned. Tried a few things. Offered animal sacrifices instead. That wouldn't do. The demon wanted a human life or no deal."

She was afraid to ask, afraid to even voice the possibility, but she worried his father had offered Sebastian's life as that human life. Worried because it wouldn't be the first time a parent had offered a child in exchange for whatever it was they wanted from a demon.

Sebastian must have seen her worry, or guessed where her mind went. "He didn't offer me, though at one point, I thought he might. The way he looked at me, looked at my mother. I thought he might. But he didn't. Or maybe he just didn't get the chance." His throat worked visibly with his swallow. "He loved her so much… He would have gone into hell for her." Sebastian met Angie's gaze. "He would have reached into hell to pull her out."

Angie let out a soft gasp she had no control over. Sebastian had done that for her. He'd reached into a demon realm to pull her out. He'd willed a portal he couldn't even see to stay open and reached into that hellscape and dragged her home.

She'd never loved him more.

And weeks later, she'd tried to leave him to stop the nightmares of being trapped in that realm.

Now that they were back together again, she couldn't quite make sense of her logic, of why she'd thought leaving him would work. It had made sense at the time, but now it just felt like she'd wasted two years when they could have been together.

That he loved her enough to have done that, and that his father would have done the same for his mother… There was something there. Something that worried Aidan enough she'd arrived to help.

"Did he have to? Did the demon attempt to take your mother?"

"No." Sebastian's jaw worked again. He focused on the wall, not looking directly at her. "He said he'd go into the hellscape to find the cure himself. That rather than give up his life, he'd just go get the cure the demon offered on his own." Sebastian let out a sound that, in another time, might have been an exasperated huff. "The demon laughed. Of course. Humans can't survive the hellscape. There was more negotiating. The demon then offered to be his guide through the hellscape."

"Oh that wasn't ever going to be a good idea."

Sebastian gave a little nod. "But my father was desperate."

She wanted to reach across the table and grip his hand but was afraid any kind of contact right then would break him. He looked so delicate. Like he was holding himself together with that vaunted will and that was the only thing keeping him together. So she kept her hands wrapped around her mug, her cooling eggs forgotten, and waited patiently for him to finish.

"He agreed to let the demon guide him to the cure. I don't know what he was thinking, why he thought that would work. Something he'd read maybe. He didn't see the loopholes in the deal. None of them ever do. My mother caught wind of the whole thing and objected, of course. When the day came, he set the circle with himself inside, intending on going into the hellscape with the demon. He summoned the beast. My mother showed up."

He sucked in a breath. And when he continued, his voice was emotionless and hollow. "I was watching, hidden inside a wardrobe. That's how I learned all of this. I spied on them. They wouldn't have told me any of it. I spied on them. And watched my mother step across the protective circle without any thought. Watched her break that barrier and free the demon into our realm because she was trying to stop my father.

"I watched her race after my father as he leapt through the breach the demon had opened for him. And I stepped out of the wardrobe as the demon sealed them inside that hellscape and turned, laughing, to me."

Angie felt the tears tracking down her cheeks, but she ignored them.

"I was only twelve," he said. "I had no idea how to fight a demon or negotiate with one. But when it lunged for me, I said, 'no' and it stopped. I was terrified for my parents. Felt the desperation my father felt in those moments. I wanted them back. And I...I told the demon to bring them back. Didn't ask. Didn't negotiate or beg. I *told* the beast to reopen the portal and let my parents out."

"And it did."

"It did," he said, so blandly it was as heartbreaking as the story itself.

And also amazing. At twelve years old, facing a freed demon, Sebastian had still willed it to do as he commanded. Only a future demon hunter, a very strong one, could have done that. Most people would have just been dead.

"When did Aidan show up?" she asked quietly.

"The demon reopened the portal. I couldn't see my parents through the gap, just the hellscape and all its horrors. The sounds of the screeching demons. A scream. I'm…I'm still not sure if the scream was one of my parents or not." His hands were trembling around his mug. He tightened his hold on the ceramic, stilling the telltale sign of distress, but not before Angie saw. "I told the demon he was going to be my guide and lead me to my parents. And…I think he would have. Though I'm not sure…" He choked a little and paused.

Angie, after carefully locking down any risk of reading him, slid her hand across the table, but stopped short of touching him. If he needed contact, he could take her hand. If that would be too much, at least he'd know she was here for him.

"I'm not sure it would have been good to find my parents at that stage," he finished. "Humans don't typically survive long in the hellscape."

No. They didn't. Never more than a few minutes before the demons descended.

"I was halfway through the breach when Aidan arrived."

"She stopped you?"

"Not in time. She had to deal with the demon that was free. I got into that hellscape and was there for a heartbeat, maybe two. Not long enough to see my parents, just long enough to take in the horrible stench, feel the heat, hear the screeches. Then Aidan pulled me out. Together we forced the freed demon back. But once it went through the portal it had opened…closed."

He met her gaze. "It was a while before I forgave Aidan

for that. Pulling me out before I could find my parents. She did me a mercy. But I thought… I was twelve. I thought I was invincible. And that I could have saved them."

"Where did you go…after?"

"An aunt, in Surrey. And Aidan came regularly to check on me."

"When did you start training?"

"Usually, we start training when we hear the call to the history keeping meeting. Where the hunters occasionally gather to exchange information, to record deaths, to tell stories that the history keepers add to the formal records. Before this most recent incarnation of the council, that was the only…structure we had. And if a potential hunter heard the call to that meeting and showed up, it meant they had the will for the job. We'd go, and meet a mentor, and start training."

"I… I didn't know that part."

She'd come to the demon hunters in such a different way. Because none of them talked about their start, she'd always just assumed they were mentored by the hunter who'd found them. She knew they kept history, and met occasionally to exchange information. Sebastian had gone to a couple of those meetings while they were together. But she had never realized *that* was when a potential hunter started training. "Does that mean Aidan wouldn't have necessarily been your mentor?"

"Not necessarily. She…looked out for me in those early years. That first year after my parents… I was so angry. My aunt didn't know how to handle me. Aidan would show up and, even though I thought I hated her, she'd…settle me. Sooth all that anger. I'm not sure things would have gone well for me without her regular visits."

"So. Did you hear the call to the history keeping meeting?"

"In the end, I didn't have to."

CHAPTER FOURTEEN

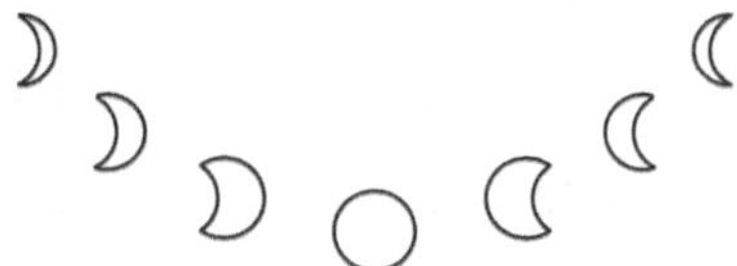

Sebastian's gaze flickered away from Angie's again, focusing on the window next to the table that looked out onto the back garden. The coffee in Angie's mug was starting to cool, and her eggs had definitely gone cold, but she wouldn't have stood and risked distracting him for anything. She knew this was a hard conversation for him to have, and that he had a reason for finally telling her all this. So she waited for him to continue and pretended to sip her coffee, her hand still resting on the table between them if he needed her.

"I started having dreams," he said after a moment, his voice quiet, "when I was…fourteen. Nightmares really. That my parents were still alive. That they were trapped and needed me to rescue them."

"Did you realize then that would have been impossible?"

"I refused to believe it was impossible. Even when Aidan

told me it was. The dreams felt so *real*. I could smell the hellscape, feel the heat. Just like that moment before Aidan pulled me out. I *knew* they were calling out to me, asking me for help."

"It wasn't your parents." Angie didn't have to ask. There were demons who could invade dreams. If there was some sort of link made with a human, there were demons who could wiggle inside their heads.

"It wasn't my parents," he said with a small nod. "That moment I'd stood inside the hellscape, there'd been another demon nearby. One who recognized my will. How strong I'd be. I didn't know it had dropped into my brain in those few seconds and bound itself to me. The dreams came so much later... I don't know if Aidan even realized since I wasn't in the hellscape that long."

He stood abruptly and went into the kitchen proper to fill the electric kettle with more water. He hadn't taken his mug with him for more tea, so she carried it to the sink and rinsed it out, letting him occupy himself with the busy work of making another cup. She recognized the stalling tactic for what it was, a chance for him to pull himself together.

"Have you ever talked about this before with anyone?" she murmured, handing him the cleaned mug.

"No one. Ever. Not even Aidan, though she knows most of it. We just don't discuss it."

"Thank you for telling me." Her voice was barely a whisper, feelings clogging her throat.

He nodded, reached out to cup her cheek with one hand.

After a moment, his hand dropped and he turned on the kettle, then went into the cabinet for another tea bag.

"The dreams became so insistent, I had to do something about them. I needed to find a way to breach the realms, to get back to where my parents were, and the dreams provided me the answer. Of course." He snorted a little at that. "Fucking demons."

"Fucking demons," she said with feeling.

That earned her a small smile, but it didn't hold long. The red in the depths of his brown eyes was brighter in the morning light coming in through the south facing kitchen windows. The lines around his eyes were deeper this morning, too.

"I thought, in the dreams, it was my father telling me how to get to them, how to help them. Showing me how to draw a circle, remain inside the circle, open the breach by summoning a demon. I didn't want to summon a demon, but my 'father' assured me it would be a harmless one and I'd just move past it to get into the realm."

"You went inside a demon realm. At fourteen?"

"Actually, the demon who'd found me had no intention of bringing me into the realm. It was just going to enthrall me inside the circle, then use me to do its bidding."

"Did Aidan know this was happening?"

"I didn't tell her. I was afraid she'd stop me."

"She would have."

"She showed up without me having to tell her. I'm not sure how she knew, though."

"Because the demon was going to break free?" That was how demon hunter instinct worked.

"No. It wasn't going to break free. That's the thing. I had control of it."

Angie blinked. "At fourteen? A demon who'd been…for lack of a better word, grooming you in your dreams. A demon you were *inside* a circle with? How?"

"Surprised the demon that my will was that strong, too. I don't think it counted on my will being fueled by my desperation. That usually weakens a hunter. With me… worked the opposite."

He took his fresh, still seeping mug of tea back to the table, but didn't sit. Instead, he stood near the window, looking out onto the mansion's backyard. The small area of well-tended planting boxes and paths one level below them was filled with a lot of light this time of day. That wouldn't last long. The shadows of all the surrounding Brownstones and the mansion itself would fill in soon. But for now, spring sunlight poured over the space.

Angie sat at the table with a fresh cup of coffee and watched him, waiting for him to continue.

When he did, his voice was deeper, and she actually felt his will in that sound. That was his hunter voice. Which surprised her in this context, when the demons were his personal history and not actual real demons.

"The beast that came through laughed, and then growled when I commanded it stay still while I went into the breach. It had told me to do that in the dream, when I questioned my 'father' about how to keep the demon from following me and closing the portal behind me. I was promised a weak demon, that the command would work if I used my will. The demon didn't count on my fourteen-year-old will being stronger than its."

Big mistake on the demon's part obviously.

"I went through that portal between worlds. Stepped inside the hellscape, convinced my parents would be nearby. That I'd be able to pull them out. I had no idea what I'd do with the demon when I got back, how I'd banish it, how I'd get my parents out of the circle. I hadn't thought that far and didn't really know enough to realize all the holes in my plan. I just knew I needed to get inside the hellscape and get my parents out."

He let out a sigh so deep, his shoulders drooped. "Of course they weren't there. Of course it didn't matter that I screamed for them until I lost my voice. I ran around that black rock, searching, afraid to go too far from the breach and not be able to find it again, but moving farther into the hellscape than a human should. Yelling and screaming."

He shook his head. And though she couldn't see his face, she could hear the exasperation in his voice.

"Of course, all that noise attracted a demon. A new one— to me—and one that was a lot bigger than the dream-invader I'd summoned. Not as clever though. This one was all brute strength and hunger. It just wanted to eat."

Angie shivered, glad his back was to her so he missed her telltale gesture. Her fear for that fourteen-year-old boy was so visceral, she found her heartbeat hammering and her pulse racing. As if this was something happening now. As if

Sebastian would tell her the boy had died even though the man he would become was standing right in front of her. Similar to some of her visions, she had a sense of the past and present happening right on top of each other, and separating them into distinct timelines got difficult.

"It pulled a very large sword from out of thin air," Sebastian said, his voice still very deep. "A sword of fire like lava."

She blinked. Sebastian had a flaming sword, one that sometimes looked like it was made of lava, that he pulled out during hunts sometimes. Not always. Usually only with freed demons when the fight could get physical as well as a battle of wills. He'd refused to use it in the hellscape, though, when they'd been trapped. Said he *couldn't* bring it out there.

"How did you end up with that sword?" she asked quietly, only realizing after she did that she'd spoken that question aloud.

He half turned toward her, but not enough for her to really see his face. "I fought the demon. And I won the sword."

"At…fourteen?"

He shrugged, and she could just make out his slight smile before he faced the window again. "It wasn't a normal physical fight. I would have lost that. But I told it I just wanted my parents back, and it offered to help me if I could solve a riddle. At this point, I still believed the messages in my dreams had come from my father, not the demon waiting back in my aunt's attic, so I thought I knew demons. From what I'd watched with my father, from what Aidan had told me, I knew they made deals and twisted those deals and couldn't be trusted. If I'd realized the creature in my dreams wasn't my father…"

He shook his head. "Well, sometimes we see what we want, don't we? In this case, though, I knew I was facing a demon and that it would lie and twist its deals. So I asked for the sword instead of its help. That's what we'd fight for. In my fourteen-year-old brain, I thought the sword would help me fight off demons while I searched for my parents."

"You were still convinced they were there somewhere. Even after seeing the place?"

"Part of me was. Part of me… Well, I was ignoring that part. And with the demon standing in front of me, I had to ignore the despairing part, didn't I?" He turned abruptly and returned to the table, sitting across from her, setting his mug down gently. "The demon's riddle wasn't as complicated as it thought it was, it wasn't as clever as it thought it was, and I won the sword."

"It didn't just hand it over?"

"Actually, it threw it at me, spear-like."

"Jesus. What did you do?"

"Stepped to one side and caught it. I think that upset the demon more than me beating it in a fight. Later, I found out the sword should have burned me the minute I touched it. That as a human, I shouldn't have been able to wield it. But because I won it fairly in a battle, I guess those rules didn't apply. It was mine at that stage."

"So… Does it remain in a demon realm when you aren't using it, or…?" She'd never asked before. She'd been very curious about his sword, but like his history and what had started him down the road to becoming a demon hunter, she knew he'd explain when and if he could, so she hadn't wanted to bug him about it. Now that he'd brought it up, though, her curiosity peaked.

"It has its own space in this realm. It's not waiting inside a demon realm, it's waiting inside its own…plane of existence. It's hard to explain. I just know it goes *there* when I don't need it, and I when I reach for it, it comes *here*."

"You said you couldn't pull it out in the hellscape, though. Because you *couldn't* or because you *shouldn't*?"

"A bit of both. Getting it back into the demon realm from its holding space would have been complicated, but also, drawing it inside the demon realm would have gotten the attention of its original owner, who would have come looking for it. I thought we had enough demons to deal with at that point."

Yeah they had. "What happened to the demon you took the sword from?"

"When he saw I could wield it, he vanished. The sword won't kill demons for me, mores the pity, but it can wound them, seriously enough to incapacitate them, and inside the hellscape, even a demon can't afford to be incapacitated or it risks being torn apart by one of its brethren."

Demons and their life really sucked a lot. So did the hellscape.

But what sucked more, was a fourteen-year-old facing all this for nothing.

"When did you realize your parents weren't there?" she asked quietly.

He spun his full, cooling tea mug on the table in slow circles. "I heard Aidan calling me from outside the portal. I didn't want to respond, to return, but she… Well, you've seen her will. And after the demon fight and taking possession of the sword, I didn't have the will to resist her. I walked back out of the hellscape crying. That part of me that knew they were gone finally overtaking the part of me that had hoped against hope."

"I'm so sorry," she murmured. Felt like she'd been saying that a lot, or feeling that a lot, during this story. But what else could she say. It hurt her very soul to think what he'd been through, to see the effects of this story in his expression.

"The acceptance finally allowed me to grieve their loss. Sometimes acceptance is better than hope."

What a painful lesson for a child to have to learn, though.

"Aidan couldn't break the circle to help me, or she risked freeing the demon I'd let out, the one who'd been getting into my dreams. My command that it remain behind had worked but with my will waning after the fight, it was breaking free and I was stuck inside the circle with it. It didn't like my flaming sword any more than the other demon had, though, so that helped. Aidan challenged it for me, a battle of wills. If she won, it had to release its connection to me, so it couldn't enter my dreams anymore."

"And if it won?"

"She'd step back and let it face me in a fight."

"That… Given you had the sword, that doesn't sound like a deal the demon would make."

"Despite the sword, it was obvious my will wasn't up to another fight. I think it fancied its chances if it could beat Aidan. That link it had to me and my dreams gave it an advantage."

"But it couldn't beat Aidan."

"It couldn't beat Aidan. It released me reluctantly, a severing that felt like a physical cut because it was a bastard, and then Aidan and I both willed it back to the hellscape. Since going back hadn't been part of the challenge, it was… reluctant to leave."

Angie huffed. Demons were such a pain in the ass.

"So then," she said, "you were back from the hellscape, with a new sword, and had successfully fought two different demons."

"Aidan became my mentor without any further steps. She cleared it with the council, who weren't the sort of…bossy assholes they are now. They weren't 'in charge' then. Just the keepers of records and history. Aidan announces she's taking on a mentee without the formality of him finding the history keeping meeting, they accept. Especially because its Aidan."

"Do I dare ask when all this happened?"

He'd told her he was thirty-nine when they'd first gotten together, before they got together actually, because he didn't want her to take the sixteen year age difference lightly. She hadn't, mostly because both her parents took issue with that age difference until Sebastian won them over. But after listening to his story, she wondered vaguely if he'd given her an age that was…reasonable but not true.

His smile was soft. "I'm not Aidan," he said. "I am the age I told you I was." Even if he didn't really look it. "This happened thirty years ago."

"Is your aunt still alive?"

"She passed away when I was sixteen. She had diabetes and didn't take very good care of herself. But at that stage, I was considered old enough to take care of myself."

"And you've been on your own since."

"Outside of the training with Aidan, yes. Typical demon hunter, though. I didn't mind. I preferred it, really. Until…"

"Until?"

"You."

Well. That hit right in the heart. "Why are you telling me all this now? It has to do with what Aidan said to you last night, doesn't it?"

"She reminded me of what my father was willing to do for my mother, for love of her, and where that had led."

"But why now?"

"Because she's afraid I'll do the same for you. That I'll go looking for a cure in the demon realms for you. And that it'll have the same result."

Angie sucked in a breath. Oh. The same result as his father's efforts would be…

She and Sebastian both dead.

CHAPTER FIFTEEN

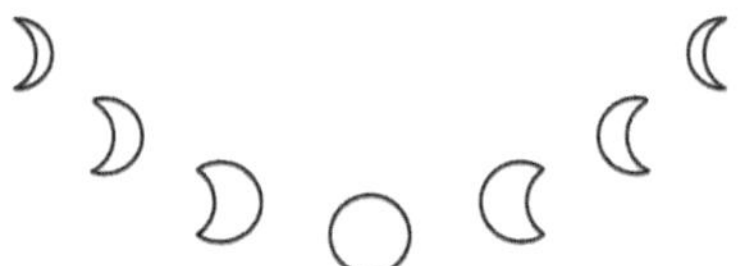

Angie sat back her seat at the kitchen table and stared at Sebastian. He returned the stare without flinching, but she could see the distance, for lack of a better word, in his expression. He was holding himself back, blanking his feelings. She wasn't sure why he felt the need to only show her a neutral expression when he'd just admitted his mentor was worried he'd get both of them killed.

Or maybe she did understand.

The spring sunlight filtering in through the kitchen windows shifted a little. Clouds passing. The morning moving on. Whatever it was, the light dimmed a fraction. The change made the red in the depths of Sebastian's eyes flare and then settle.

Yeah. Just the change in light that made that happen.

"You know," she started, then had to swallow. "You know, dealing with a demon to save my life won't cure me. I know you know that. So what is Aidan really afraid you'll do?"

"My father didn't die during the deal. He died inside a demon realm. They both did."

"So." She cleared her throat. "Aidan thinks you'll… what? Find a way into the demon realms again on your own? Go looking for a cure for me there?"

"It's one of her worries. Yes."

"Would you?"

"If I thought there was a cure there somewhere…" He blinked, but he didn't move his gaze from hers. "If I thought I could help you, I would."

"I'm not dying."

That wasn't really the point. Well, maybe some of the point. They didn't *know* if she was dying or not. And really, everyone died eventually, so yes, she was, technically, in a human sense, on her way to dying. Eventually. But not necessarily because she'd picked up demon magic.

According to Morty, she should have been dead already. But Morty didn't know any more about what was likely to happen to her now than she did. He'd been trying to scare her. Or maybe trick her into making a bad decision. Whatever the reason, he'd definitely been lying. To her, but also to Sebastian. Because Morty was afraid Sebastian would pick Angie over his mission as a demon hunter.

And now, the hunter who knew Sebastian best, worried not only that he would pick Angie over the hunters, Aidan worried he might do something he *knew* wouldn't work in order to keep Angie alive.

"There's no cure in the demon realms," she said, firmly, because she needed him to believe that. "If there was, the diarist's demon witch would have found it."

"That's a leap. Even you don't know why she was going into demon realms, what 'medicine' she was looking for. She could have been looking for a cancer cure for her lover. She could have been doing what my father was doing. Just with more knowledge base."

He was right. Still. "There are no cures there. For anything. She never found what she was looking for or the diarist would have said something. *I* would have seen it."

"Are you sure?"

No. "Yes."

"You don't lie well."

Fuck. She knew that. At least to Sebastian, lying was not her strong suit. "There is no cure *for me* inside the demon realms. They're the problem. Not the answer."

"Sometimes the answers can only be found inside the problems." He raised a hand when she opened her mouth. "I will not try to find a way into the demon realms to hunt for a cure that may or may not be there. Wandering the hellscape at random with no plan and no idea what I'm looking for would be suicide. I recognize that. I'm not interested in dying right now. And not in that way. Does that help?"

"Did that help Aidan?"

He glanced away, before meeting her gaze again. "Aidan worries too much."

Angie actually snorted a sound that could have been a

laugh but there was no humor in it. "Only when she has something to worry about."

"I will not be going into a demon realm," he said again, firmly. "Unless we have some compelling evidence that I can help you there, I will not go. I promise."

"Just…" She shook her head hard. "Just don't do anything, anything at all, without talking to me, without us agreeing on a plan. Don't attempt to fix things alone. Okay. We do this together. Anything that needs to be done, we do together."

That was the only way she could think to save him from himself, to insist they do everything together. He'd think twice about going into a demon realm if he knew she'd be there too.

"Please," she added. "Promise me. No going off on your own. We do this together, whatever needs doing. Promise me."

"Aidan's worried we'll both end up dead. Doing things together isn't going to prevent that worry."

"It'll keep you from running off on your own and getting dead," she said firmly.

Even saying those words out loud caught at her throat and made her panic. She tamped down the fears. She wouldn't be able to think straight around that fear, and right now, she needed to think straight. This wasn't negotiating-with-a-demon dangerous, but she needed to know Sebastian wouldn't try something on his own. And she needed to make sure that was clear and there were no loopholes in his agreement.

"No running off on my own," he agreed, though reluctantly. "At least in this."

"What's that mean?"

"That I might have to go hunt on my own. It's not safe for you to go on a hunt at the moment."

"It was never safe because I was never a hunter. But technically, I still am a hunter and you're still my mentor. Which means I go when you go."

He made a face. "That's a farce and we all know it. Even Gabriella is going to have to give up this idea."

"She hasn't, though, has she?"

"No."

"And now Jacob, who wanted me out, is keen that I stay. As myself instead of attempting to be a hunter, but still."

"He wants you to assassinate demons."

"Which, yeah, I'm not going to do. But I don't see any of them leaving me alone in the immediate future. Not with… what I brought out of that realm with me."

Beyond the fact that she could kill demons now, she also now had powers they couldn't predict. They'd want her watched. Monitored. She wasn't going anywhere, or leaving the demon world to the hunters, anytime soon.

She thought of Sokolov, and his boss, and the target on her and Sebastian's backs. So long as she could do what she could, so long as she had this demon magic in her, neither of them was safe.

A part of her still wanted to shut it all down, to cut off all her demon related powers. She might have to settle for less power as a witch, she might even lose her psychic ability, but she'd be rid of the demon world.

Maybe.

That maybe had been the reason she'd hesitated to cut off the demon witch thread of magic. With the demon magic, she probably didn't even have the option anymore. But there was still a part of her that considered the possibility. That wondered if maybe she could do that still. Something she'd been looking for in the hunters' secret files, though she hadn't been conscious of that fact until just now. She'd been looking not just for information about other witches who might have picked up demon magic. She'd been looking for a way to get out of *all* of this.

"I haven't finished going through everything the hunters have," she said. "Most, but not all. It's possible I'll still find an answer. Gabriella said I could come back today for the last of it. If this fails…we'll come up with something else. Someone knows something. This can't be the first time this has happened. Especially knowing other demon witches have gone into demon realms." Multiple times for at least one as it turned out.

"Sokolov's demon might know more," Sebastian said carefully.

"No meetings with him! He wants you dead. No."

"You met with Morty knowing he wanted you dead."

"Morty is a human. A demon hunter but still human. Sokolov is a gangster and his boss is an actual demon. There will be no help for us there. Only destruction. No demon help. Remember. They can't be trusted. And I shouldn't have to tell you, of all people, that."

"They can't be trusted. But they can be manipulated."

"And so can you."

He gave her a look.

"Right now, when it comes to this, because it affects me, you can be manipulated. That's why Aidan is here."

"She's right," Aidan said from the doorway, making Angie jump.

Sebastian didn't, so either he'd seen her already, or he'd been expecting her to arrive. Angie hadn't even realized the hunter was still in the house. Though where she'd have gone, Angie had no idea. Of course she'd stay here while in town. That's what this place was for.

"See, even Aidan agrees with me," she said to Sebastian to cover her startled reaction.

His mouth ticked up a little at once side, an acknowledgement of her surprise and her attempt to cover it, but then he got serious again. "You're both assuming I'll run off without thinking. I will not do that."

"It's the thinking part I'm worried about," Aidan said. "You'll *think* you've come up with the best solution. But your thinking is clouded when it comes to Angie. It always has been."

That was an insight Angie wanted to ask more about. But maybe not now. It might derail the conversation.

"At any rate," Aidan said, "we can argue more over this later. Sebastian, are you ready?"

"Wait, what?" Angie's gaze jumped between Aidan and Sebastian. "Ready for what? Where are you going?"

Aidan gave her a small smile. "I told them you weren't a demon hunter." She shook her head. "Don't feel it, do you?"

"Feel… Oh shit. No." She faced Sebastian. "How long have you?"

It was the call to a fight, the tug that sent demon hunters moving because somewhere there was a demon about to escape.

And Angie never felt that tug. She'd never once felt that tug.

Sebastian's mouth flattened, pulling at his goatee. He let out a long breath. "All morning, but we needed to talk and it wasn't very urgent at that point."

"You could tell I didn't feel it."

"We both know you wouldn't."

She cursed. "Why not tell me?"

"We needed to talk first," he repeated.

"Escaping demons take precedence."

"It's not escaping this minute," Aidan said, in an attempt to rescue Sebastian from Angie's wrath no doubt.

Well, Angie had enough wrath for both of them in that moment. "Someone should have spoken up earlier." She stood to put her coffee mug in the sink and turn off the coffee machine. When she turned to face the hunters again, though, they were exchanging a look. "What?"

Aidan raised a brow at her. Sebastian sighed.

"What don't I know?" She scowled at them both.

"It will be better if you go to the archives today and finish your research," Aidan said. "For you, that's the important thing. We can handle this demon. There's no need for three of us."

Angie stared at Aidan for a long moment. Aidan showed her nothing. There was nothing to read in her expression or body language, no hint that she was hiding something.

She was absolutely hiding something.

"This is a trap," Angie said. "You both know it, too. This is a trap. For who? Sebastian? Me. Both of us?"

"It's not a trap."

"Don't lie to me."

"You're making assumptions without evidence. How could you possibly know if it was a trap or not?"

"I'm a psychic," she reminded Aidan.

"You're not touching anything relevant right now."

"Stop. I'm not stupid either. You wouldn't be here if this wasn't a trap. You knew before you got to New York."

Aidan threw Sebastian another look.

He shrugged. "I told you," he said, his accent thicker in that moment.

Aidan sighed. "Should have known neither of you would make this easy." She faced Angie again. "Sebastian isn't going to be alone. I won't let anyone trick him or trap him. That's why I'm here."

"You weren't here when Carmen lured him into a trap in October," Angie said, then winced.

That wasn't fair. Demon hunters were always spread thin.

It was rare two went hunting together because there weren't enough of them to congregate in one place without it risking some other demon escape somewhere else. What was happening with Aidan being here now had to be even worse than the Carmen thing, even though the Carmen thing had set up their current disaster.

"Sorry," Angie mumbled. "That was…unnecessary."

"I wasn't here in October," Aidan said. "And I probably should have been. But I was dealing with something. You both survived."

"And that situation directly led to this one," Angie said. "But I blame Carmen for that so it isn't right to try blaming you, too."

"You have a right to be angry at all this, Angie," Aidan said.

"Stop trying to counsel me. I'm going with you on the hunt. I will have your backs. As always."

"That's not a good idea."

"Why?"

"This is a trap," Sebastian said.

"Told you—" she started before Sebastian interrupted.

"For you."

All Angie's righteous anger and determination stuttered at Sebastian's quiet insistence. Still, she felt the need to argue.

"You can't know that," she said. "You can't know it's a trap for me."

"We can," Sebastian said, his voice quiet in the bright sunny kitchen.

Why was it so sunny? When bad things were happening shouldn't it be dark and stormy? "I'm the psychic, not you," she said, again. Pointlessly. She already knew they were right, even if she hadn't before. She didn't need to be touching anything for her instincts to zero in on Sebastian's insistence and accept the truth of what he was saying.

She just didn't like it.

"Aidan's here to protect you as much as me," Sebastian said quietly. "This is a trap. It's a lure for me, but it's a lure for me to get to you. They won't expect Aidan to have my back. They'll expect you to show up. It's a lot harder to manipulate you, using me, if you're not there."

"I should still be there," she said, but mostly out of stubbornness, not because she believed that statement. "Do you know what they plan?"

"Can't," Aidan said. "Just know who should be there and who shouldn't. And you shouldn't. And I should."

"Fuck." Angie put her hands on her hips and hung her head. "It is going against every cell in my body to let you two go without backup."

"We're each other's backup." Aidan chuckled. "You do know we've been hunting demons since before you were born?"

Angie made a face. She rarely remembered she was the youngest person in the room with these two, but she was, by a lot, and that was weird if she thought about it.

"We've got this," Sebastian said quietly. "You need to be safely inside the archive. They won't even know where you are while you're there."

That was interesting, and probably shouldn't have been surprising. "I don't wanna," she said, even though she knew she sounded childish.

Sebastian's expression softened into a smile. "I'd rather go read books with you, too," he said. "But we'll be fine. And you need to be out of their reach. That's how we avoid their trap."

"They aren't expecting me," Aidan said. "I'm supposed to be somewhere else. We'll be fine."

"Element of surprise." Sebastian stood and came to her, gripping her shoulders. "I need you safe so I can concentrate on not falling into any traps. Aidan has my back. I will meet you at the archive when this is done."

"Gabriella will let you in?"

"I checked with her last night, or more like early this morning."

"You knew last night this was happening?" She scowled and wanted to shove him, but that felt childish, too. "Why didn't you tell me?"

"You were asleep."

That took the irritation out of her sails. Still. "You could have told me this morning."

"Already mentioned why we didn't. Ang, we have to go. And you need to go to the archives. I will be there soon. Before you notice I'm missing."

"Not likely," she said, then pulled him close and kissed him hard and didn't even care that Aidan was standing right there. It wasn't like Aidan hadn't seen them kiss before. "You stay safe. And listen to Aidan. She's in charge because your perspective is compromised."

"Yes, general," he said with a finger to his brow solute.

She rolled her eyes. "Don't be an ass. You know what I mean."

"I do." He set his forehead against hers. "And I will be careful. You too."

"I'll be ensconced in a giant library only a handful of people can find. I'll be good."

He kissed her this time. Then released her and walked out of the kitchen without looking back.

She met Aidan's gaze. "Take care of him."

"I will," Aidan said. "Take care of you."

"I will."

Angie stood in the kitchen for a long few moments after she'd heard the door downstairs open and close and knew the house was now empty. She remained in place, waiting. Though she wasn't sure what she was waiting for. A sign that she should follow them? The call to the hunt that every demon hunter is supposed to feel? Some inner knowledge that she'd made the wrong call?

None of those things happened, though. She remained in the kitchen for a full ten minutes waiting, and nothing but the cooling clink of the coffee pot and the sound of birds outside the window. She blinked at the sunshine outside, the blue sky she could just see past another building.

Such a beautiful spring day. Given her mood, it really should be raining.

But she wasn't calling lightning or thunder without

meaning to. That was a good sign. If she wasn't losing control of all that magic in this moment, when a low level of panic was crawling through her stomach and all she wanted to do was race after Sebastian and Aidan to ensure they were safe, then her control was solid.

Small comfort when everything else felt so far out of her control.

CHAPTER SIXTEEN

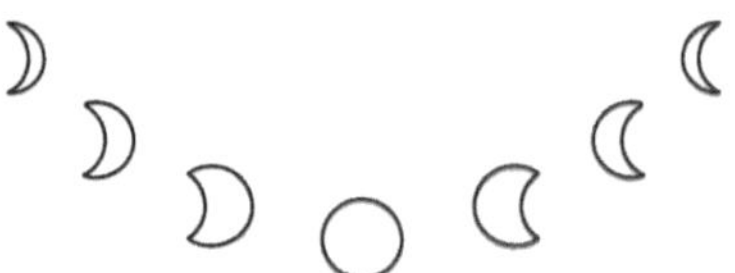

Angie blinked hard a few times and refocused on the pile of aging documents on the table in front of her. It was proving a lot harder to concentrate than the other two times she'd been here. She wanted…needed to get through the rest of these documents today. Three visits to the records room, the chance to go through everything the hunters had on demon witches, was more than she'd expected. She knew she and Gabriella were pushing the council's tolerance with multiple visits. She had to take advantage of each in case it was the last, and that meant she had to focus on the documents she was attempting to read and not continuously let her mind drift into worry.

Her mind drifted to worry again.

Gabriella had wandered off, still somewhere in the archives but giving Angie time alone. She probably should have been suspicious of that. Gabriella hadn't once left her alone while she'd been here before. And Sebastian wasn't even here to keep an eye on Angie. Angie could quite literally wander around throughout the records room without Gabriella even noticing.

Or maybe she would. Angie had no idea. But the need to get up and move had her springing from her chair and pacing around the small nook where all the demon witch artifacts and documents were. Worry and restlessness. She'd just get some of this out of her system and then she could focus. The pile of papers she was reader were handwritten accounts of a demon hunter scribbled onto pages he'd had to hand after a battle with a demon witch. This one wasn't named, and it was the only account of her, according to Gabriella, but there was something niggling at the back of Angie's mind in this account, something that made her instincts sit up and take notice. The pages held something of importance, she was sure.

If she could just focus.

She wandered outside the nook, strolling along the wall, idly studying the books lining the shelves. She pulled a few off, put them back. Nothing really caught her attention, but she wasn't looking closely at the books or their titles. She ran her hand across the spines, keeping her psychic sense closed down. Reading some of these books unexpectedly, picking up either their contents or knowledge about someone who'd recently touched them, seemed like a bad idea, given where she was. Without Sebastian, or even Gabriella, around to ease her out of a vision, she risked being overwhelmed. The temptation hovered in the back of her mind, but the cost and potential downside outweighed her curiosity.

She didn't want to end up incapacitated when Sebastian was out there somewhere in danger, possibly fighting his way out of a trap even as she paced safely inside this archive.

Folding her fingers into her hand, she forced her rising nerves back under control, clenching and unclenching her hands until she could think around the tightness in her gut again.

A cabinet of artifacts caught her attention and she wandered closer. These weren't in the demon witch section of the records room, so she hadn't really noticed them before. But she needed distraction, so she got close and looked through the glass covering to the shelves.

The contents looked a lot like old scientific instruments to Angie. An arched copper piece that looked like a protractor. A tube with a glass covered end that could have been a microscope or very small telescope. A small brass globe with etchings on it. A rolled-up piece of parchment capped at the ends by elegantly etched copper end pieces. A glass pipet with something red inside—she suspected blood but since it was still red, it was either blood from someone magical or it wasn't blood. Either way, she was reluctant to ask. There was also a glass beaker with a stopper in it, but the stopper looked to be made of cork or wood instead of plastic, and the inside of the of the beaker looked empty. Since it was inside the secret demon hunter archive, she was going to assume that looks were deceiving and there was something dangerous inside that beaker. Something that it was better not to mess with.

In a cabinet right next to the scientific equipment, also behind glass, were shelves lined with pretty glass balls, like ornaments. She squatting down in front of the case so she could see them better. Not a lot of them. Maybe a couple dozen or so. Some the size of a Christmas tree ornament and some the size of beads. They all looked hollow. And when she looked from the side of her eye, she could just see movement inside, like fog or shadows.

That was…weird and interesting. She'd never seen anything quite like these, and her curiosity almost had her calling out for Gabriella. But since she wasn't ready to go back to reading, and she thought Gabriella might make her return to the area she was allowed to be in, she kept quiet.

One of the larger glass balls was swirled with blue and red and a little purple, and for reasons she couldn't entirely pinpoint, those colors called up the image of her web of power. The shape on the ball didn't look like a spiderweb. But the colors all wrapped together in a circle of lines… Yeah, that reminded her of the web. She closed her eyes and looked at her magic.

With her at the center, threads of light streaked out and around her, forming the spiderweb. Most of the threads were blue, bright blue and pulsing with her ordinary witch magic. A few had become mostly purple from the time before she'd gone to retrain with Esmerelda, when her powers had been… blending.

And then there were those three red threads, shooting out from her chest, straight through the web.

One, the original red thread in the center, had always been with her, even before she had this visualization. That was her demon witch magic, the magic that let her open portals into demon realms by looking through the right natural shape in a tree trunk. Now, she could open portals directly, just by grabbing hold of that thread. The other two red threads were the newer demon magic, absorbed inside the demon realm. She'd been very careful not to *touch* those threads since returning home. She wanted nothing to do with that magic.

Mainly because it made her feel *too* powerful.

She'd always been a strong witch, and, though she never wanted to admit her teachers were right, she'd always shied away from tapping all that strength. She'd had to lately, had to learn to control it and access it. When she was focused on her witch magic… Well, she was fine with that mostly. But when she looked to these three threads… Nope. Too much fear still. So much power she was afraid of what she could do with it all.

Her web looked perfectly ordinary and fine in that moment. As it had since she'd returned. No strange behavior. No blending of the threads to form that strange purple magic. Everything looked as it should.

She opened her eyes, looked at the glass ball again. Huh. Why had that ball made her want to look at her magic? It still reminded her of her web, though she wouldn't have been able to explain why, but other than that, the blue and red globe didn't seem to be doing anything. What was inside those glass spheres?

Standing, she looked over the central shelves and cabinets to see if Gabriella had returned and caught her wandering around. So far, no sign of her. Angie risked wandering a little more. The movement and distance from what she'd been trying to read was helping. She still had the crawl of anxiety in her gut, worrying for Sebastian and Aidan, but she didn't feel like she was going to crawl out of her skin anymore.

She made her way back to the demon witch nook and all things demon witch. She wanted to study those documents closer and with her full focus. She felt like she could now, so hopefully she'd be able to make more progress.

The first-person account of the demon hunter's fight with the demon witch was actually fascinating when she could pay attention to the writing. She was tempted, more than she'd like to admit, to opening her psychic senses to this account so she could see what the hunter wasn't saying out loud. There was an undercurrent in the retelling that spoke to secrets being kept. But whose?

The hunter had come upon the witch in the woods, which wasn't surprising, but she'd done what the diarist's witch had done and opened more than one portal, one of which wasn't linked to a tree. The hunter couldn't see the portals of course, he just knew they were there because of the demons attempting to crawl out of them—the reason he was called to the fight. The demons were far enough into this realm they became visible to witnesses. Though, the hunter would have seen them sooner than an ordinary human would have.

Angie was having trouble pinpointing the time period for the documents. The paper looked old. But there were no dates associated with it, and the hunter hadn't bothered to record things like clothing and specific location. She assumed a date of some kind was somewhere in here, but she'd have to ask Gabriella about that when she wandered back this direction. But based on the language use, Angie assumed this was several hundred years ago. Written in English, so the hunter spoke English. The location of the portals and details of the fight with the demon witch were murky too. Which didn't help.

Honestly, Angie had always assumed the hunters did a better job of recording their history. That's the point of the annual meeting. To record these things properly. How had this collection of documents ended up in the archive and yet didn't have any mention of dates or location?

She flipped to the last page in the pile, just to see if the hunter had signed off with that information. Nope. The writing just trailed off…

And that was strange.

She read the last page. Oh. Oh shit.

She flipped back to the earlier pages and started reading faster, skimming over the old language usage to get the gist of what had happened.

It seems the witch had moved inside one of the two portals while the hunter was dealing with the demons she'd unleashed. The demons stopped coming once she went into the portal, so the hunter had assumed that closed both breaches. Since he couldn't see them, he couldn't be certain of course, but had assumed they were gone because when he stepped through the area they'd been, he didn't move into a demon realm. This was after he'd banished the three demons who'd made it into this realm.

On his own. Banished all three. That was…impressive. According to both Morty and Jacob, that was something only Aidan and Sebastian could do now. The hunter didn't record exactly how he had, which wasn't helpful—this was not the time for modesty, man!—but he did claim he'd forced all three back into a demon realm. Then he'd searched the area for the witch. Searched where he knew the portals had been. Searched all around the area, particularly where there were trees with the right shape. He hadn't been sure how the witch would get out of the demon realms and, after about an hour with no sign of her, he decided she'd died inside the realm.

He'd begun the trek back to town—unspecified town (sigh)—and been about a mile from the location of the fight when he was ambushed. He didn't see her move out from the trees. He didn't see the breach open. One moment, he was walking along an animal trail, the next the witch was standing in front of him.

And there was someone else with her.

Another woman. A woman who looked… The hunter didn't do a very good job of describing her. She apparently looked very pale and wild. But that was the best he'd managed. Pale and wild? What the hell did that mean? But anyway, she wasn't the demon witch who'd unleased the demons. The demon witch stood in front of her, but they'd both stepped out of thin air, he assumed from a demon realm, at the same time.

The second woman just stared at him with blank eyes that had a great deal of red in them, more than his own eyes—that was his best effort at description. The demon witch's eyes were also red now, but more like a demon's, fully glowing red, not like just the hints that happened with demon hunters.

Though he didn't go into detail—because of course he didn't—the hunter did say that the demon witch looked almost more demonic to him in that moment, like she was glowing red and the heat in the woods went up just by her presence. That might have been literary license, but since he kept shunning descriptions, maybe it was a fact?

The witch pointed at him, said something he took to be a spell, and cut the air with her finger. There were gestures he couldn't interpret—though if he'd recorded them in detail Angie was certain she could have figured out the spell the witch used. Her own witch magic worked with a combination of words and hand gestures—and words hissed, and then a bolt of fire shot out of the witch's hand…

Killing a demon that had come up behind the hunter.

The hunter had missed one of the escaped demons. And the witch saved him.

By *killing* a demon.

Angie sat back in her seat and blinked at the document. Another demon witch had harnessed the power to kill demons. What had happened to Angie *had* happened to another witch. At least once before.

Holy shit.

Morty must have known this, must have seen this record. Right? Gabriella had to know. Was this what Morty had been thinking about when he'd seen Angie kill a Molder demon? Had he remembered this story?

Why hadn't Gabriella pointed out this document? Did she even realize this was a record of a demon witch *killing* a demon?

Had this happened to more than just this witch?

She leaned forward to finish reading up to the last page. The hunter had come to take care of the freed demons, that's what called him to the fight, and he wrote that he felt he should—could?—banish the demon witch as well. But then she'd saved his life. So he asked her why she'd been releasing demons into this realm.

"They wouldn't have escaped, had I not been forced to flee you," the witch said. "'Twas not your place to interfere."

"Interfere? I am bound to prevent demons from entering this world. Of course I will interfere when they are freed, lest they become a plague upon this world."

Angie wondered if this dialogue was accurate, given it was recorded after the fact.

The witch laughed. "You have no idea what a plague the demons are. The infections they cause. Do you not see? Can you not imagine how we have become as we are? She will die if we do not return soon. This is our only way now. And yet, I still search for the cure."

Angie's heartbeat picked up speed as she read. This story, the two women, searching for a cure… Could it be the same witch? The diarist and her lover? It seemed too much of a coincidence for it not to be.

"Cure? Of what do you speak, woman?"

Angie rolled her eyes.

"I passed my infection to her, you see," the witch said. *"I must now cure us both. And the only hope left is in a realm so difficult to reach…"* The witch stared with her red eyes at the hunter. *"I have seen this realm. Most demons cannot even approach it. But I have seen this realm. The realm of the gods."*

"The gods?"

"Demon gods."

And here, the hunter went on about how they'd suspected the presence of a demon god realm based on some information from demons that they didn't trust. But this was the first time someone who was not a demon had referred to the place. The hunter didn't want to believe the witch, but admitted that a thing that was both demon and god would be terrifying to contemplate and this was why he resisted the idea.

Angie couldn't blame him. The presence of demon gods somewhere in the realms was accepted fact now. But fortunately, those gods showed no interest in this realm and so the hunters never had to deal with them. She'd also understood that moving between a demon god realm and her own realm was virtually impossible. Not a straightforward portal. Couldn't get from here to there directly.

Which she'd always been grateful for since she couldn't control which realm she opened.

A thought niggled at the back of her brain, an idea that maybe she *could* choose which realm she opened now? Was that what this witch was doing? She seemed to know more about the realms than Angie did. And she moved in and out of them easily.

Or maybe Angie was conflating two witches because their stories were so similar. She honestly couldn't be sure this was the same witch that the diarist had loved and disappeared with. This could be two other women in a different time and place since neither document had dates or specific locations.

That was frustrating and something she'd have to ask Gabriella about.

Where the hell was Gabriella, anyway? Angie had been left alone for much longer than she'd expected.

She'd go look for the hunter in a moment. She wanted to make sure she'd understood the last page of the document and that meant finishing the earlier pages.

The hunter went on to record that the witch claimed she could breach the god realm, but it required a special spell and a very large tree from this realm. Either that or movement through multiple demon realms, which risked the life of her companion. The companion, for her part, the hunter said, remained silent throughout the exchange and just stared. He thought her maybe in shock or maybe her mind was diseased —his words—so she was no longer aware of her surroundings.

There was no way for Angie to know which, or even if, any of those guesses might be the case.

The hunter warned the witch to trend no more with demon realms, blah blah blah, and then the witch said, *"I shall have my cure in the realm of the gods and then ye who would have killed her, killed us, ye shall suffer..."*

That didn't sound good, to either Angie or the hunter. Who then tried to kill the witch.

He didn't say how, he didn't describe the fight. He just said he attempted to rid the world of her for fear she would unleash the demon gods onto this world. He feared she had become a demon herself, that her companion was actually a demon disguised as a human woman, and he attempted to banish the disguised demon while destroying the witch.

He'd woken two months later, still healing from injuries he had no memory of receiving, with a permanent mark branded into his chest. A circle with a triangle etched in the center of it.

Angie closed her eyes as the memory of the triangle the diarist's witch had formed with the three different portals. The triangle itself had seemed to serve the purpose of a protective circle, keeping the diarist from entering.

Angie hadn't been aware of a circle around that in the vision, and the diarist hadn't mentioned an outer circle. But now that Angie thought about it, that made sense. An extra layer of protection. A circle around the triangle.

She blinked her eyes open, her hand hovering over the last page.

The last thing the hunter had written was that he was having nightmares about a realm he couldn't actually remember upon waking, and that he was dying. There were drops of brown on the last page, brown that Angie was pretty sure was blood. The writing trailed off with the hunter saying the eyes of the gods were on him and he would be damned. And then…

Nothing more.

CHAPTER SEVENTEEN

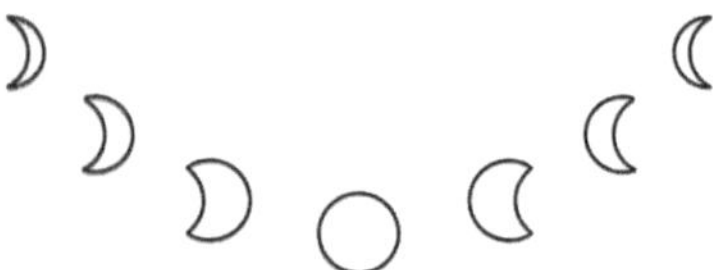

$\mathcal{A}$ngie stared at that last page of the pile of documents for a long moment, the silence in the surrounding archive almost loud in her ears as her thoughts chased around each other, possibilities and options and worries and half-formed fears.

And she knew, if she touched this last page, opened herself to it and allowed herself to *see* what had happened, she knew she'd find an answer there.

She was terrified of the question, though.

"You okay?"

Gabriella's sudden voice in the otherwise quite archive, when Angie hadn't even known where the hunter was, gave her such a start, she jumped.

"Sorry," Gabriella said, sounding prim but also a little apologetic. "I thought you heard me walk up."

"I need to read this document." Angie looked up at Gabriella. "I need to read it. Psychically. But I need you to stand there and pull me out if things get too… Just, I need you to pull me out."

Gabriella frowned. "How?"

That she didn't question, or even try to prevent Angie from doing what she needed to do, left Angie very grateful. "Just repeat my name. Only touch me if you have to, and then only briefly. I'll read you in that moment, but if the touch is light enough, brief enough, I will be too much in the vision to pick anything up from you. It'll just shock me out of the vision."

"Fair enough. Have you tried this while I wasn't here?"

"No."

"Why?"

"Because I'm afraid I won't be able to get out or the vision will make me collapse."

"Okay." Gabriella settled in a wide-legged stance across the table from Angie, her hands clasped loosely in front of her. "I'll pull you out if necessary. Did you find anything on your wander around the archives?"

Angie let out an almost chuckle and rolled her eyes. "I should have known you'd be aware of what I was doing."

Gabriella didn't dignify that comment with an answer. "Did you?"

"I'd like to know more about the colorful glass balls in the cabinet by the science equipment."

Gabriella's gaze turned inward, then she nodded. "We can discuss it later."

"That's…" Unexpected? "Not the answer I thought you'd give me."

"I didn't say I'd tell you what they were. Just that we could discuss it."

With a snort, Angie shook her head. Then dragged in a deep, trembling breath. "Thanks for the moment of distraction. You ready?"

"Are you?"

"No."

She let her eyes drift half-closed, her full focus on the loose pages in front of her, the yellowing paper, the dark ink, the spots of brown that reminded her of blood. She let her hand hover over the top of that page for another breath, two, then very gently, set her fingertips down on the paper.

The vision came immediately…

DARKNESS, TREES, THE SOUNDS OF A DISTANT NIGHT BIRD, probably an owl. The scent of blood strong in the air. On her clothes. Everything was always blood.

The man in front of her, looking terrified but trying not to.

Angie frowned in her real body, wondering why she was seeing this through the witch's perspective. The man had written the document. This should be his view of this scene.

Behind her, her love stood silently. The rot was worse in this realm. But she couldn't leave her behind any longer. They approached if she wasn't right there. They tried…

things. She was so close. They only needed one more realm. She knew *knew* the cure was there. In the god realm.

A plan opened up in her mind, the exact way she needed to open the portal. She needed to be here to do it. This wasn't one she could open without the anchor of a tree. She needed the stability to get this portal open, needed the shape.

Always triangles and circles. There needed to be a triangle. And a circle.

"You can't go there," the demon hunter said, drawing her attention back from her thoughts. "If such a place exists, ye cannot tread there as a human. You will die."

"She will die if I don't. We both will. I've infected her."

And gods help her, Eloise was the last person she'd wanted to infect. She didn't even know how she'd done it? How it was possible. But that hardly mattered. She had to cure them both. She had to cure Eloise. No matter what happened.

"There are other options…" the hunter started, but she cut him off with a sharp hand gesture.

He flinched, which made her sigh. "You're a hunter. You should not show me your fear."

"Not fear," he said. "I'm drained. The three freed demons were difficult to get back." He glanced behind him. "And I obviously missed one."

Her turn to wince. "I did not mean to leave you with them. It… It happens sometimes, they get out. But I don't leave them if I can help it."

"Did you…banish that one?"

She could see he didn't believe that, but hoped what

she'd done was just banish. She should lie, tell him what he wanted to hear. Instead, she told him the truth. "Killed. I killed the demon."

"'Tis not possible."

"The infection, you see. It's the infection."

The hunter blinked at her. He was older, though that was hard to discern with hunters as they could affect their impression with their will. His dark hair, pulled back into a low tail, was threaded with gray. Creases around his eyes and mouth, though that could have been from his exhaustion. His trousers and doublet were plain but of good quality, dark and well matched to the night. He carried no weapons—why would he?—and the flare of red in the depths of his brown eyes was strong in the weak moonlight.

He was alive, so he was a powerful hunter. But the fight tonight had weakened him. She regretted that. The world needed the demon hunters.

It was only a shame there were not such hunters for the human men who acted as demons.

Eloise moaned quietly and Betha cursed. "I must get back. We cannot attempt to reach the god realm tonight. She is too weak now."

"You...you must not attempt this. If you unleash something from that realm here..."

It was her fear, too. She couldn't always keep the demons in. As evidenced tonight. Not while protecting Eloise. Some snuck out. And she had to leave Eloise to either lure them back or destroy them. But with each death, with each killing, she succumbed further to the infection. The disease spread. She could not keep killing without consequence.

And if she was destroyed, who would save Eloise?

The hunter took a step toward her, hesitated. His gaze jumped between her and Eloise. "We must speak again before you do this. Please."

She was about to refuse. But the please…

So few had engaged in even common courtesy with her. The last hunter who'd entered her life had demanded and ordered. Called her cursed and insisted she lock herself away for the safety of all. And then been killed when between them they could not banish the demons fast enough. That's when it had happened, the infection. But too late to save the hunter.

Betha tried not to think too closely on that night. The infection felt like a curse from the hunter, though she knew they didn't tangle in such spells. She was sure some demons had escaped that night, too. She was still…confused on the details. But she was certain they had not gotten every single demon freed.

Because that was the night when she'd seen the god realm for the first time. She'd not opened a doorway directly to it, of course. And hadn't seen it with her own eyes. But she'd had a vision of it. Through the portal, beyond many realms. There. Looming.

The vision had come from a brief brush against one of the demons, before the fight had taken her attention again. She wasn't sure if she could even trust the vision, though it haunted her nightmares. And she'd never seen the demon she'd gotten the vision from. But moments after that, things had gone very bad in the fight. Her distraction from the vision had kept her from helping the hunter, whose will had been taxed beyond endurance. The hunter had ended up dead. Because of her.

So the infection felt like punishment. For that night. For her failures, many as they were.

But now that it had infected Eloise…

She must find the cure. Even if it killed her. She must save Eloise. She'd not survive her love's death anyway.

"You cannot talk me out of it," Betha told the hunter. "It must be done."

"But…you should not do it alone."

Betha blinked at the man. "I am always alone but for Eloise."

"Not in this." His gaze flicked to Eloise again.

The compassion in his expression broke Betha. She'd experienced so little of it in her life. So little empathy. No understanding. She should say no. She should do this alone.

But she'd been trying to solve everything alone. And had failed again and again. She should not turn away honest help. For Eloise's sake, if not her own. What was pride and wariness to the life of her beloved?

"Two nights hence on the full moon." The moon phase wasn't necessary. But it made for better light.

"I will be here."

Whether that be a threat or a promise, Betha would know soon enough. She opened a portal at their backs and stepped through with Eloise.

CHAPTER EIGHTEEN

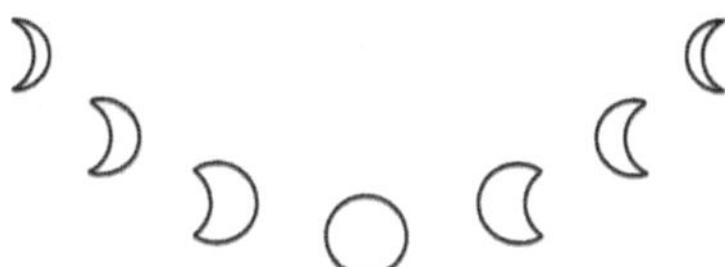

*A*ngie gasped as she was shoved out of the vision. Not by Gabriella or any distraction. It was like Betha had shoved her away so she wouldn't enter the demon realm with them.

"Are you okay?" Gabriella, beside her, not touching her thankfully.

Angie's hand hovered over the page again, her touch broken the moment the vision broke, though she hadn't been aware of removing her hand from the paper. Images from the vision still danced in her mind and it took her a few breaths to separate herself from it, from Betha and all Betha's emotions.

So much guilt.

"I'm okay," she said when Gabriella leaned in closer, afraid the hunter would touch her. "I need a moment." She breathed slowly through her nose, letting it out through her mouth, settling her nervous system, reorienting to her body, her world.

That vision was one of the most vivid she'd ever had, and she'd been so *inside* Betha's experience.

But…

"She didn't brand him that night." Angie had assumed, the way the written document ended, that Betha was the one who'd etched the brand of circle and triangle on the hunter's chest. That Betha was responsible for his eventual death.

But in the vision, they'd been forming an alliance that night. An alliance to save both women.

And…if Angie had picked things up right, she suspected Betha was also a touch psychic, like her.

"The diary," Angie said, waving a hand, still too inside what she'd seen to form proper sentences. "Please," she managed, because Gabriella was scowling at her.

She was glad she didn't need to clarify more than "the diary" because she didn't have the brain space for it yet. Gabriella set the correct diary down on the table next to her without a word.

Angie hovered her hand over the diary. "This witch, the one the diarist talks about…" She hovered a hand over the pile of loose papers. "And this witch, the one the hunter talks about… They're both the same witch. Her name was Betha—that's how she thought of herself, I'm not sure if it was short for anything. The diarist's name is Eloise. I don't know what the hunter's name was. I assume you do?"

Gabriella gave a short nod, but her brow was creased as

she listened, without comment, her gaze jumping from Angie's to the two different records.

"And Betha didn't try to kill the hunter, the way it appears with his recording. In fact, he agreed to help her that night. They met again after this. She refers to the magic she pulled into herself in the demon realm as an infection. And she claims she passed the infection to Eloise. In the vision, the diarist does look very…very bad. She never spoke, she looked hollow and absent, and her eyes were very red."

That got Gabriella's attention. Her frown deepened. "She carried demon magic, too? There's no indication she was also a witch in the diary."

"There's not, and I didn't get the impression from Betha that Eloise was a witch either. It could have just not come up, but…from inside Betha's perspective, I didn't *feel* like Eloise was a witch."

"So how the hell would she pull in demon magic?"

"I don't know. That's maybe why Betha thinks of it as an infection, though. Because she thinks she passed it to Eloise. She's searching in the demon realms for a cure. But also, Eloise has to stay there. Too long in the human realm, and she'd die."

"A human living in a demon realm? Impossible."

"Lot of things that are supposed to be impossible are happening in this witch's life. She and Eloise spend most of their time inside the demon realms, since going in. They… Living probably isn't a great word for how they survive, but they survive there."

"Two human women just…hanging out in a demon

realm? Without ending up dead?" Gabriella shook her head. "Have your visions ever been wrong?"

"About future stuff? Yes. That's the point, really. The future is ephemeral and what I see of it is usually the possibilities. Depending on what everyone does before then. But past visions? No. I've never been wrong—where I've had the evidence to double check. I can't say for sure here, of course. Happened too long ago. But I'm going to say the vision is showing me an accurate scene from the past."

She told Gabriella, in detail then, about the rest of the vision and Betha's thoughts as she spoke to the hunter. She kept the part about Betha maybe being a touch psychic to herself, though, glossing over the detail of how Betha had first learned about the god realm, of how she'd "seen" it. Angie wasn't certain about Betha being a touch psychic anyway—the information could have simply been fed to her by the demon she brushed against for some demon reason. But, though Angie couldn't articulate why exactly, she didn't want Gabriella to know there might be a similarity between Betha and Angie's powers. Not yet anyway.

Gabriella's mouth compressed into a tighter and tighter line as the retelling proceeded. At the end, she said, "I'd like to know why Yusuf didn't record this part of the story."

"Maybe because of what happened the next night they met." Angie rolled her lips into her mouth, her gaze on the diary. "Do you think she really could access a demon *god* realm?"

Everything they knew about those in modern times said the god realm couldn't be reached directly, that it required going through several demon realms to access, and that even a lot of demons couldn't get there.

Gabriella shook her head. "I doubt she could have, where no one else can. Not even the gods can get here directly without a huge sacrifice in power. Moving through the other realms is possible for them of course. So I suppose a human woman *could* navigate various demon realms to reach the god realm—if she could survive, and obviously this witch had the skill for surviving inside demon realms. But getting *into* the god realm? No. And if she did, it would have broken her brain."

Of that, Angie had no doubt.

"She said she could only access it from this realm, using a tree. That was what she and Yusuf were going to do the next night."

"Either she was lying to kill him—"

"I didn't get that impression from her," Angie cut in. "She could have killed him immediately, or even easier, let the demon kill him before she destroyed it. She didn't need to lure him to a second night of demons to kill him."

Gabriella shrugged. "Then she was lying to herself. There's no record anywhere that a demon witch can access the god realm."

"There was no 'record' of this woman's name or the fact that she lived in the demon realms to save her love's life, either," Angie pointed out. Without her visions, they'd still assume an unnamed demon witch had attempted to kill Yusuf and Yusuf had tried to destroy her.

For that matter, Angie was very curious *why* Yusuf would

leave that impression of the witch when she'd saved his life. Why allow that assumption in his record?

What had happened that next time they met?

She stared at the spots of blood. She'd assumed those were the hunter's blood, that he'd written all this in a hospital or medical facility or whatever passed for that sort of place all those centuries ago—based on clothes she was guessing sixteenth century but she was no historian so she wasn't sure. At any rate, she'd assumed the record was taken well after the fight but while Yusuf was still healing, based on his opening paragraphs. And she'd also assumed that the blood on the last page had been his from his wounds.

But she'd seen that vision through Betha's eyes, lived it in Betha's head. How was that possible when the documents were written by Yusuf? Or at least recorded *for* Yusuf. Someone else might have been doing the writing. A caregiver of some kind, nurse or whatever.

Angie frowned harder, staring at the table but her gaze turned inward as she remembered the *sense* of Betha in the vision.

Was it possible? Had she been the one to transcribe the document for Yusuf?

Even if that was possible, what did it mean? That she'd survived, of course, but…had Yusuf survived really? He must have or how would these loose pages have made their way into the demon hunters' archives?

"Yusuf would have handed these documents over himself, yes?" she asked, just to be sure.

"Or they would have been passed to another hunter who

then passed them to the history keepers at the annual meeting, if Yusuf died from his wounds."

"Did he?"

"We've no record of that." Gabriella scowled. "He died, of course. We have records of all the hunter deaths. That is rather the point of the history keepers. But..." Her gaze turned inward, as if she were searching her memory. "I'd want to double check, but as I recall, Yusuf died several years after this event, in another fight. One that didn't involve a demon witch."

"He claims to be dying at the end of this document."

Gabriella shrugged. "Literary license?"

"From a demon hunter?" The man wouldn't even describe clothes and location in any detail.

"Maybe he thought he was in the moments he wrote this? I don't know. But I'm almost positive he died years later."

"You told me all the demon witches you have records of died. They all loosed demons and then were killed. Did that happen here?"

"We had no idea the diary entries and Yusuf's record of these events were related to the same witch. We didn't know her name. We don't know her fate. We only know the fates of the witches we have names for. And they all did die, either from demons or during the fight to return the demons they'd unleashed. But, obviously, we have holes in our records."

Angie couldn't argue with that. There was nothing in either of these records, without her visions, to indicate these two documents were related. And nothing in them to indicate the fates of the demon witches. No names for them. No idea it was even one witch and not two different ones. No hints of their ends. Which was, she supposed, why these records were stored here. There was information here that the council didn't want the general population of hunters to know. But not nearly as much information as Angie had uncovered in her visions.

She hovered her hand over the spots of blood on the last page of Yusuf's record. If she touched those spots specifically, what would she learn? Blood was…tricky. It held *a lot* of information. There was no telling what sort of information she'd get. Or how intense the vision would be. And she might not get anything clear enough to make sense of. Nothing new or useful.

Still…

The last vision hadn't managed to drain her, though it had left her disoriented. She could risk another, with Gabriella standing right there, she could risk going in again. If she dared.

Gabriella must have guessed her thoughts, because she said, "Are you sure you want to chance it?"

"I'm not certain, no," Angie said. She pulled her fingers back and folded them into a fist as she stared at the document. Then she reached down into her purse, set at the base of her chair, and pulled out her cellphone, checking for any texts from Sebastian. He and Aidan were out on a hunt. If they needed Angie, she didn't want to be drained so much she couldn't help.

But there were no messages. No texts or voicemails. No hint what was happening with them.

She glanced up at Gabriella. "Would you know if they were in trouble?" She didn't have to specify who "they" were.

"I'd know if something got out that wasn't supposed to," Gabriella said.

If that happened, it might well mean both hunters were dead. Or would be dead soon. That didn't reassure Angie at all. "The danger here is a demon who's freed already. Would you...sense anything around that?"

Gabriella shook her head. "Unless he unleashes more demons and they break free... No, I won't know until it's too late. When another hunter is called to replace the...the ones who failed."

The ones who died. Angie appreciated Gabriella trying not to be quite that blunt. But that was the only outcome to failure for a hunter.

That brought her back to Yusuf ending up in medical care. He hadn't died in a demon fight. Which meant he hadn't *lost* a demon fight. The document implied the wound came from the witch and he'd lost a fight with her—which, yeah, hunters might survive that. Betha wasn't a demon. But...something about that. That he'd survived and ended up in a hospital or whatever instead of dead by demon...

She stared down at the blood spots on the last page again. They might not be blood. Brown ink stains were possible. They could be spilled soup for all she knew. But she didn't think so.

There wasn't anything she could do to help Aidan and Sebastian in that moment, without even knowing where they were and with Sebastian being very clear he wanted her away from this fight. But she could attempt to get more information about this. Maybe find an answer to what Angie had done to herself. If Betha had done the same thing—and it very much looked like she had—then Betha was the key to finding out where this demon magic would take Angie.

"I want to try to see more," Angie said. "Same procedure. If I look like I'm in distress, a light touch and call my name to pull me out."

"I'm here."

Angie looked up and held Gabriella's gaze. Then she looked back at the spots of blood.

A deep breath.

Fingers lightly on the spots…

CHAPTER NINETEEN

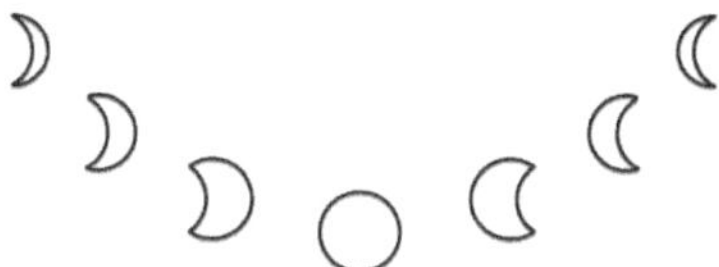

For a surprising moment, nothing happened. Angie thought maybe she'd been wrong. That the brown spots actually had been something as innocuous as spilled soup or dripped ink. She was about to feel silly and ridiculous.

And then the new vision hit her.

This one hit her hard.

She was inside Betha again. The giant tree before her with the natural split trunk forming a V was closed off inside a circle, Betha and Eloise on the inside. Yusuf was there, behind her somewhere. She'd left him outside the circle, despite his protests. He couldn't help her from out there, he'd said. She knew that. She didn't want him stopping her. And if demons got out this time, they'd be stuck in a circle. He could better control them that way, send them back easier.

"To a god realm?"

"Better than without the circle. If they kill me, you will not have the doorway to work with. You will have a more difficult time with them. This is the only way." At least, she hoped so. This was a realm where the rules were not certain. There was no way to know if this would really work.

She began a spell. A simple one. Not for opening into the realm. This was a protection spell for Eloise. She grew sicker by the day. Remaining inside the demon realms was destroying her, but leaving them sped up the process.

Yet, there was no way for Betha to access this god realm from within the demon realms. That required moving through many different realms, passing through some that she would not be able to survive—the heat or cold too severe for a human body, even one infused with the demon's infection. And there were no trees inside the various demon realms that led to this place.

But a tree inside the human realm could, given the right circumstances and the right focus, open onto the god realm.

She hoped.

She'd explored the brief vision she'd gotten from the demon, studied the images she'd picked up from it. The realm itself wasn't a place she wished to trek, but it held the key to curing Eloise. A bit of the sand, mixed into a potion. She'd discovered the potion from a demon in an ancient realm she'd finally found access too after months of searching. She had to go through the fire-lava world to get there, open a gateway from there, but she'd made it. And found a demon willing to talk. It was…the chatty type when it thought it was due a meal at the end of the conversation.

She'd disappointed its hopes of a meal—she'd learned well how to negotiate with demons to avoid their traps—but she'd learned what she'd needed to. Gotten the formula for the potion.

The only sticking point… She required sand from a realm impossible to reach.

She might have despaired if not for that brief vision she'd received, if she hadn't *seen* through that demon's eyes, the very realm of the demon gods.

So she'd studied the vision, the…mind of the demon. What she'd picked up of it in the brief moment of touch, what she understood—there was much she didn't and was grateful not to—and the answer was there in its thoughts even if it didn't understand the answer. It didn't *know* that was the answer.

The demon had come here through her gateway to avoid losing power. It had been in the god realm. Lived there. Was of that place. Betha had no idea if it was a god or not. Though had it been one, she thought the world would have known about it by now. Because there wouldn't be a human realm still standing. That the world still existed for her to return to, left her confident whatever the creature had been, it had not been one of the gods.

Still, it had moved through the doorway she'd opened with other demons and its thoughts presented an image, an image of the doorway into its old home.

A V shaped doorway inside a circle.

A symbol of one of the gods maybe? That part she hadn't understood. But the shapes…she had understood the shapes.

There was writing around the circle, but in a language that if she tried to even perceive the letters, made her nose bleed. She didn't focus much on the letters after trying twice. The language was incomprehensible to her. She wouldn't be able to reproduce that language to open the gateway, so she had to hope it wasn't necessary.

The shapes. The shapes were important. Required.

She could make those shapes, and using the power born of infection, she knew she could open that gateway.

She had been tempted to leave Eloise behind in what she laughingly called their "home" world, but she wanted her love nearby so that she could prepare and minister the potion the instant she had the final ingredient. The rest was ready, waiting inside her leather satchel a few feet away.

Only a moment. Just long enough to scoop up the sand. That was all she needed. She didn't need to risk going *inside* the realm. She was afraid that would shatter her soul. But lean in long enough to get what she needed... She could do that.

She could do this.

She pulled in a deep breath, most of her fear burned away months ago, but an edge of it still settled in her stomach. That was fine. Fear fed her powers just as the rage did. And she had so much rage to fuel this gateway.

Squeezing Eloise's hand, she said, "Stay behind me, far away from this place. It will not be good for you."

Eloise nodded, her eyes so red now there was barely any of the beloved blue left. Her dark hair was matted. Her skin translucent, blue lines beneath, so emaciated, she seemed skeletal now. There was no time left for her. They both knew, this was the last chance. If Betha failed tonight, Eloise died.

Without arguing, Eloise moved to the edge of the circle, close to where the hunter hovered. He'd promised to protect Eloise if he could. Yusuf. He'd said his name was Yusuf. That he'd given her a name at all was a level of trust she had not expected. Even if it was not his real name. Any name given a witch like her could be used against him.

The name and the promise had gone a long way toward settling Betha's worries that he would interfere. She should not have invited him here tonight, and yet, she was grateful for him.

She turned fully to face the tree, huge and sturdy and with a perfectly split trunk. The V formed by the split was as perfect as if she had written it in the air. It required a circle around it—not her protective circle. That was something different. This one required the shape built of smaller windows onto other realms.

Very specific windows onto very specific realms.

Not a place she could access easily. Never on accident. No. Going here would take effort, and concentration, and purpose.

She opened the first window at the top of the V shape in the tree. Followed that to the east with another window. Again to the east with another window. Four on that side all together. Four different realms. Then a southern window at the base of the V. Four more moving up to the west. Until all ten windows opened onto the different realms and closed around the tree's V-shaped trunk.

Finally, with a deep sense of concentration, with the sounds of screaming and demons and that…chittering that set her skin on fire, she looked into the V, looked into the realm that opened beyond.

Angie!

The world was nothing Betha could understand. Her brain simply couldn't make sense of what lay beyond. There were sounds. There were images. But not things she could force into patterns she might comprehend.

Angie! You have to come out. Now.

Betha stepped close to the tree. The encircling windows filling the air with the sharp acrid stench of brimstone and blood. But she willed those windows only partially open. The barriers thin from this side, while inside the ten realms, no demons should see them or be able to get through. It was a delicate balance. But it meant when she braced her hands on the tree with the split trunk, she did not risk a demon from the southern window reaching out to grab her.

Angie, dammit. Close the damned portal.

Betha frowned. Shook her head. Then leaned as far as she dared into the realm. Pain screamed through her head, like sound as pressure and fire all at once, burning her from the inside, pressing so tight against her soul, she thought she'd burst apart.

Reaching into that incomprehensible rage of pain hurt more than dipping her hand into lava. How could she grab the sand she needed without her hand. She closed her fingers around…something solid. And stumbled away from the opening.

But dragging her gaze from the tree felt impossible.

Oh no! She must close the gateway. She had to look away. She had to close them all before anything got through.

Scrambling with the power from the infection, she gasped. Someone yelled her name.

Angie!

A touch on her arm. The feeling startled her so sharply she looked down. Eloise. No…someone else?

She blinked.

And Angie startled back into herself in the archive.

To see an open portal not two feet away.

With a demon trying to crawl out.

CHAPTER TWENTY

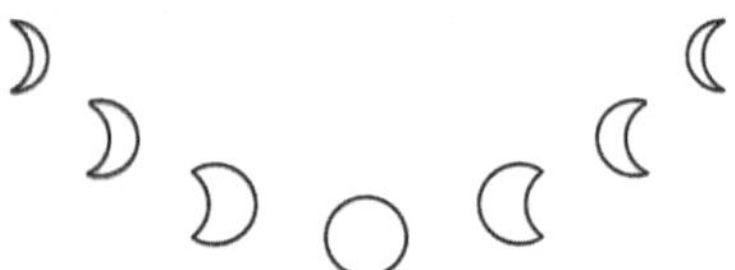

ngie stumbled out of her seat, stumbled backward from the portal. Gabriella remained where she stood by the big oak table, her focus fully on the demons trying to crawl out of the breach between realms.

"Close this damned thing," Gabriella said, her voice a growl. "I can only hold off these bastards for so long."

Shit shit shit. What had happened? What was going on?

Angie shook her head hard. Questions later.

She took hold of the demon witch thread in her magical web, realized she had touched it already. Careful not to access the actual demon magic, she concentrated on the portal she'd opened. A gateway she'd had to swing open with effort. Not just automatically, like she did when she looked through a tree's naturally split trunk. This was like the one she'd used to get out of the demon realm. A shoved open door.

Which meant just looking away wouldn't close it. She had to consciously close it.

She hadn't done this since that night in New Mexico. She hadn't opened a portal since then. And closing that one had taken effort. There'd been demons piling up against it, too, demons Sebastian had barely been able to hold off.

Gabriella was not as strong as Sebastian.

Shit. Shit. Shit.

Concentrating, pulling in the magic of that red thread and balancing it with her blue witch magic, she took a deep breath…

And shoved the doorway closed.

Demons screeched. There was resistance to her push. But she continued to close the door, letting the demon witch magic flow into the process. The power there was immense. The circular opening into the demon realm shrank, a red line of fire around it closing down. More resistance, more screams of protest. She barely felt them. The demons, even with their bodies in the way, were no barrier.

The circular opening whirled smaller and smaller. A demon hand reached through the shrinking space, red skinned, fingers tipped with glittering white talons. Angie snarled at the demon. The demon hand disappeared back into its realm.

And the portal snapped closed.

The screeching sounds cut off abruptly and left the archive in ringing silence. Angie's head felt like it was stuffed with cotton for a moment, dizzy with disorientation, her senses unable to process everything around her properly.

Her skin felt cold and hot at once. Her breathing was sharp. The scent of sulfur and ordinary books mingled weirdly.

She blinked hard a few times and looked at Gabriella. Then sank slowly to her knees.

"What the fuck happened?" she said, her voice very deep and scratchy. As if she'd been the one yelling and screeching, not Gabriella and the demons.

"You opened a fucking portal while you were in the vision is what happened," Gabriella said. She knelt beside Angie but didn't touch her. "Do you need something?" Her voice was unexpectedly gentler now. "Water? Food?"

She couldn't stomach food yet, but, "Water would be good."

Gabrielle moved to Angie's bag and retrieved her water bottle, setting it on the ground next to Angie so they didn't accidentally touch. Angie drained the entire bottle. She could use more, but this would do for now.

The cool water wet her dry throat and made speaking easier. She stared at the spot where the breach had been. "I've never done anything even close to that in a vision before," she said. Her voice was still scratchy but not as deep as a moment before. That was good. The magic was receding.

She turned to Gabriella, who was kneeling on the floor beside her again. "The visions aren't... Sometimes I see what's happening like I'm floating above it all, or standing beside the person. Sometimes I see things from inside their heads. I've been having these visions from inside Betha's head. But... I've never had visions of another demon witch before. Especially not with a link to their blood."

"Blood?"

"The brown spots on the last page of the document. That's Betha's blood. Not Yusuf's. I thought it was Yusuf and figured I'd see more of this…story? More of what happened from his perspective. But I was still in Betha's head."

"She opened a portal in the vision, so you opened one here." Gabriella's tone was grim.

"I didn't do that any of the other times she opened portals in my visions, though." She had considered if she might, when Betha looked between a tree's natural V, but Angie's worry had been somehow opening a portal inside the vision. When she didn't, she assumed she'd have no effect on the visions. She'd been right.

She just hadn't considered if the visions would have an effect on what was happening in the real world around her.

Gabriella glared at the floor, her gaze turned inward. "Betha's blood shouldn't have been on that document." She faced Angie again. "Yusuf woke up in one of our hospitals with the brand on his chest. He was brought in by a concerned citizen who'd found him on the roadside, and Yusuf had just enough awareness to tell his rescuer where to take him before passing out again. The hospital is run by staff knowledgeable about demons and demon related injuries."

"Is? Not was?"

"It still exists now, in different forms, of course, and there are different branches around the world. But we still have a hospital."

"Why didn't I know that?"

"How often has Sebastian been injured enough to need a hospital while you were working with him?"

Angie startled at that. For all they'd been through, every fight, every close call… "Never," she realized. "His injuries, if there have been any, have usually been superficial. It was mostly just exhaustion and drained will after bad fights."

"Exactly. Aidan has only needed the hospital once, too. That I know of. Honestly, if a hunter is injured enough to need the hospital, they usually die before they can take advantage of it. But the facility is there in case they don't. In case they can get to help."

Wow. This surprised Angie almost as much as the fact that the council knew less than she thought they had about her kind. Only this was…nicer news. Yes, nicer. To know they'd take care of their own.

"So," she said, getting back to the topic, "Yusuf ended up in the hospital."

"And that's where he transcribed this story. Dictated to a trusted scribe, one of the hospital staff. And then a history keeper came to collect and store these documents. The incident with the witch in these pages was over and she was gone. Dead according to Yusuf's account. How would she have bled on the page?"

"She saw the documents after the history keeper took them? Yusuf wrote this at a different time? Or she wasn't dead and came to the hospital to see him. Maybe after he finished the dictation? Maybe just before he finished."

"All possible," Gabriella said, her nostrils narrowing with her deep inhale. "And since we had no more information about this incident than was here, no way to know for sure. Unless you see the answers in another vision, which, I'm going to ask you not to attempt yet." She glared at the spot where the breach had opened. "At least not without more hunters here to help if that happens again."

"Shit." Angie shook her head.

"Tell me the rest of the vision. What happened that night?"

"The end got jumbled a little, because you had to pull me out. I don't know how things ended. But Betha opened a portal into a demon realm that made her head feel like it was going to explode and made her nose bleed, and I'm gonna say it was the god realm."

"Fucking hell," Gabriella muttered. "Tell me."

Angie did. Everything but the details of *how* Betha had opened the portal. She skimmed those, said the details were fuzzy. They hadn't been. Angie was scarily, terrifyingly positive she'd be able to open one of those portals now. The information was there, in her head. It took effort and more than one breach, which meant there was no way for her to do it on accident, thankfully. But if she needed to, she could.

Not that she could conceive of a reason she might *need* to. Even through the barrier of a vision—which apparently hadn't been enough of a barrier if it made her open a portal here!—the power and strangeness and incomprehensibility inside that realm had hurt her brain. Not just Betha's but her own, the part of her who'd still been Angie inside the vision. She had *no* desire to ever open something like that ever.

Betha had braved pushing her hands inside the realm,

though. Absorbed all that pain to grab what she needed for Eloise.

"But I have no idea if it worked," she finished. "I'm not even sure if the portals closed when Betha looked away from them." She nodded to where the breach in the archive had been. "That was like the portal I opened coming out of the demon realm. It's…physical. I have to open it, and I have to close it. With conscious effort. Or well, I suppose unconscious vision effort will work too. The point is, most of the portals I've opened over the years have been effortless. Sometimes too effortless. And all it took to close them was to pull my gaze from the breach."

She shivered and said, "That's how we ended up trapped in the demon realm. When I was…pushed inside, I fell forward and my gaze wasn't on the portal and stayed off the opening for too long for me to hurriedly open it again. It closed. We were trapped." She pulled in a deep steadying breath.

That moment, that realization that they were trapped in a demon realm, replayed in her nightmares a lot. Not enough time had passed for the shock and terror to have dissipated much. She wasn't sure there was enough time in the universe to dissipate the fear of that moment.

With effort, she returned to her explanation. "The portal I opened to get out of the realm took effort. Not a lot. It wasn't…hard. But it needed me to do something more than just look between the right shaped tree or touch my demon witch magic directly. This was more like opening a door. I had to give it a shove open. And then I had to give it a shove closed."

"You're worried this god realm required more effort to close than just looking away."

"I'm not sure. I didn't see that far. I got the impression from Betha's fears that she had to look away from the tree to close it. But since she'd been moving through portals in and out of demon realms for, I think, months at that stage, I'm not certain. I couldn't tell. I'm pretty sure what she thought of as the infection is the same thing as the demon magic I absorbed. But I have no idea how Eloise got 'infected' with it still."

Or if the cure worked. Or if anything had come through that portal, or any of the portals, that night. How did Yusuf end up with the brand on his chest? How had Betha survived?

So many more questions. And Angie was sure she could find the answers in another vision, especially anchored to Betha's blood. But… She glanced at the place where the breach had been. Yeah, not yet. Not without more hunters, like Gabriella suggested.

"That will have to wait," Gabriella reiterated, echoing Angie's thoughts. "You need to recover first. And we need more backup."

"Sorry to interrupt the research," a new voice said.

Startling both Gabriella and Angie into turning. Angie automatically started to build a shield, even before she spotted the speaker. When she did, though, she dropped the spell before finishing it.

"Aidan?" She scrambled to her feat, searching the

archive. "Where's Sebastian? What's wrong? What's happened? Is he okay?" The panic rolled in so fast and hard, she nearly ended up on the ground again when she got dizzy.

"First," Aidan said, her voice level. "Breathe. Calm down. You're no good to anyone passed out."

Angie made a face but did as the hunter suggested because she was going to hyperventilate soon. "What's happened?"

Aidan's mouth flattened, before she said, "Things went pear-sharped, and I need your help."

CHAPTER TWENTY-ONE

Angie nearly dropped to her knees again as a series of potential catastrophes raced through her head, the room around her blurred, and dizziness made her wobble. Gabriella reached a hand out to steady her, but stopped mid-gesture to avoid touching Angie, and it was one of the kindest things the hunter had every done for her. Angie could not have taken touch in that moment.

"Sebastian?" she asked, her voice hoarse.

"Is keeping an eye on things," Aidan said, the hunter speaking slowly and clearly. "Not hurt or dead. Just ensuring no one else gets hurt. He's okay."

Angie sucked in a deep breath and let it out slowly. She blinked hard to shift the spots dancing behind her eyes. Panic receded. Her brain switched back on again. She'd already been overwhelmed, her nerves tensed and sensitive after the vision and opening a portal on accident. Now this.

"Tell me," she said, steadying herself with another deep breath.

"The demon about to escape was…more than one demon. Summoned by Sokolov at his boss's behest. They actually are contained. They used the trick Carmen had used on Sebastian to lure him to the hunt—of using a weakened circle. But Sokolov knew how to strengthen it back up when we arrived so the demons didn't get out."

"How is this 'gone pear-shaped'?"

"Sokolov has…hostages. People he's going to sacrifice to the demons. If we don't bring you."

"People?" Angie could feel the panic creeping back in and the spots dancing at the edge of her vision as her adrenaline spiked again. "Who?" A sudden thought had her asking, "Carmen?"

She didn't think Aidan wouldn't know Carmen on sight, but Sebastian would have told her about the witch. And Sokolov's boss was after Carmen. If Carmen hadn't gotten out of town or disappeared after warning Angie about the demon's intent…

"Not that Sebastian saw," Aidan said. "There were a dozen people in a tight grouping inside a circle. We weren't allowed to see them all. Just that they were there. And so far, safe."

"So… So you don't know if they're people I know."

Aidan's mouth flattened. "Sokolov implied you'd want to save some of them."

"Fuck." Angie knees wobbled again. "My family?" They

were all in New Mexico, but still. With Sokolov's reach, it was possible.

"No. That was the one thing we were sure about. Sokolov made a point of saying that was his…payment to you for saving his life. Your family aren't involved."

Angie wasn't sure whether to be grateful about that or not since they were threatening to kill other people, and had threatened to kill Sebastian. Who had done more to save Sokolov's life than Angie had.

"But…" Aidan started, then trailed off, let out a long sigh. "At least one of the hostages is a coworker from Dana's Cauldron."

"Who?"

"Sebastian said her name was Laura."

Angie braced a hand against one of the nearby shelves. A mistake as a flash of a vision started. Something about a bonfire and dancing and blood and it was all too much.

She snatched her hand from the cabinet, then stood perfectly still with her eyes closed and put a lock on her psychic vision.

"Where?" She snapped her eyes open.

"A warehouse in Queens. Heading out toward Long Island. It'll take time to get there. We have to leave now."

Angie snatched up her oversized purse and dropped the strap over her head, across her chest, following Aidan without another word.

"Wait," Gabriella said, stopping them before they could go far. "I have something for you." She disappeared into archive.

Angie frowned at Aidan who shrugged at the unspoken question.

Gabriella returned moments later. Carrying one of the glass balls Angie had seen in the case next to the one with the instruments that looked like laboratory equipment. Not the ball that had reminded Angie vaguely of her spiderweb. Another one. This one mostly green with threads of gold and red through it.

"Make sure you're not going to read this before I hand it to you," Gabriella warned.

"I've locked that down. I won't. What is it?"

Gabriella held it out. "It looks more delicate than it is, but still be careful with it until the time is right. This is Sokolov's demon's sanctuary contract. The agreement he made with the hunters that's allowed him to remain free and functioning in this realm. He's violated the terms of his sanctuary by going after a hunter."

Aidan narrowed her eyes but didn't comment.

So Angie did. "Technically, he hasn't 'gone after' a hunter. Yet." She didn't think tricking hunters into going to a specific location necessarily counted, if he hadn't hurt them. At least, she didn't think so. She wasn't honestly sure.

"You're a hunter," Gabriella reminded Angie. "Even if you're a crap one."

That earned a startled laugh from Angie. That she had a laugh—short and choked as it was—surprised her as much as Gabriella's comment. "Told you so."

Gabriella let out a small smile that dropped away a

moment later. "He's set up a situation to lure you to him, for nefarious purposes no doubt. His terms of sanctuary mean he is not allowed to lure, interfere with, or kill a hunter. Any hunter. The fact that he's involved three hunters in his scheme just adds a cherry to legal ice cream. He's broken his terms of sanctuary." She shrugged. "I can make a fair argument for that with the council anyway. None of them will fight too long in his favor."

None of the hunters liked freed demons. But he *had* received sanctuary and a deal with the hunters. Sokolov's boss, Will Fredericks, wasn't one of the more harmless demons who just wanted to live quietly in this world and not get eaten by another demon. He was one of the powerful ones. One who made no attempt to hide how dangerous and powerful he was. Which meant he was strong and dangerous and had killed hunters before the sanctuary deal was struck.

He was the kind of freed demon that had Jacob and his faction of hunters looking for ways to strengthen all their wills. He was the kind of demon none of the hunters wanted to tangle with, but one they all hated had sanctuary here. No hunter would spend a lot of time defending the demon's right to that sanctuary.

"What do I do with it?" Angie said, taking the glass ball from Gabriella and holding it carefully. Even without her psychic senses, the ball buzzed lightly against her skin. She could feel the magic in the glass. The vibration of whatever was inside against her palm. It was a strange sensation, like static electricity, and made her want to put the ball down.

Beyond the feel of it, she also got the impression that the colors swirling over the surface aided the magic. She wasn't sure how. While she saw her spiderweb of power in colors, color magic wasn't the basis for her witchy practice. Colors, like aura reading, were more Laura's purview.

A sharp rush of fear for Laura and the other hostages pulled her attention from the glass ball itself and back to Gabriella.

"When the time comes," the older hunter said, "break it. That breaks the contract."

"Is there a trick to breaking it? Just...drop it on the ground? Crush it with my hands?"

"Slam it against the nearest hard surface. Like anything glass. You will need to put effort in. The things are sturdier than they look. But it won't be like trying to break open a plastic ball. The glass will shatter."

Angie nodded, her gaze on the swirling fog she could see through the green, red, and gold exterior. "What's going to come out of it when I break it?" She raised her brows at Gabriella.

Gabriella gave a little shrug and exchanged a look with Aidan, who remained silent but her brows were raised, too. Gabriella said, "A small essence of the demon, held as a guarantee against violating the rules of sanctuary. When you break the glass, the essence is destroyed. It...weakens the demon a little. Not much of course. They're all too strong for that. But it's a moment of weakness you can exploit while they're recovering from the break."

"How long a moment?" Angie asked warily.

"Depends on how strong the demon is. In this case…" She sighed. "A moment is probably a few seconds. No more. The weakness isn't the point."

"Says the person who won't be standing in front of a powerful demon telling them they no longer have sanctuary here."

Gabriella rolled her eyes. "The *point* is that once this is broken, you're free to send Sokolov's boss back to his realm." She made a face. "He was one of the higher order demons. You'll be better off banishing him to one of the realms deeper in the circle."

"What?"

Gabriella blinked at her. Then cursed. "Damn it. I forgot your focus was… You never got to the circles, did you?"

"What the hell are you talking about?"

Angie knew there were many demon realms. Obviously. She'd learned about those early on, when she'd first started backing up Sebastian and, occasionally, Aidan on hunts. They'd taught her there were different realms and some were more dangerous than others. And her reading about the demon witches here, as well as the visions she'd just had confirmed there were a bunch of demon realms, including a demon *god* realm. And she'd learned in her research here that some witches had mapped some of the realms. At least the realms they knew of.

But circles? There were circles involved? "What?" she repeated.

Gabriella sighed. "Okay, quick primer. We don't tell all the hunters this, because frankly, they don't need to know.

They can't choose which realms to banish a demon to. Usually, we just banish them back to where they came from because that's the link they have when they're inside summoning circles. But think of it like Dante's circles of Hell." She spun her finger in concentric rings. "There are levels, layers. Moving toward the center. The god realm is at the center."

Angie let out an involuntary shudder at the memory of that realm.

Gabriella narrowed her eyes but otherwise ignored the gesture. "That's why it's hard for even some demons to reach. They have to move through the levels. They can't just jump from an outer ring on the circle to three levels deeper into the circles. They have to move through them. For the strong demons, moving through the levels, the layers, isn't all that difficult. The lower-level demons find it much harder."

Gabriella glanced at Aidan, then gave her head a shake. "There's more, but we can discuss that later. You have to go. Remember to break the glass at the appropriate time. You'll know. Or Sebastian will and will tell you. And if you can, try to send the bastard back to a realm that's hard for him to return from. Hard to be summoned from."

"How do I do that? Exactly?" She'd never attempted anything like that. She didn't open specific realms on purpose. She'd only just realized she might be able to thanks to her visions and the documents here in the archive.

"Just…" Gabriella swirled a hand in the air. "Just concentrate on it. Will a deeper realm to open."

"I do magic not will, remember?"

"Oh stop. You're will is strong and you're perfectly capable. You may be a crap hunter but you're an excellent witch and an unfortunately powerful demon witch. You'll figure it out."

Both the compliment and the confidence in her abilities were so unexpected, Angie could only stare for a moment.

Then Aidan said, "We need to leave." And Angie shook herself out of the daze.

She opened her purse. "If I put this inside, will it break?" She looked at Gabriella and Aidan. "I don't want to walk around on the subway with it in my hands."

"I've got a taxi waiting," Aidan said.

"But it should be fine," Gabriella assured. "Like I said, it's not as delicate as it looks. It'll take effort to break."

Angie narrowed her gaze. "I feel like you're not telling me something. Tell me whatever it is now. We don't have time for these games."

Gabriella scowled, her mouth flattening into a straight line. "I've told you everything you need to know."

"Tell me the part you think I don't need to know."

Gabriella let out a huff and looked away.

"Tell her," Aidan said. "We don't have time for this."

Gabriella narrowed her eyes at Aidan. "How do you know?"

Aidan just raised her brows at that.

"Fine." Gabriella let out a huff. "The ball won't break if the demon hasn't *really* violated sanctuary. That's part of the…deal. We can't just randomly send a demon back if they haven't done something to deserve it. *We* can't," Gabriella emphasized. "The hunters. A non-hunter can do whatever they want."

"But, as you keep reminding me, I *am* a hunter right now," Angie said.

"And that's the point. This demon has come after you and Sebastian. He's manipulated circumstances and endangered someone you care about—your coworker. All these things indicate 'coming after and interfering with a hunter' for the purposes of sanctuary. Sanctuary *has* been violated. The ball will break."

"Does that mean it will break *early*, though?" Angie asked. "Like will it break in my bag."

"No. You'll have to break the glass in the presence of the demon."

Angie looked at Aidan for confirmation, which made Gabriella's scowl deepen. But Aidan nodded, so Angie put the ornament-like ball into her purse. She snatched up her water bottle, which was empty but she liked it so she didn't want to leave it behind, stuffed that into her purse carefully next to the glass ball. Then followed Aidan toward the area where she knew there was an exit even if she couldn't see it herself.

"Stay safe," Gabriella called.

Again, Angie found herself startled, and she looked back at the older hunter.

Gabriella shrugged. "We have more to discuss. And you have a lot more ways to annoy me than we've fully explored yet. Harder to do that if you get killed."

Angie almost smiled. "Thank you."

Words she never thought she'd say to Gabriella and mean so deeply.

And if she got Sebastian and Laura and the others out of this mess alive, she looked forward to annoying Gabriella more.

CHAPTER TWENTY-TWO

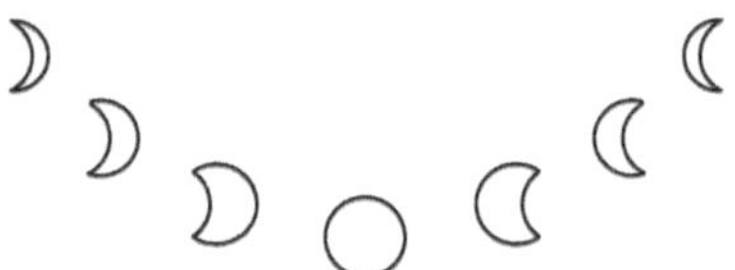

The warehouse in Queens was actually an old, converted Catholic church now used as a storage facility. The irony of a demon using an old church as their hostage location was not lost on Angie.

Though, honestly, the attachment of religious significance to demons wasn't as strong as people thought it was. Sometimes consecrated ground and religious symbols worked on demons, if they were summoned using those symbols. The method of summoning always contained the clues for banishing, and if the summoner used a particular religion as the basis for their ceremony, those same symbols worked to banish the demon.

But this wasn't always the case. And when it came to freed demons, all bets were off. You could flash a Christian cross and throw holy water at them all you wanted and it had no effect. So a demon taking up residence in an old Christian church sent a signal as much as anything.

You can't get rid of me that easily.

The church was one of the older, gray stone structures, with a beautiful arched doorway at the top of gray stone stairs. The peaked roof was tiled in dark gray slate, and the windows at the front of the building were remarkably intact stained-glass. The only sign this was a storage facility instead of an active church was the anachronistically modern sign over the beautiful wooden doors that said *Harvey and Son's Storage* in big block letters on a dirty white background. The metal sign seemed out of place against the gothic gray stones.

Aidan led them around to the side of the building after the taxi dropped them off outside the front of the church. The surrounding neighborhood felt worn and neglected. Many of the narrow, two-story houses looked quiet and currently unoccupied. Middle of a work day, that made sense. There was a strip of shops and fast-food restaurants two blocks away. The dollar store lined the sidewalk with a rack of clothing and a shelf of bins filled with plastic shoes and fake flowers. There were enough people walking around to worry Angie, but thanks to it being the middle of a work day, she hoped no one noticed what was going on in the old church.

There were no subways out here, just buses that hissed passed on the main road. And the car traffic on a nearby highway made a constant drone of noise in the otherwise quiet neighborhood. The day was bright, and warming, and completely at odds with the danger Angie found herself walking into.

Her gut churned with worry as she followed Aidan to a small wooden door at the side of the church. Almost without thinking about it, she started to stack up a water spell and an illusion spell. The problem with her witch magic was always that it took time. She had to say words, do hand gestures, build the spell and cast it. She couldn't just shoot raw power from her palm the way a wizard could. Though, with the power she'd drawn into herself in the demon realm, she had managed to shoot that from her palm twice. She did not want to take a chance on not being able to do that again.

So she defaulted to her most familiar powers, the magic she'd been working with her whole life. She'd trained herself a long time ago to hold a couple of spells at once, at the point where only one word and a single hand gesture would finish them and cast them. But until recently, she'd only ever been able to hold two spells at most in this way.

Since New Mexico, she'd found she could hold as many as four spells in the wings, close to completion, ready to be cast. The effort was no more difficult than holding two had been, and maybe even a little easier. The magic from the demon realm seemed to have enhanced her ordinary witch powers, which, she wasn't sure how to feel about.

In this circumstance, she was grateful for the extra strength. She was going to need everything she had.

Holding four spells did take more concentration than holding two, though, so she stuck to only two spells in the wings. That allowed her the focus to cast another spell and room for any spontaneous spells she might need to build, depending on the situation.

Once she had the illusion and water spells stacked and waiting, she cast a shield spell, murmuring the words quietly as she formed the necessary shapes with her fingers. Aidan waited for her to finish before opening the unlocked side door. When Angie gave the hunter a slight nod, Aidan pushed into the dark interior of the building, Angie going in close to her side so she could hold the shield in front of them both.

Out of the bright sunshine, the dark interior of the church came into clearer view. They stood in a small room which looked like an office now, with a cheap, wooden desk pushed against one wall and a series of gray metal filing cabinets against another. There was a small table with a coffee maker on it, a thin inch of black sludge left in the bottom of the glass carafe. The room smelled faintly of dust, old coffee, and paint, though the walls here were paneled in wood, so the paint smell must be from some other part of the building.

There was another door that led from the office into the rest of the church. Aidan went right for it, but paused with her hand on the doorknob, as if listening for something or waiting for some signal to go through.

Angie held her tongue and didn't ask any of the questions she wanted to. This wasn't her first rodeo with Aidan. She trusted the hunter.

The moments ticked by with Angie straining to hear whatever it was Aidan might be listening for. Her nose twitched from the dusty, old coffee smell in the office, but so far, she didn't smell that telltale hint of sulfur. Was that good or bad?

Aidan finally looked up at her and nodded, then slowly

opened the door, peeking out into a dark hallway beyond. She signaled Angie, and they both went through the door together, Angie's shield in front of them. The hallway wasn't as dark as it had looked, but the lighting was low and there were stacks of plastic crates lining the walls, coming up to Angie's head, which seemed to suck out the light.

The crates narrowed the hallway, making it impossible for Angie and Aidan to walk side by side, but to keep the shield in front of Aidan, that meant Angie had to go first.

Aidan leaned in close to her shoulder, and whispered, "Straight ahead, you'll come out into the transept of the church. We're heading toward the nave, the main area in the center of the place. There are boxes everywhere, like here, but mostly metal and wooden crates inside. The hostages are in the very center of the nave, inside one circle. Sebastian should be somewhere in that same area."

Angie nodded.

"Once we hit more open space," Aidan continued, in a whisper so quiet, Angie had trouble hearing her, "I'll move next to you again. It's better if I'm leading the way by the time we see Sokolov and the demon."

Another nod, then Angie started forward. The hallway wasn't long, but there was no door to pass through out into the main building here. The hallway dead ended at a sharp turn into the main church. At the dead end, more boxes against the stone walls, and above them what had probably once been a chandelier, though now there was just a brass plate.

They turned at the dead end and the entire nave opened

before them. As Aidan had warned, more boxes stacked around them, mostly large metal crates, and smaller wooden ones. The main part of the building was open with none of the benches or other decorations that had probably been here when it was a working church. Even the lighting overhead had been changed to lines of hanging florescent lights from whatever had been there before. The harshness of florescent lighting made Angie squint.

There were stone columns down the sides of the nave, and at the front, where the altar would have been, was just more boxes. The light from one of the stained-glass windows did drop some pretty colors onto a few of the crates near the front of the church, but otherwise, the interior was nothing but boring storage and dust. Obviously, nothing stored in here had been moved for a long time.

They edged around a stack of boxes, and finally Angie got a look at the center of the nave.

And the hostages.

A large circle had been drawn in chalk on the wooden floor, right at the very center of the open space. There were candles at the cardinal points in the circle, and a few symbols around the edges that Angie couldn't see from the distance. A standard containment circle. But it had to be a strong one to keep the humans in.

Especially since more than one of those hostages was a witch.

Angie closed her eyes, very briefly, and tried not to let the fear and overwhelm roll her under.

Not just Laura. Two of the psychics from Dana's as well,

her friends Bianca and Rachel. One of the witches who worked the floor, Talvin, who'd only started at Dana's six months ago. And Moon Star, a mundane human who also worked the main floor. Five people from Dana's. Held captive, under threat by a demon.

Because of her.

No. No. She wasn't taking the blame for this. This was the demon. And Sokolov. They could have left her alone. They could have ignored her. This was their doing.

And she intended on getting her friends out.

There were another six people as well as the people from Dana's. She didn't recognize four of them, but two were regulars at the store, though she didn't know their names. They didn't do readings with her, but they'd been at the shop often enough she'd nod and say hi to them in passing.

Were all the people from Dana's?

She let Aidan lead the way toward the circle, though she stayed close enough her shield was still safely in front of them both. She only spotted Sebastian when they neared, and he stepped out from behind a stack of wooden crates. Angie nearly collapsed at seeing him safe and uninjured.

"You okay?" she mouthed.

A brief chin bump of a nod.

Good enough. She hunted the area, looking for the demon, for Sokolov. For more guards. They had to be here or Sebastian would have freed the hostages already.

Her gaze fell on a spot on the floor that was shimmering slightly. Like heat rising into the air. Not an obvious anomaly. If she hadn't been looking, she might not have noticed it. Or might have thought it was heat rising from a heating grate in the floor—there were some of those around the edges of the room and down the center of the nave. But the heat wasn't on in here. The air inside the church was actually quite chilly.

Angie turned her head slightly to look at the waving air from the corner of her eye, and spotted the shimmering magic. A kind of glamour, she suspected. A spell? Or Fae magic? She doubted Fae. They didn't tend to deal with demons and she'd rarely encountered one anyway. Not a lot of them came into the modern world, especially the Fae with extreme iron allergies. So this was likely a witch's spell.

She started toward it when another movement caught her attention. Across the circle from Sebastian, opposite him, Sokolov moved out from behind another set of crates. The two men stared at each other wordlessly for a moment, before Sokolov turned to Angie.

He smiled, a small, slight expression that still managed to be weirdly friendly. "Angela Jordan. It is good to see you."

"It is not," she said. "Why have you kidnapped my friends?"

"To get you here, of course. This would have been easier had you just met with my boss. None of this was necessary."

"None of this was necessary period. I gave your boss my answer. No."

"You don't even know the question yet."

"I don't have to."

"You might be more interested in what he has to say than you assume."

"He's a demon. I have no interest in anything he

proposes." She glanced to the people inside the circle, met Laura's gaze. "You all okay?"

She nodded. "My fault," she said. "Should have spotted his aura. We were at karaoke."

"Never your fault," Angie said. "I'm sorry I missed karaoke night."

Laura smiled faintly, but there were lines around her eyes and mouth. Her steel-gray hair had come loose from the braids she'd tied it back in. She was wearing a green paisley blouse and a pair of fitted leggings, an almost modern look compared to her typical work attire, which leaned toward Sixties and Seventies hippy-chic.

Angie's other work colleagues were also dressed in fancier clothes than they usually wore to work. Well, except for Bianca who always wore diaphanous gowns and amazing bustiers that showed off her curvy body. Rachel, who usually wore glamorous, silky attire to work, was dressed in jeans and an off the shoulder blouse heavy with sparkling sequins. Moon Star and Talvin were also dressed up in fancy trousers and skirts and sparkling tops.

Her friends and colleagues just out having a fun night together and Sokolov used that against them.

She was not a happy witch.

CHAPTER TWENTY-THREE

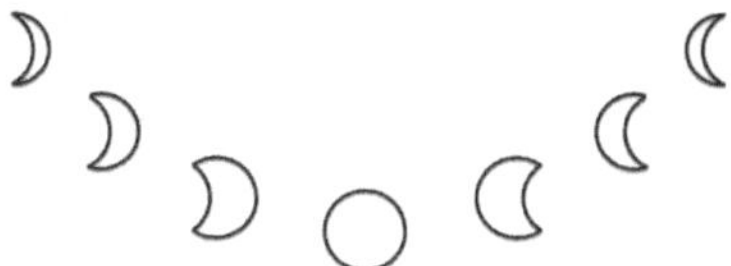

ngie turned her attention back to Sokolov, who was watching her like someone might watch an interesting bug. Angie snarled at that, and at him. "All I have ever done to you is save your fucking life. And help your sister's sick child. And this is what I get for that? My friends kidnapped, their lives endangered. Fuck you and your boss."

Sokolov shrugged. "The world is a harsh place, Angela. And powerful people do what they must."

"Remember that was something you said. Not me." Because she wasn't the one without power here.

"We could have made an arrangement at Halloween. We would not be here now. Your boyfriend insisted on refusing my offer of…friendship."

"For good reason. We are still not friends. And this will not end well for you."

"We'll see." He waved a hand, in the general direction of

the shimmering air, murmuring something under his breath which Angie assumed was a spell.

The waving air cleared. To reveal Carmen. With a demon's hand around her throat.

Because of course.

Angie let out a long, pained sigh. "We have to stop meeting this way," she told Carmen.

Carmen rolled her eyes, but didn't speak given the large, red, claw-tipped fingers around her neck. The demon wasn't the same as the one Carmen had used to threaten Sokolov. But other than that, he'd recreated the position she'd put him in six months ago, with Carmen duct taped to a chair, a demon behind her.

This demon had a long tail that it had also wrapped around her body, the spike at the tip of the tail pointing at her temple. The demon's skin was a purplish red, with scales covering his arms and tail and black horns coming out of his horse shaped head. The sharp sharp teeth it flashed from that horse mouth was so incongruent it made Angie's brain flinch away from the sight.

Searching her memory, Angie came up with a name for this demon. An Icheik. Not a pleasant creature but not one of the smart ones. All brute strength and hunger. There were way too many demons that were all strength and hunger.

But the smart ones were the really terrifying ones.

Speaking of…

From behind another set of boxes, a third man stepped into view. Sokolov's boss—Will Fredericks. The man who'd brushed against her on the sidewalk just a few days ago, and made sure she knew he was a demon.

He presented himself as a large man. Taller than Angie's six foot, wider than Sebastian. He had a demonic form—he'd shown Angie in the vision what he really looked like when he wasn't showing the world this human face—but to blend in, most freed demons who could, maintained a human appearance. The stronger ones rarely let that human appearance lapse. And Will Fredericks was a strong demon.

His human appearance spoke to his power. His black suit was immaculately cut to his larger frame, the white shirt beneath crisp. His black silk tie perfectly knotted, the pattern so subtle, Angie would have to get close to see it. Which she didn't intend to do. He had short, buzzed brown hair, a skin color that was pale but tanned, the kind of tan a person got spending too much time in the sunshine. He'd allowed some weathering to his face to give gravitas, his jaw line was heavy, his lips thin.

Some demons insisted on handsome human appearances. Some used ordinary ones that blended in. The most powerful used Fredericks's sort of appearance—not handsome, but compelling and oozing with strength.

This was the kind of magnetic "human" who drew people to him, to follow that power and bathe in his wealth and status. And Fredericks knew it.

He smiled at Angie, a hard smile. And allowed his brown eyes to flare red.

From inside the circle of hostages, she heard a few gasps. She couldn't afford to look away from the demon to check on everyone, but their fear was Fredericks's point. And that just pissed her off.

"We finally meet, Angela Jordan." He spoke with a deep, blandly American accent, unlike Sokolov's mild Russian accent. For some reason, that surprised her. Since he was known to run a Russian based group of mobsters, she'd assumed he'd give himself a Russian accent. Then again, he'd given himself a very bland, ordinary American name to go by as a human, so maybe bland American was what he was going for.

She didn't respond to his greeting, other than with a stare. He'd forced her here, they both knew it. She had no greetings for him. And she was too worried about the people in the circle for snappy comebacks.

"You can drop your shield," he said after a silent moment. "It is unnecessary."

"No."

He waited another beat, then his smile deepened. "Chatty."

She just stared.

"You have no questions for me?"

"You've forced me here. I assume you have questions for me."

"I do." His gaze flicked to the people inside the circle. "Do you want them to hear this?"

"If you hurt them, I will…" She cut off the comment, worked her jaw to keep from threatening to kill him. He was a demon. And she shouldn't be able to do that. And if there was any chance he didn't know she had killed demons, she intended on keeping that to herself. She didn't think there was much chance of that, though. Not after what Sokolov had implied at Dana's.

"I never intended on hurting them," he said, softly. "But you are stubborn and refused a meeting."

"Your man threatened Sebastian. Even though we saved his life." Her gaze flicked to where Carmen had a demon's clawed hand wrapped around her throat. "And that doesn't look like you don't intend on hurting anyone."

Fredericks's gaze flicked to Carmen. "That is a different situation. Your friends, work colleagues, they aren't under serious threat."

"I think you're lying about that."

"Why?"

"Because that's what your kind do."

"Many of us don't lie. We don't have to."

"Manipulate the truth then? Either way, they've been brought here against their will, and you have them held inside a magic circle, and none of that is good. So no, I don't take your word that they're not under threat."

He nodded faintly and pursed his thin lips. A thoughtful expression. Without the red in his eyes that he was making a point of revealing, he looked like a perfectly ordinary man. A powerful one, to be sure. But there were no other hints of his real nature. Which, she knew, spoke to his strength.

"If I release your friends, will you agree to hear me out? I just want a conversation."

Conversation? Sure. That's all he wanted.

But aloud, she said, "You release them, allow them to

leave, and I confirm they're safe… Fine. I will listen to you talk. That's all. Nothing else. No agreement to anything else. No deals of any kind. You get to talk while I'm in the same room. That's it."

"You realize this is a deal you're making," Fredericks said with that slight smile.

She wanted to snarl at him. "A limited, no loopholes one with two hunters here to witness the limits involved."

"Three."

"What?"

"Three hunters here." When she frowned, he said, "You, Ms. Jordan. Or has something changed?"

"I can't be a witness to my own very limited, no loopholes deal, which is that I'll be in the same room with you while you talk in exchange for releasing my friends and the people from Dana's and allowing them to go safely back to their lives without any repercussions or follow up threats to them."

She felt her cheeks warming at her slip. She never thought of herself as a hunter. But one of the reasons Fredericks's sanctuary was being revoked was he was a threat to her. Because she was a hunter. And if she forgot that, she risked… Well, she wasn't sure. The glass ball that was his contract not breaking when she dropped it, maybe. Maybe his sanctuary wouldn't be revoked if she somehow forgot she was a hunter?

She wished she knew or could ask Aidan or Sebastian about this. Fucking up here could get too many people killed.

"You're very specific with what our arrangement will be," he said.

"You're surprised?"

"No. Impressed."

She nearly snort-laughed at that. He didn't look impressed by her. Given her near slip and how off balance she was feeling, she didn't blame him. She wasn't particularly impressed with herself in that moment.

Fredericks considered her, his head tilted to one side. The look made her feel a bit like an ant, and he was considering if he'd step on her or let her carry on. And either option carried the same level of emotion for him.

Then he nodded, swirled one finger around and cut down sharply with that finger.

Gasps behind her had Angie itching to turn, but she didn't want to look away from Fredericks because he was still staring at her.

Aidan leaned in and whispered, "He's released the circle. Your friends are freed from that."

"Get them out of here and make sure they're safe."

"You really want me to leave you alone with that guy?" Aidan asked.

"No. I want you to come back and help. But I need to know they're all safe first."

Aidan nodded. Then looked at Fredericks. "No talking until I get back."

Fredericks's head came up and he glared at Aidan. But he didn't speak.

Which was interesting.

Laura came up beside Angie then and Angie nearly collapsed in relief. Because Aidan was so focused on Fredericks, Angie felt free to turn to Laura and give her a hug. "You're okay?" she murmured in her ear.

"We're all okay. No one was hurt," Laura assured. "But this is…not good."

"I know. It's okay. We'll take care of it."

"Do you want me to stay. Aura reading isn't my only skill."

Angie leaned back and met Laura's gaze. "I love that you're willing to help. I need you to make sure everyone else gets away safely and remains safe." She flicked a glance to Fredericks. "You…understand what he is?"

Laura nodded and issued a brief, sardonic laugh. "Met one or two in my lifetimes. Dirty auras. This one's aura is so big, though, I can't really read it."

"He's…powerful."

"Mmm. That's a word for it."

"There are always loopholes," she whispered to Laura even though she was sure Fredericks could still hear her. "I've made a deal I think will work to keep you safe, but… But there are always fucking loopholes, and I…" She shouldn't be making deals. She knew she shouldn't. But these were her friends, innocent people she needed to have safe. And frankly, she might have panicked a little. "So what I really need is for you to ensure everyone is safe and there are no…repercussions." She held Laura's gaze. "Do you understand that?"

Laura nodded. "Like I said. I've met one or two of his

type before." She glanced past Angie to Aidan, who was still staring down Fredericks. "Dana's would be safe," she murmured. "We'll go there. All of us. And stay there until you say we can leave."

"If you don't hear from me by the morning, assume there's been a disaster and take all necessary precautions, use all the spells and wards and protections you can get your hands on."

"You do that now." Laura flicked a glance at the demon. "I don't want to leave you here."

"I love you, too," Angie said. "That's why I need you to help me by ensuring everyone's safe. I'll be able to focus and concentrate better that way."

And not make any more potentially disastrous deals. This one was worth it if everyone got to safety. But if she didn't focus, she would get herself killed—or worse, end up enthrall to a demon. And with so many innocent people in danger, it was very hard for her to focus enough to navigate a conversation with a demon.

Bianca and Rachel came up behind Laura. "We're here too, if you need us," Bianca said.

"You've got a lot of backup," Rachel said.

Angie smiled and hugged them both. "I'm so sorry this happened. Thank you. The best way to help me is to ensure you and everyone else is safe. I promise I'll handle this better if I know you're all okay."

"Dana's then," Laura said. "But I'm a text away—"

"We're a text away," Bianca said.

"We're all a text away if you need us," Laura finished.

"Thank you." Angie gave the three women a last hug then hurried them toward the front door of the church where Sokolov had gone to push it open for them.

Laura, Bianca, and Rachel took charge of the group and herded everyone out the door. Aidan followed last, only taking her gaze off Fredericks when Sebastian replaced her next to Angie, his gaze on Fredericks.

There was some underlying hunter thing going on there, Angie was sure of it. Tests of will that weren't formal fights but…well, tests. So she didn't interrupt to ask questions.

"I'll ensure they get off safely, without being followed," Aidan said. "Then I'll be back." She flicked a glance at Fredericks. "Everything waits until I return."

Then she was gone.

The church fell silent then, with Sokolov returning to stand next to his boss.

Angie looked at Carmen. And realized she was still stuck inside a circle, a demon's hand around her throat, duct tape securing her to the chair. She hadn't been included in Angie's deal apparently. Shit. Angie had been too worried about everyone to notice she hadn't specifically asked for Carmen to be freed. Since Carmen wasn't her "friend" or one of Dana's customers, she'd been left out of the deal.

Dammit. A stupid mistake. Making a deal was a mistake, Angie knew, but she'd tried to mitigate the damage. And still she'd forgotten something.

Well, this was a mess Carmen had gotten herself into. Angie would just have to find another way of rescuing her without making another demon deal.

She shifted a little closer to Sebastian so her shield was protecting him now, too. And then waited in silence for Aidan to return.

The creaking and settling of stone and wood around them, the sound of a heater ticking as if it might come on. The fact that all this was happening in the middle of the afternoon, on a normal weekday, and not at night with the moonlight outside the stained-glass windows struck Angie as strange. Her encounters with demons almost always happened at night. That wasn't strictly necessary. Demons weren't vampires who were weakened by sunlight and so never came out into the sun if they could help it. But most humans used the cover of night to summon demons, so dealing with demons seemed to happen mostly at night.

Fredericks's mouth moved a little, but he continued to hold his silence as they waited. His expression didn't give away how he felt about the enforced wait. She couldn't tell if he was annoyed or just biding his time with an infinite amount of patience.

She was not a patient person. She wanted this conversation done and over with and she wanted to find a way to get Carmen out of this alive. But she didn't start the conversation. It would give him an excuse to break Aidan's edict—one she had a feeling Aidan and now Sebastian had enforced with their wills—and Angie didn't want to undermine what Aidan had done.

So Angie held her tongue and they all stood silently, staring at each other. Even the demon with its hand around Carmen's throat seemed to be waiting patiently. Unlike when

Carmen had done the same thing to Sokolov and the demon had spent the day trying to rip the mobster's head off. Sebatian had spent that day in a separate circle, willing the demon to *not* rip Sokolov's head off, and exhausted himself in the process. Angie was glad they weren't reliving *that* part of Carmen's scheme.

Carmen should be grateful too.

Angie glanced at the witch, but Carmen's expression was closed up, her gaze straight ahead. Hard to tell what she was thinking. Or doing. Carmen wasn't without talents. In fact, Angie wasn't entirely sure what most of Carmen's skills were beyond telekinesis and a will strong enough she could have (might have?) been a demon hunter. As Angie continued to glance between Carmen and the demon, she wondered if Carmen weren't doing something to keep the demon from ripping her head off, rather than the demon just being patient.

When Aidan finally returned, it felt like only about ten minutes had passed, which seemed quick for getting enough taxis to get everyone out of here, especially in this part of Queens. Aidan had probably willed the taxis to them.

She came up next to Angie, on the opposite side from Sebastian. "They're all safe. I sent them to the store with another hunter."

Another hunter had arrived? "Who?"

"Jacob."

Angie glanced sharply at Aidan. She knew Jacob had been involved in the New Mexico disaster. They did *not* trust Jacob.

"He showed up as I was getting cars to get everyone

back. He offered to help." Aidan met her gaze. "He was sincere. He was called here. Like Sebastian and I were."

That was surprising. There weren't enough hunters for *three* to be called to the same potential fight. Sometimes two —this wasn't the first time Sebastian and Aidan had been called to the same hunt—but those were usually the near impossible hunts with more than one freed demon. Three being called at once just never happened. Never.

The only time a third hunter might be called to a fight was when the first two had been killed. Hunters were never sure if that was the case until they arrived, so Jacob wouldn't have even known Sebastian and Aidan were here. Or that Angie was here.

Shit. She'd forgotten again. She was the third hunter here. Jacob the fourth. But *she* wasn't called the way a hunter was. Something she couldn't admit to or insist on right now.

At the very least, she knew Jacob couldn't have shown up because this was something to do with her, so it meant he had shown up sincerely.

Though, now that she thought about it, Angie wasn't sure what was bringing the hunters here. Unless the demon holding Carmen was about to escape. Otherwise, while there'd been a hostage situation and there was a dangerous freed demon right there, the hunters were only usually called when a demon was about to escape confinement. Was Carmen's demon captor about to escape? Or was Fredericks doing something to manipulate all this?

If so, he'd managed to drag some very powerful hunters into this audience. She couldn't imagine why he'd do something that would *also* bring Jacob. There was more going on than met the eye. But what did Jacob have to do with it?

"I think…" Aidan lowered her voice. "I think it's better Jacob's not present for this conversation." As if answering Angie's unspoken question. "Your friends will text when they are safe. And Jacob has agreed to stay with them. Laura told me if he means any harm, he won't be able to remain inside Dana's. So that will work out either way. He can stay, he'll help protect them. He can't, we learn something."

Aidan, like most hunters, was almost too pragmatic.

But she wasn't wrong either.

Angie pulled her cellphone out of the depths of her purse, and opened it so she could watch for the text. Given traffic and distances, they had at least another half hour wait, probably closer to an hour, unless Jacob willed traffic out of the way. Adrenaline had kept her upright so far, but Angie's energy was waning. She'd bolted a protein bar on the way here, but that wasn't nearly enough after all the energy used up during her visions. Her grumbling stomach and body were going to have to wait. But this was one of those *very* inconvenient moments when her need for so much food got in the way.

Still. She could have used a seat. Her gaze flicked to Carmen. Or maybe not.

Neither Sokolov or Fredericks had spoken since Aidan returned. Continuing to wait until Aidan gave the say-so. Angie couldn't tell if that was Aidan's—or even Sebastian's—will, or if they were just waiting for the distraction to be over. Maybe even a good-faith pause so Angie was assured her friends were safe.

Both kidnapping them to get Angie here, and then releasing them so easily and letting her assure herself they were safe, was some pretty top-class manipulation. She'd be more inclined to view the demon as not *that* bad because he'd allowed her friends to go free.

If she didn't know demons so well.

And understand that the show had all been a manipulation that could work for the demon on multiple levels. She'd made a deal with him—limited as it was—and that opened her up to more potential deals. And he'd made himself look generous, reasonable. Not out to kill everyone and everything.

Which, honestly, he had to know they *all* knew was a lie.

The silent wait was excruciating for Angie, and she thought maybe for Carmen, too, given the demon hand wrapped around her throat the whole time, but the others seemed to have infinite patience and no one even wobbled as they stood for nearly forty minutes. No one but Angie that was. And eventually, she just gave in and sat on the floor.

But she drew a protective circle around herself and Aidan and Sebastian first.

The only response from Fredericks was a slight smile.

When the text finally came, Angie was glad she was sitting down. The relief was intense. She exchanged a few texts with Laura, learning that the owners had arranged to lock the place down for the rest of the afternoon and evening, and the people who had to stay inside, the former hostages, were going to be fed and taken care of so everyone would remain safe.

She also learned that Jacob had been able to come into the store without feeling uncomfortable and was doing a good job at keeping everyone reassured and calm— particularly the non-witchy customers. Laura said his aura was soothing and not hectic or dark, so she thought they could trust him to keep them safe from demons.

Angie wasn't as confident. Jacob had shoved her into a demon realm. She did not like the man. But even she had to admit, he'd done so because he was afraid demons would escape and he wouldn't have the will to banish them. He'd panicked, which wasn't good, but he'd had practical and realistic reasons for that panic. Escaped demons were bad.

Still, she wasn't happy about *him* being the hunter looking after her friends. It was better than nothing. But Angie would have preferred if it was someone like Gabriella, who she trusted a smidge more.

When the text exchanges were finished and she was satisfied everyone was as safe as they could be, she reached up and Sebastian gave her a hand, helping her to her feet without ever taking his gaze off the demon and Sokolov.

Neither hunter had looked away from Fredericks and Sokolov during the entire wait. Sokolov had looked away once, to check his phone—which made Angie nervous. She was glad Dana's was on lockdown. The demon had kept his gaze on Aidan and Sebastian, a slight smile tipping up his mouth. No other signs of his mood.

Angie returned her phone to the depths of her purse and

used the action to check the glass ball was still there and still unbroken. She believed Gabriella when she said it would be hard to break. But honestly, having a glass ball in her big purse with all the different things she kept in there knocking against it was a little nerve-wracking.

"Okay," she said, finally, her voice sounding loud inside the quiet church-turned-warehouse. "Talk. Why are we here?"

The demon glanced at Aidan. Aidan gave a slight nod.

That was a fascinating exchange that Angie didn't get a chance to dwell on, because Fredericks began his pitch.

CHAPTER TWENTY-FOUR

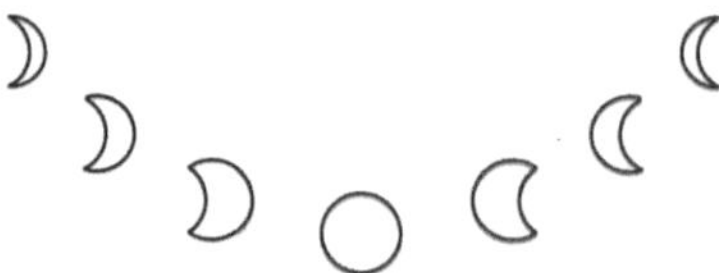

"As you are all too aware," Fredericks started, "there are several very powerful freed demons walking this realm."

The statement, given it was a fact they all knew, and that they were standing in front of one of those powerful freed demons, felt like a weird way to start, but Angie kept her mouth shut. Let Fredericks say what he needed to say. No matter what, she intended on saying no to him. But she'd made a deal that she would listen to him talk, so she was going to listen to him talk.

Even if he had started with a self-evident statement.

The light coming through the church-turned-warehouse's stained-glass windows changed as the sun got lower in the sky, taking them into the evening. It was darker in the interior of the nave now, with dark shadows filling in the high rafters and the space around the boxes and crates as the fluorescent lights overhead seemed to dim. That dimming felt a little ominous. Like this entire time, instead of waiting for Angie's friends to message that they were safe, they'd actually been waiting for dusk to fall. For this conversation to happen at night.

Because that was when horrible deals with demons were made. At night.

"Some of these demons are…not the sort of people any sane hunter would want walking around," Fredericks continued.

Angie dropped her chin and gave him a look. She couldn't help it. The irony was rich.

Fredericks gave a little head tilt in acknowledgement. "Fights happen among those powerful demons sometimes," he said. "And that is… That is bad for business."

Whose business? she thought, but kept her mouth shut. Still abiding by her part of the deal and listening.

"I understand, Ms. Jordan, that you've acquired a new and interesting talent. A very useful skill."

She neither confirmed nor denied his comment, but the tiny bit of hope she had that he might not have known about her ability to kill demons vanished. It had only been a tiny hope anyway. Given his lead in, though, she was starting to see where this was all going. And she didn't like it.

"I think," Fredericks said slowly, "that we can all agree, this new skill has…potential. Potential to rid your world of some very dangerous demons."

The *like you?* comment was on the tip of her tongue, and she only barely held it in.

"I have many enemies," Fredericks continued. "Most of whom are of very little concern to me. They aren't strong enough to touch me. Or my operation. Gnats, buzzing around. A nuisance but nothing to worry about. One firm swat, and they're no longer an issue."

Sokolov shifted from one foot to the other, his only movement during his boss's speech.

"But there are some of my enemies that are not so easy to just swat aside. A few I'd like to have gone. Those few, it would be to your benefit, to all the hunters' benefit, to have gone as well. Dangerous, horrible people. This realm would be safer without them in it."

He was really pushing her buttons and making it hard not to comment at the understatements mixed with irony floating through this conversation.

Which…

Angie thought back to the deal she'd made. Was there a reason Fredericks was trying to get her to do something other than listen? Would that somehow nullify their deal? Demons were forever twisting and turning through loopholes in deals. Had she missed something, even with such a simple and straightforward bargain?

She couldn't see anything in the wording, but now that she realized there might be something there, her determination to remain silent and hear him all the way out without commenting got stronger. He wanted to talk, he could talk.

There was nothing he could say that would make her want to be a demon assassin.

She carefully ensured her protective circle was still in place, though.

"I could make you a rich woman," Fredericks said, "in exchange for…doing a good deed for the world. Ridding this realm of beings who should not have been allowed here in the first place."

Aidan spoke up there, saving Angie from talking, though whether by design or not, Angie wasn't sure.

"The beings who are here have been given sanctuary by the demon hunters," Aidan pointed out. "Hunters can't go after them unless they break the terms of their sanctuary. Have any of these demons broken their deal with the hunters?" Aidan held Fredericks's gaze as he turned toward her, not so much as wincing when the red in his eyes flared.

Aidan had not so subtly reminded Fredericks that he had broken the terms of his sanctuary. Or at least come very close. Technically, Angie realized, he might not have yet. He'd…lured hunters here for a conversation, which could be interpreted as "interfering" with them. But so far, he hadn't attacked any of them. Not even Angie. And he hadn't threatened to kill them.

Angie wanted to curse again. Because, *technically*, she wasn't sure this counted as a breach in the sanctuary deal. The glass ball wouldn't break if it wasn't. Which meant they weren't in a position to banish Fredericks yet.

And the demon with its hand around Carmen's throat didn't count. Carmen wasn't a hunter.

But Aidan had still reminded Fredericks he was treading a thin line here.

Fredericks rolled through the moment without losing his cool. The red in his eyes settled, and he let out that faint smile. "I'm sure we can find something they've done to break their sanctuary. Shouldn't be too hard."

"Speaking from experience?" Aidan asked, tilting her head to one side to consider the demon.

His smile widened. "So far, I haven't broken the terms of my arrangement with the hunters."

"You're a threat to Angie."

"Ms. Jordan isn't really a hunter."

"She is. Technically. And we all know how much you guys love a good technicality."

Angie kept her lips pressed tight together so she didn't huff out a laugh that. Especially since she'd just been thinking along the same lines.

She wasn't happy that Fredericks knew her demon hunter skills sucked. That she wasn't *really* one. How had he known that?

His gaze drifted from Aidan to her and he said, "You didn't come when the others did," he said, answering her unspoken question. "You weren't summoned to the hunt."

She wasn't the only hunter in town who hadn't been, though. Gabriella, the other council members... None of them were here. That couldn't be how he knew Angie was a crap demon hunter.

Defending that point would require her to speak though, and she still thought it might be better if she didn't. Something was nagging at the back of her mind, some instinct that said, let Aidan and Sebastian do the talking. That her speaking would be her walking into some kind of trap she couldn't see.

She did take a moment to make sure all the magic in her web was locked down. She was safely inside a circle with her hunter companions, so she figured she could risk that moment of checking internally. Everything looked fine, every thread in place, nothing blending, nothing stretching or shivering in ways that weren't supposed to happen.

Though…

She focused in on the two red demon magic threads. Keeping her eyes open as she did meant she couldn't see the visualization representing her powers as clearly as she would have with her eyes closed. But she'd swear there was something happening with those two threads. A slight… bending? Not toward Fredericks, as she might fear. It was difficult to tell, though.

Argh. One more thing. She really hadn't needed one more thing.

The silence stretched. She stared at Fredericks while keeping an inner eye on those two threads. Neither she, nor Aidan or Sebastian, responded to Fredericks's claim Angie wasn't really a hunter. They all just stared at him.

Eventually, Fredericks was the one to break the silence. "At any rate, the demon witch isn't bound by the sanctuary arrangements, even if the demon hunter is. There's no reason the witch can't…act. Especially with this new skill. And really, it would only take…one powerful demon to send a message. The rest would back down, go into hiding. Leave this realm in peace."

"Except you," Sebastian said. The first time he'd spoken.

And the sound of his deep, powerful voice sent a wave of assurance through Angie. That comforting sound gave her some space from her fears and worries.

Enough space to realize Fredericks was not asking her to assassinate a bunch of demons. Not yet.

He had someone very specific in mind. One demon. One who's death would let all his rivals know they needed to back down and go away.

Who? Who was powerful enough to send that kind of message to all the other demons?

Fredericks spread his hands, his gaze on Sebastian now. "That is, after all, the point." His gaze moved back to Angie. "But you would be *very* well compensated for your participation in this endeavor."

"She doesn't need money," Sebastian said, answering for her so she didn't have to speak. Both he and Aidan must have sensed some trick to the demon trying to get her to talk, too. Because they were saying aloud the things she was trying to avoid saying.

"Is this true, Ms. Jordan? You have no need of money at all? Why do you work?"

She just stared, keeping her mouth shut. The more he tried to make her react, along with the way Aidan and Sebastian were speaking for her, the more she was certain he had some trick up his sleeve.

"Finish your pitch," Aidan said. "Then we're done."

"I have finished." Fredericks held Angie's gaze. She stared back. "A...mutually beneficial working relationship.

To end the reign of some of the worst freed demons on this planet."

"No." The first and only word Angie had spoken. And her answer. She hadn't agreed to anything but listening. And now her answer had been given. That *should* be the end of it. Except that this was a demon and demons were never that easy.

Fredericks ignored her single word response to his offer, which she should have expected. "Wait until you hear my first candidate. A wicked demon who lives here under the name Sharia Bakari. The outer guise of this demon is as a female banking CEO, but I can tell you her…loans are not what they seem. Do you care what happens to children, Ms. Jordan? Because Bakari does not."

Angie snarled. Children in trouble was a soft spot. And she now had a name she intended on taking up with the hunter council. But she *couldn't* be the one to go after this demon. Fredericks might take that as a deal—even if unspoken.

"No," she said again. It would be the only word she gave him.

"No, you don't care about the welfare of children? My my. How unexpected."

So so close to snarling at him. She held her neutral expression but only barely. How dare he?! But she couldn't afford to lose her cool because she'd made that stupid bargain with him. And she just knew if she did more than say no, she'd somehow end up in a worse situation.

Because he was smart and he was pushing the right buttons.

Her gaze flicked briefly to Carmen when the demon inside the circle with her made a small movement that Angie caught in her peripheral vision. Nothing inside that circle seemed to have changed when she looked, though. The demon's claw-tipped hand was still firmly around Carmen's throat and its spiked tail was still pointed at her temple like a gun. And Carmen still looked both pissed off and terrified.

She caught Angie's gaze and managed to give her head a very tiny shake. A warning.

Angie wasn't entirely sure what Carmen was warning her about, but since all of this was bad, Angie figured the warning was universal.

"How about the freed demon who delights in polluting this planet with chemicals that will take a millennium to clean?" Fredericks continued. "They're ensuring your government continues to strip resources and destroy this world piece by piece."

Angie's mouth worked as all sorts of comments and questions piled up against her tightly closed lips. She kept them inside.

"Nothing?" Fredericks asked. "What a terrible witch you are, not even caring about the health of this planet."

No pretending he wasn't trying to push buttons now.

Sebastian moved an inch closer to her, though he didn't touch her. Her touch psychic skills were locked down. She couldn't afford any accidental readings. Especially after the earlier visions. But she appreciated Sebastian's show of support.

Fredericks titled his head to consider her. Again, it was that "looking at a strange bug and considering if squashing it was in order" look. Angie didn't very much like being the bug in this situation.

Unfortunately, Fredericks hadn't given her a reason to break his contract yet. If she pulled out that glass ball and attempted to smash it now, and it didn't smash, she'd have not only shown her hand, she'd probably get herself and her companions killed. The irony of which would be that then the glass would break. But it would be too late for Sebastian and Aidan and Carmen and herself.

Not a great plan.

She needed to get Carmen and get out of here. How, though? How to get Carmen free without making another deal? Without saying something that got Angie trapped in some unseen loophole in her deal with Fredericks.

She was afraid to say anything but no. Afraid to even ask about Carmen. And while the two hunters had been doing a good job of doing the speaking for Angie, she had a feeling they were also exerting a lot of will to keep things on a neutral level and not tipping over into an actual fight.

How much longer could this go on before she was officially free of the deal she'd made?

She thought back on it. She'd agreed to remain in the same room with him and hear him out in exchange for the release of her friends. Agreed to be in the room while he talked.

She hadn't set a limit on how long he was allowed to talk before the conversation was done. Which was a mistake. He could literally drag this out for days. And she was already wobbly and in need of food and rest. She'd come into this wobbly and in need of food and rest.

What other mistakes had she made?

He'd switched to describing yet another horror of a freed demon, out in the world doing horrible things. She half ignored him, because the two insidious examples he'd already dropped were more than enough. She now understood Jacob's drive to ensure the hunters were strong and able to banish these high-level demons. Why he was so driven to ensure they didn't free any more. Freed demons like these, these powerful ones who destroyed hunters before the sanctuary deal and then continued to brutalize humans afterward with no consequences, were an abomination. An insult to everything the hunters tried to do.

Listening to Fredericks, Angie definitely had more sympathy for Jacob's cause. She still didn't like Jacob. Or trust him. But she could see his reasoning.

"You're determined to keep the gift you've been given to yourself," Fredericks asked, "instead of using it for good? You could destroy so much evil, Ms. Jordan."

Classically, demons were known for their temptations. And in reality, tempting their victims really was one of their specialties. That was how you got loopholes in bargains. By offering temptations the summoner, or deal-making human, couldn't resist.

Getting rid of so much evil in the world with this power

she'd brought out of the demon realm was absolutely, hands down, one of the best temptations this demon could have offered her. She knew he was tempting her, attempting to trick her into another bargain. And still she was lured. Still she wanted to get rid of the evil he was offering her up on a platter.

The world would be such a better place without these demons. Safer. And all she had to do was take them out. To destroy them as they'd destroyed so many lives. To…

Become just like Carmen where the ends justified the means no matter what it did to Angie's own soul.

Her gaze flicked to Carmen again, but this time Carmen made no small, warning head gesture. Probably because this was the exact bargain Carmen herself had wanted to make with Angie. She also wanted Angie to start killing freed demons, to rid them from this world.

They all wanted her to be an assassin. The hunters, the demons, Carmen… Everyone.

And after some of the things Fredericks had described, she finally, finally understood why Carmen did what she did, too. She finally understood that temptation to take matters into your own hands to destroy the bad guys.

But in doing so, Carmen had endangered countless innocent lives over the years. Including children. Including babies.

Did Angie really want to become that?

No. No she did not.

This was a stance she'd come to years ago with her magic. To do no harm with her magic. To be careful what she put out, knowing it would come back. It was a difficult line to walk. Harm was often, unwittingly, inevitable. But she did her best, tried her hardest, walked that line. Because it was important.

As a witch.

She hadn't officially come to this position with the demon magic yet. There hadn't been time. She had mostly been focused on finding a way to get rid of it, to remove it from her other powers. To maybe even remove the demon witch thread, though she wasn't sure she could.

She hadn't had time to make the same commitment with the demon magic as she had with her witch magic. But in the end, that commitment was no different. She did not want to go down the path of revenge and killing and death to justify an end result. Humans were too fallible. *She* was too fallible. She could easily make mistakes, kill the wrong people, destroy more lives than she saved. Because she wasn't perfect. She didn't know everything about everything.

And it would be entirely too easy to make mistakes once blinded by blood lust.

That was the path the hunters had feared she'd take *before* the demon magic. She wondered if they feared that still.

Or might they end up on Fredericks's side of the equation, the way Jacob was, because this was about killing demons.

"No," she said. Again. To all of it.

There was no other answer if she wanted to remain herself. If she wanted to be able to look herself in the mirror.

The crimes of the freed demons would have to be dealt with in another way. Something she could discuss with Gabriella and maybe the rest of the council. But she would not be the one exacting those consequences.

She was a witch. Not an executioner.

"Perhaps, you just need clearer…motivation," Fredericks said.

The words were barely out of his mouth, with no time for Angie to react. When another circle popped into view. Opposite Carmen and her demon.

Holding someone who looked like a very annoyed human.

But who smelled, very distinctly, of sulfur.

CHAPTER TWENTY-FIVE

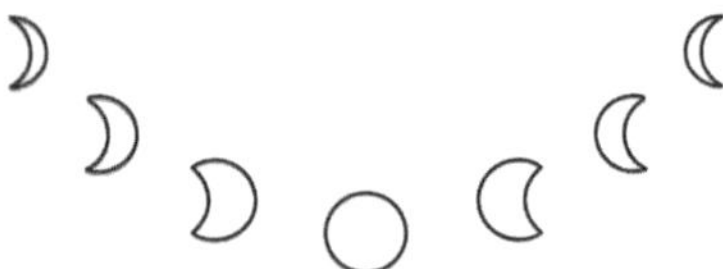

"A smaller, but no less wicked enemy for you to consider, Ms. Jordan," Fredericks said, his attention turned to the newly visible circle and the human-looking demon standing within.

Sebastian and Aidan both moved up a step away from Angie. Aidan placing herself more in front of Angie now. Sebastian moving to stand between Angie and the newest circle.

Angie wanted to be annoyed that they didn't trust her not to give in to this lure, but knew she was too close to that edge, and wasn't surprised they knew it too. Was actually much more relieved than annoyed that they were taking precautions to ensure she didn't do something stupid. Or that Fredericks didn't do anything more aggressive than he'd already done.

The human-looking demon stepped up to the edge of the

circle he was in, smiled as he nudged the very edge of the chalk line, now visibly drawn onto the church-turned-warehouse's wooden floor. "As promised," he murmured. "Weak."

And then the demon changed forms. A woman stood inside the circle now. One who looked vaguely like a young Carmen, though with darker hair and bright red eyes. She wore a slinky black dress that wasn't like anything Angie had seen Carmen in before.

"She taught us the trick, didn't she?" the demon said, smiling at Carmen, still firmly trapped by another demon. "How to lure the hunters. Such fun. But I'm not happy about my part in this game, Will." The demon set her full mouth into a pout.

Fredericks chuckled. "Then you shouldn't have gotten indebted to me, should you." Fredericks shifted his gaze to Angie. "You've met a Khymir before? They're an interesting species."

The demon changed shapes again, this time looking exactly like Fredericks. It let out a chortle. "Interesting," the demon said imitating Fredericks's voice exactly. "Is that what you call this? I call it coercion."

Fredericks ignored the shifting demon. "It has caused much pain and suffering in its time. Summoned and banished over many centuries, always just on the edge of escaping before a hunter shows up. No one would dare let this demon out. It can be…anyone. Anyone at all."

The demon shifted again, and now it was Laura. "Don't

trust him," the demon said in Laura's voice. "His aura is dirty. You can't trust someone like that."

This last was the image that nearly made Angie lose her façade of indifference. The demon sounded *exactly* like Laura. And if Angie hadn't known better, she'd swear that demon *was* Laura.

That was absolutely terrifying.

"It's the demon," Aidan cautioned. "Don't let it fool you."

Angie nodded, her gaze remaining on Fredericks now, so she didn't have to see what form the demon took. Hearing it use different voices was enough.

Fredericks's smile widened. "Carmen has been very helpful, teaching my associates how to lure hunters. Not something I thought I'd have use for until…you. But there you go. You never know when an interesting fact will come in handy, right?"

Angie scrambled at that comment. The demon had said something similar. And said the circle around it was weak.

Fuck. That shapeshifting demon was on the verge of escaping. That's what all the hints were about.

She started to say as much out loud, only to realize Sebastian and Aidan would already know. Their demon hunter instincts knew. That's why they were here. They might have even been aware of that third demon this whole time. There hadn't been an opportunity for them to mention it without Fredericks overhearing. Maybe they wanted him to think they didn't know about it.

Telling them something they probably already knew

might give too much information to Fredericks—especially the fact that Angie did not know what a demon hunter should. He knew. They all knew she wasn't really a hunter. But the technicality still mattered for whether or not he'd broken the rules of sanctuary.

She hated demons.

His expression of smug triumph made Angie want to snarl. But she needed him to keep talking—better him than the Khymir since it could speak in any voice and that might freak her out again.

Fredericks didn't talk, though. He just stared at her, as if waiting for…something. Her to speak maybe?

She got the distinct feeling she was missing something. Something important. And he was waiting for her to figure it out.

When Sebastian snarled, drawing her attention—because he rarely let out that kind of emotion during a fight—she realized the shapeshifter demon looked like her now. And wasn't that freaky and weird. Almost like looking in a mirror. Though her mirrored-image's expression was a taunting smile and not the more horrified expression Angie was sure she had.

But seeing herself inside the circle…

The demon looked at her, with her own eyes, smiled wide. And shifted again. This time taking on the form of Jacob.

And Angie gasped. "Shit. They've already freed one. It's with the others."

She dug out her cellphone even as Fredericks and the

Khymir laughed. Even as she heard Aidan made a noise like tsking and Sebastian stepped to the edge of Angie's protective circle.

And the Khymir slid its foot against the weakened containment circle that was keeping it out of this realm. The chalk smudged.

The circle would collapse soon.

And all Angie could think about was the danger her friends were in. Locked into Dana's with a demon!

She fumbled with her phone, hunting for the texts she'd just exchanged with Laura. Rapidly trying to get to the right number to make the call.

"Now what, demon witch?" Fredericks asked, conversationally. "You've a conundrum on your hands. So many people in danger. Probably enough hunters around to handle it. Maybe." He paused. "But maybe not."

Laura's cellphone rang out. Angie cursed again and hit the button on her phone that automatically dialed Dana's Cauldron. That phone rang out, too.

More cursing. Panic bubbled through her. She couldn't get there fast enough. They were so far away and she was out here with another demon about to escape, one with a hand wrapped around Carmen's throat, and a smug already freed demon with one of his minions laughing at Angie's distress.

Gabriella. Angie tried that number next.

"None of them can help," Fredericks said. "You'll have to deal with the situation as it is."

Angie's pulse thumped so hard she could barely hear the rings on her cellphone. She was panicking so much now she couldn't think straight. So much, it took her several more seconds to realize the Khymir hadn't escaped yet. And she still had two hunters here.

She narrowed her eyes at the Khymir still looking like Jacob. It hadn't seen him come in. How did it know what he looked like? Was the other Khymir at Dana's in Jacob's guise? But if so…Jacob would have been uncomfortable in the store. Laura would have seen his restlessness.

The Khymir could *be* Laura. And everything Angie thought was happening had been a lie told to her by a freed demon.

But she'd hugged Laura. Even with her touch psychic skills hard locked down after the earlier visions, she'd have known she was hugging a demon and not her friend. Wouldn't she?

Gabriella didn't answer either.

Who else. Who could she call?

She tried Bianca and then Rachel. Neither answered. That was bad. Very very bad. In desperation, she tried her boss's house number.

Then nearly collapsed when Dana herself answered. "I'm sorry to bother you in the evening at home, but I think we have a situation at the store. Have you heard of a Khymir demon?"

It took exactly two seconds for Dana to catch on—much quicker than it had Angie—and because Dana and her partner already knew the situation, it took Angie exactly one minute to ensure *someone* was heading to the store to check on the impending disaster and take care of the problem.

She knew Dana and Omar were strong witches. They set the protection on the store themselves yearly. They'd been in this business, knowing supernatural entities were likely to show up at their store, for longer than Angie had been alive.

She'd trust them now to look after the others.

Taking a deep breath, she faced Fredericks again. Her heartbeat was still hammering and the adrenaline rush of panic had left her dizzy. But she'd done what she could on that side of things.

Now it was up to her and Sebastian and Aidan to take care of this side of things.

"Feel better?" Fredericks asked.

Angie didn't answer.

"It won't matter," he said. "They'll just all die."

She swallowed her growl. Because his taunt, his attempt at making her lose her temper, had possibly given her a weapon. *She* might have just been given a loophole in their deal. Fredericks couldn't have really done that. Could he? She thought back over her words to him again.

"He has," Aidan said quietly, most of her attention still on Fredericks.

Angie didn't have to ask how Aidan could possibly know what she was thinking. The hunter had been dealing with demons for a very long time. She understood their deals, their loopholes, and the problems and consequences of dealing with them.

She'd probably realized Fredericks had fucked up the minute he had, a few seconds before Angie realized.

Angie went through the words in the deal she'd made

again. And aloud, said, "…you talk in exchange for releasing my friends and the people from Dana's and allowing them to go safely back to their lives without any repercussions or follow up threats to them."

She met Fredericks's gaze. "Without any follow up threats or repercussions. To them."

Fredericks raised a brow but otherwise hid his reaction to that well. Angie felt the shift in the room, though. The change in balance. He'd agreed to a deal that protected the others from any follow up threats. A Khymir in their midst was a follow up threat. Planted ahead of time. Among the hostages inside the circle. Or even in the guise of Jacob.

That Khymir was a definite threat. A continued threat. When there shouldn't have been any follow up threats. According to the very specific words of the deal Angie had agreed to.

"I win," she murmured.

Because whether Fredericks had meant to or not, she was *technically* a demon hunter, and *technically* what they'd just done had been a challenge fight—any deal made with a hunter could absolutely be viewed as a challenge, from a given angle. And *technically*, he'd lost because he'd broken the deal.

Which meant…

Technically, Angie could banish him now.

CHAPTER TWENTY-SIX

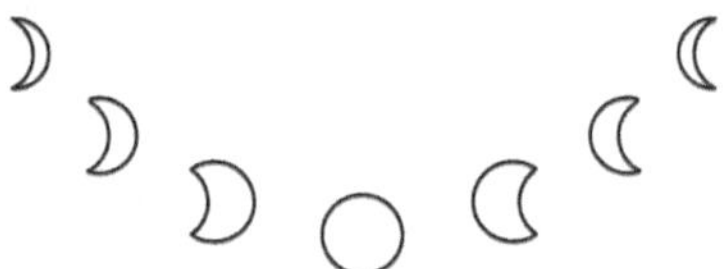

"It wasn't a challenge," Fredericks said, though he wasn't smiling when he said it. "I don't challenge hunters. It goes against the terms of my sanctuary."

"Making a deal with a hunter is a challenge fight. A fight of wills. That's why you were trying to get me to talk, wasn't it? I agreed to listen. Just listen. Not argue or debate or even comment back while you had your say. That's the trick, the loophole with the deal I agreed to. Once you said you were finished with your pitch, I could speak, but there was nothing in the deal to say you couldn't keep talking. And I'd have to keep listening. But now… The deal is broken. By you." She smiled, but with a vicious edge to it. "I win."

"We never set terms. What did you win but a hollow victory?"

"What would I have lost if I'd spoken earlier?"

Fredericks gave a brief shrug. "It hardly matters now."

"Uh huh. Meaning there was something you intended to take if I lost. So, there is something I can take now that I've won."

"And what will that be? Banish me? My colleagues will just summon me again." He glanced at Sokolov. "It's true I won't have free reign here anymore. That would be unfortunate. But not something I couldn't work around."

"You sought sanctuary here for a reason. Running amok and killing hunters couldn't have been that tiresome. You chose negotiation instead of bloodshed." And Angie had no doubt it could have been a bloodshed. "What did you get with your freedom here? More importantly, what were you escaping?"

"Is that your prize, then? Answers?"

She shook her head. "No. Just hoping you'd bad-guy monologue."

Fredericks's eyebrows shot up. Sokolov made a noise that sounded like a cough.

The barely trapped Khymir shifted to Bianca's form and let out a high, sweet laugh. Angie wanted to throw something at the demon for daring to take Bianca's shape. But she kept her attention on Fredericks.

"No…bad-guy monologuing today I'm afraid. If you want those answers, I will give them to you, but they'll be your prize for winning our battle."

She grinned. "Glad we agree it was a proper challenge."

"It was," Sebastian said, though his focus was still on the Khymir.

"It was," Aidan added. She had her attention divided between Fredericks and the demon holding Carmen.

Fredericks spread his hands. "It was. And I failed. So. A prize. Banish me, then, is it?"

She narrowed her eyes. Banishing him would get him out of their hair. Might even put him back in the way of whatever had pressed him to seek sanctuary in this realm. It wouldn't be the end of him, though, as he'd said. He still had an entire crime network and loyal minions here to do his bidding. And he'd find another way through.

But it would complicate things for him. And make it more difficult for him to harm her friends.

It would not put her friends beyond the reach of Sokolov and his people, though.

She could make that her prize. None of her friends, acquaintances, family members, anyone she ever knew, could be targeted by him or his people.

Somehow, she had a feeling he'd find a way around that. It was too open and vague. Maybe by torturing strangers in front of her just to prove she'd lost after all. That would be a very demonic thing to do.

She could get him to recall and banish the Khymir he'd already freed. The one that was likely amongst her friends even as they spoke. She had no doubt Fredericks had some sort of control of that demon. He'd have hardly agreed to this arrangement with a Khymir otherwise.

Rescuing her friends and getting rid of that demon did tempt her as a prize. But she had to trust the witches and

Jacob—which was harder to do than she'd admit in front of Fredericks. Still, Angie couldn't be in two places at once. The others knew what to do.

So, what prize?

Her gaze flicked to Carmen. Carmen's eyes widened. Angie sighed. Yeah. Yeah. That's what she wanted.

"Carmen freed from her current predicament inside that circle. Carmen free from the circle. Carmen officially off your hit list. That's my prize."

From the corner of her eyes, Angie saw Sebastian's shoulders tighten, him move a step closer to her. But he didn't comment or make a noise that could give away how he felt about what she'd asked. Neither did Aidan. Aidan didn't even move, except for her gaze sliding between Carmen and Fredericks.

"You don't banish me as a consequence of losing? That's…unusual for a hunter."

"We've all established I'm an unusual hunter. But you have another prisoner that I want free. We can deal with you after that."

"Deal with me? I do still have sanctuary here."

It was the first time he'd said that so boldly. But he'd challenged a hunter and lost. He'd lured hunters here—even if she hadn't heard it—and he'd tried to hire her as an assassin, which, really should count as "interfering" with a demon hunter. And yet…

Angie still wasn't sure. She got the feeling he'd skirted the line of all this so closely but still stayed on the side of safe. And that if she tried to break the glass ball tucked inside her purse, it wouldn't break. She couldn't ask the others. Gabriella's assurances were…not as reassuring now as they'd been in the archive. Not while Fredericks was smirking at her. And Angie knew if she jumped the gun, she could cost them their only advantage.

She should probably have banished him. The challenge was a way around the sanctuary. Probably. It had to count. Right? Damn she wished she understood this all better.

She really was a crap hunter.

"Depends on what you do after you release Carmen," she said, to hide her uncertainty. And because they were saying the quiet part out loud now, "You've been skirting the line of your sanctuary agreement all day. By luring the hunters here. By luring me here. By threatening people close to me."

Who were still in danger and she wasn't there to help them because of all this crap and really she wanted to be there to help them. She trusted the witches of Dana's. But she hated that she wasn't there to keep them safe.

Fredericks shrugged. "My sanctuary is at an end anyway. She'll be here soon. You've summoned her. There's no way to avoid it. Unless, of course, you decide to go another way."

"A way that saves you?" She snorted. "Who's this 'she' I've supposedly summoned. Since I haven't summoned anyone. And why is Carmen still inside that circle with a demon's hand wrapped around her throat. You're not abiding by the challenge rules."

One thing a demon did, like it or not, was abide by its deals and by the challenge rules. But often because they'd worked some loophole into their deals. They were bound to the challenge rules, same as hunters were. The fact that he hadn't feed Carmen yet was…odd.

Fredericks waved a hand at the circle. The demon slowly, slowly released its grip on Carmen's neck, moved its tail spike away from her temple, and stepped away from her.

She was still taped to the chair, so she couldn't get up or leave the circle. But at least the demon wasn't right there so close to being able to kill her. It wasn't enough space and she wasn't free yet, though.

"You okay?" Angie asked her, because she hadn't spoken this entire time.

Carmen made a sour face and nodded, her mouth pursed. Then jerked at the tape holding her wrists to the chair and raised her brows. Angie in turn raised her brows at Fredericks. But in the back of her head, she wondered why no sarcastic or annoyed comment from Carmen.

Fredericks considered Angie a moment longer. Then glanced to the demon still inside the circle with Carmen. "She's really caused me a lot of trouble over the years. It's tempting to let Sokolov have his revenge."

"Challenge forfeits must be paid."

"Yes, but thanks to you, all the rules have changed."

"I don't think so."

Fredericks smiled. "You really don't realize, do you? Well, I suppose you wouldn't. No one is still alive who could tell you."

"I hate demon games," she muttered.

"Shame then that they just love you."

"Real shame. Release Carmen."

"If you insist. Release her I will." Fredericks waved his hand again. "But you should know, this will not end well."

Angie cursed, but before she could do anything, the demon inside the circle with Carmen surged forward and drove its spiked tail through Carmen's chest.

CHAPTER TWENTY-SEVEN

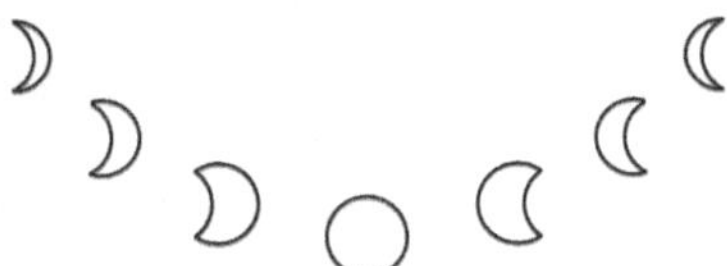

Angie screamed in denial even as she *knew* she'd fucked up. This was her fault. She hadn't phrased her forfeit right. She *knew* better. She knew this was her mistake.

That only increased her anger.

Anger and guilt that had her acting out without thought. On instinct.

Reaching for the demon magic threads. Throwing that power at the demon who'd just killed Carmen.

A red streak of fire shot from her hand. Cut through her own magical circle. Cut through the circle surrounding Carmen as if it wasn't there.

And slammed into the center of the Icheik demon's chest.

The demon screamed. A flash of bright white light. An explosion that rocked the church-turned-warehouse's stone walls.

And then it was gone, in a red mist.

In the silence that followed the explosion, the Khymir demon giggled. A sound that was like none of Angie's friends or acquaintances, thankfully. But the sound still grated across her raw nerves.

Angie's entire body shook as Carmen slumped forward in the chair, her bonds still holding her in place. Red dripping down her chest and pool on the floor under her chair.

Everything inside Angie rebelled at that sight. She didn't even *like* Carmen. Didn't even know her real name. And yet the pain and guilt and anger at seeing her killed…

Angie growled as she faced Fredericks. "Fuck you."

She wanted so badly to take her anger out on him, even though she knew she was to blame. She'd left room in her demand. "Free" didn't mean safe and alive to a demon. "Free" and "release" could mean freed and released from life. Dead meant Carmen was no longer in the predicament of being held captive by a demon.

Angie *knew* these things. But with everything else…she'd forgotten. She'd fucked up. And she was never going to forgive herself.

And she wanted to punish Fredericks for it. Wanted to make him pay.

"Your eyes are red now," Fredericks said. "Fascinating to watch. I…escaped the last time before I witnessed the full extent of the carnage first hand. I can see now that was wise."

"I don't know what you're talking about." Her voice was very deep with her magic and barely sounded like her.

Sebastian didn't move any closer to her, but he didn't

move away. And Aidan hadn't even flinched. Had they known what was coming? Why hadn't they stopped her and ensured she didn't fuck that all up?

She wanted to cry and scream and hurt Fredericks. She wanted to feed all this pain and guilt into him, cut through him like butter.

She'd spent all this time trying not to let that anger out. Trying to ensure she stayed in control of her power. Her magic. Her demon witch ability to release a plague.

This ability to kill demons… It made that control harder. And in that moment, Angie understood Carmen so so well. Understood how tempting and *easy* it would be to take revenge for a wrong, when that revenge was meted out on someone truly evil.

There were no innocent bystanders here. Aidan and Sebastian were safe. She could keep them safe. Especially if she killed Fredericks and the giggling Khymir demon. Sokolov wasn't much of a threat without his demon boss. But she could kill him too. She could kill them all.

Angie blinked hard a few times and gave her head a shake. Tears leaked over her cheeks.

"Ang?" Sebastian, a quite murmur that cut through the chaos and anger. The *guilt*.

"I'm not okay," she said.

"I know." He did move closer then. Not touching her. But enough that he was standing at her shoulder. And if she needed to, she could take hold of his hand.

"I want him dead."

Sebastian shrugged. "You wouldn't be the only one."

That response startled a snort out of her. Not a laugh really. But a burst of some emotion that wasn't the guilt. And it managed to lessen the grip of her own anger. Not fully, not even much. But just enough…

She took a deep breath. Let it out slowly through her mouth. Kept her gaze on Fredericks so she wouldn't see Carmen's slumped form.

Aidan remained where she was, a position that managed to block Carmen from Angie's peripheral vision if she was careful. That the hunter hadn't said anything at all during all this baffled Angie. And she wanted to ask why? Why Aidan hadn't stopped her making that mistake? Why Aidan had let her fuck this up so monumentally that she'd gotten someone killed?

Why hadn't Aidan stopped her?

Why had Aidan let her kill another demon?

The last… Well, neither Aidan nor Sebastian could have stopped her in the moment. Angie hadn't even thought about what she was doing. It had all happened so fast. Sebastian had even seen Angie do this before and hadn't had enough time to stop her.

But would the hunters have even if they'd been forewarned? Their job was to rid this realm of demons. And as Jacob had pointed out, dead demons were so much better than just banished demons who could always come back. Jacob *wanted* Angie to go around killing demons.

But then, so did Fredericks.

Fuck. "Did I just kill one of your enemies? Did I do you a favor?"

She'd hate that as much as she hated the fuck up that had gotten Carmen killed. That she'd have just done the thing Fredericks wanted her to do. She suspected he'd had Carmen killed specifically to see Angie lose control. And she'd been stupid and angry and guilty enough to oblige him.

So many mistakes in such a short period of time.

"You proved the rumors were true," Fredericks said. "There was a moment of doubt there. A moment when I thought maybe you couldn't really do what was being claimed. I mean…what are the odds? Two humans in one millennium? Very improbable. But obviously, not impossible."

"I really don't know what the fuck you're talking about."

"I realize that. I'm still coming to terms with it all myself."

The hints and insinuations without answers made her already raw nerves and delicate temper spike again. Why couldn't he just fucking say what he was trying to say? She hated demons so fucking much.

Sparks of magic, her magic this time, the witch magic, danced around her fingertips. She wouldn't mind giving Fredericks a nice, solid hit with her shock spell. Something about the idea of using her witch magic, not the demon magic, to hurt him felt very satisfying.

But she reined that in, too. She pulled in all the magic that was pushing at her control, pushing her to lose control. The need to unleash her fury and guilt all over this church-turned-warehouse was so strong she shook.

She wasn't thinking either. The guilt, the anger, they were

all clogging up her brain, making any sort of logical thought impossible. She was going to unleash that anger without understanding any of this and that would be yet another mistake.

The demon had done all this on purpose. Fredericks wanted *proof* that she could kill a demon. He'd set her up, thrown her off balance. First by having her friends here, and Carmen captured by a demon the way she'd done to Sokolov. Then letting her friends leave with a freed Khymir demon in their midst. Revealing that he'd freed the Khymir only after she'd relaxed enough to think her friends were safe. Throwing her so far off balance, without her even realizing how much, he was able to get her to make yet another mistake after their unofficial but still very real challenge.

And then he'd killed Carmen.

To get Angie to *prove* she could kill a demon.

What had he said…? Two humans in a millennium. Two.

She blinked and straightened her shoulders. The demon witch from centuries earlier, Betha. The one who'd been searching for a cure for the thing that allowed her to kill demons, the thing that had infected her love.

The one Angie only knew about because of the visions.

The hunters hadn't known about Betha. Not her name anyway. Only a random pile of documents from an injured hunter to say that a demon witch had killed a demon before. They hadn't even known the diarist and that random pile of documents from Yusuf were about the same witch.

But Fredericks knew about her. Hell, Fredericks could have been there.

Even if he wasn't, he knew. He knew something. And he'd set all this up to confirm the improbable had happened again. With Angie.

Why, though? What was his end game? Just to make her kill his enemies? He'd claimed his sanctuary was at an end anyway. So what could he possibly want from her now?

And did any of that really matter?

The end was the same, no matter his goal. Carmen was dead. Her friends at Dana's were dealing with a demon in their midst. The shapeshifting demon was giggling irritatingly enough she wanted to smack it with a shut-up spell. And Fredericks was smirking at her.

Short of killing Fredericks and Sokolov, banishing the Khymir demon, what else could she do here?

The sense of doom. Of overwhelming failure hit her hard. So strong she blinked again. Because, while she had failed, while the guilt choked her, the sense of failure, of inevitably losing everything, of blackness, of bleakness, was so intense it didn't feel like hers.

She snarled at Fredericks. "Stop it."

She wasn't sure how he was doing it—she didn't know enough details about his particular species of demon—but there were demons who could force emotions on humans. Fredericks was obviously one of those.

The bleakness cut off abruptly. Nothing stopped her guilt, not with Carmen right there. But the hopelessness that had started to swamp her stopped instantly.

"Tipped your hand there," she murmured. And rebuilt the protective circle around herself and the hunters. She'd cut it when she'd killed the demon. That it had taken her this long to remember and rebuild it wasn't entirely surprising, but it didn't speak well of her self-preservation instincts in those moments.

More of the doom and overwhelm eased. Giving her more room to think.

Did it matter that Fredericks knew there'd been another demon witch who could actually kill demons? It did. Because he was doing all this for a reason. And that reason would cost more lives if she didn't figure it out.

So she wasn't going to kill Fredericks just because she was angry. That way led directly to her own destruction. Like it or not. She couldn't afford to go down that path, tempting though it was.

"You knew her?" Angie asked. "Or did you just hear about her?"

Fredericks paused for a microsecond. Not long. Not too obviously. But long enough Angie realized she wasn't supposed to have known about the other witch. That made sense. The hunters hadn't known about her. Fredericks had been dropping hints without thinking Angie could have any way of making sense of those hints. She'd only just learned about Betha in the last few days. Had this confrontation happened any earlier, or if she hadn't attempted to get visions from some of the documents in the archive, she would have no clue what Fredericks was keeping from her, no way to even guess at what his hints meant.

But she did know. And that had surprised him.

"You knew her," Angie said. "Did she almost kill you?"

Neither Sebastian nor Aidan reacted to what Angie was saying. Sebastian had probably already caught up, might have even figured out what Fredericks was saying earlier, when Angie was still too compromised by her emotions to understand. Aidan might have figured it all out earlier, too, but it was always hard to tell what Aidan knew and didn't know.

So the fact that it was Aidan who answered and not Fredericks mildly surprised Angie. "He was there. He knew. He saw."

Angie worked hard not to react to that, the same way the hunters hadn't been reacting to her comments. But she did blink a few times. Angie had known there was more to Betha's story. But how much more? What had happened in the end?

And how the hell did Aidan know about it when none of the other living hunters did?

Fredericks's lips pursed and he shrugged. "It's impossible to forget that sort of encounter. Even for a demon. I did not expect to witness it a second time. Not so soon."

She was still missing something, Angie realized. There was still something she didn't know.

Before she could ask, though, the demon inside the circle, the Khymir demon who'd been giggling, said, "This is all soooo entertaining. But you promised me freedom. Like my brother. And it's time to pay up."

Fredericks sighed and looked at the demon. Who shifted to look just like Fredericks, flashing him the patient and irritating smile that Fredericks had used on Angie a few times.

The real Fredericks narrowed his eyes. "I realize you think you're funny. But I'm not a demon you want to toy with."

The Khymir demon immediately changed forms again, this time to look like a random man who wasn't anyone Angie had seen before. A Hispanic man, medium height, dark hair, casual clothing, little older and thick around the middle. A man who would blend well in this neighborhood and go completely unnoticed walking down the street.

"Better," Fredericks said. "You understand the terms? They are the same as your brother."

"I understand," the demon said, its voice now a neutral American accent like Fredericks's but with a little roll in vows.

Fredericks turned his head just enough to indicate a glance at Sokolov without actually looking at his minion. Sokolov went to the circle containing the Khymir.

"No!" Angie edged forward. "You can't release another one of them." One was enough. "That violates your sanctuary."

And there was no waffling or questions, no had-he or hadn't-he about it. He wasn't allowed to release a plague of demons. That wasn't a loophole the hunters would have ever allowed in a sanctuary agreement. Or this realm would have been overrun by demons a long time ago.

Fredericks also couldn't just say it was his minion freeing the demon, not him. Not with two hunters witnessing him give the order… Three, she corrected. Still, technically, three hunters. He was blatantly showing them he was no longer under the binding rules of the sanctuary agreement. He'd said as much earlier but this was not something he could walk back or talk himself out of. This was absolute.

Angie removed the glass ball from her purse.

Fredericks saw her hold it up. Met her gaze over the top of it.

And smiled.

CHAPTER TWENTY-EIGHT

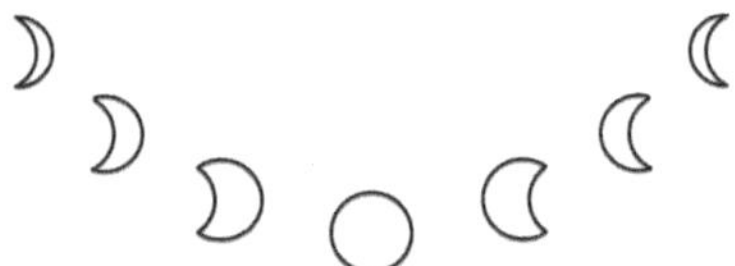

Fredericks's smile gave Angie pause. She held up the glass ball that represented his sanctuary contract with the hunters, but didn't smash it immediately against the church's wooden floor. Why was he smiling? What was she missing?

She'd missed a whole freaking lot during this interaction. More than she should have. She'd made so many mistakes. What if this was another one? What if she was playing into yet another of Fredericks's machinations?

He'd violated his sanctuary. Many times over now. She didn't need to keep waffling about that, or questioning if he really, *technically* had or not. He had. She could break this glass, destroy the small part of his essence he'd left with the deal, and weaken him enough they could send him back. Without games, or challenges, or anything else that might fuck things up even more than she already had. She could open a portal and send him into a demon realm, and they could end this.

But… That smile.

And neither Sebastian nor Aidan were giving her any guidance. They'd let her screw up, multiple times in this interaction. So badly, she'd gotten Carmen killed.

It finally, finally sunk in that Sebastian and Aidan had been…really focused this whole time but not actually speaking much. And Aidan hadn't willed the demon holding Carmen not to stab her. Why hadn't Aidan willed the demon not to stab Carmen? She had been focused on that demon this whole time. She was strong enough to do that. Angie had *seen* Aidan do things like that.

Something was wrong.

Something had been wrong this entire time. Something she couldn't see.

Something else was going on.

"Aren't you going to break the glass?" Fredericks asked. "You brought that all the way here. I have violated my sanctuary. Time to open a portal and banish me."

"Why are you in such a hurry?" she asked.

From the corner of her eye, she saw Sokolov pause beside the shifting Khymir's circle, waiting. He didn't cut the circle, as she'd assumed he would do immediately, but looked back to his boss, waiting.

The Khymir snarled at the delay and pressed his fingers to the containment field. Flames erupted around the demon's human-looking hand, but it didn't notice or seem to care. Most of its attention was on Sokolov.

"Things here are done," Fredericks said. "As I said. I don't want to be here when she arrives. And I don't want her to be able to trace me."

"She…who?"

"The bringer of death. The destroyer of worlds."

Angie wanted to both roll her eyes and also panic because what the hell kind of horror would earn the name "bringer of death and destroyer of worlds" from a demon? That… couldn't be good.

"These hints and games for fun, or are you going to tell me what you mean by that?"

He considered her for a long moment. Then, "No. I don't think I will."

"Then why bother hinting?"

"Maybe to irritate you?"

She snorted. "Good job. Well done. You're great at it."

He smiled. "I'm sorry we didn't meet earlier, Angela Jordan."

"I am not."

"Break the glass. My time here is over."

She narrowed her eyes. To Sebastian, she said, "Why does he want me to do this?"

Sebastian, his attention focused on the shifting Khymir, said quietly, "Break the glass, Ang. It's okay."

His voice sounded strained. And when she risked a glance at the side of his face, his jaw was tight.

"Aidan?" she asked, though her attention was still on Sebastian.

"Break the glass," Aidan said. "And then open a portal."

That was more advice than either of them had given her this entire time. But she realized Aidan sounded strained, too. Reluctantly, Angie pulled her gaze away from Sebastian to look at Aidan. She never could read the hunter's expression well. She still couldn't. But Aidan's shoulders were stiff and her attention focused on the place where Carmen's body still slumped against the tape in the chair.

But…why? Angie had killed that demon.

What the hell was going on?

"It's okay," Aidan murmured. "Break the glass. We're out of time."

Angie turned her attention to Fredericks. She hated that she had no idea what was happening. But fuck it. She raised the glass ball and threw it against the wooden floor.

The glass shattered, shards of green, red, and gold scattering. The church shuddered and shook, dust filtering down from the ceiling. A rumbling through the ground, like the subway passing beneath their feet. Then a flash of bright white light. A hiss.

Green gas rose up from the shattered glass, filling the air with the scent of rotten eggs.

And before she thought too long about what was happening, Angie pulled at the demon witch thread of her magic and opened a portal. A single breach into the demon realm. The portal opened with a push, like a doorway. A circular cut in spacetime.

Beyond the opening, a land of lava and blackness. Shadows and screeching and flickering red light. The sky was red. The horizon picked out by belching volcanos. This was a land Angie had opened onto before, many times. It was the demon realm her magic called to. The one that, when she reached, answered.

She realized, as she held the door open, that she understood how to open into other realms now. The information that she'd *seen* in Betha's head while experiencing the vision was still there. She could focus the portals, open into specific places.

The knowledge was so surprising, so…there, that before she thought about why she was doing it, she opened a second portal. This one into another realm entirely. This realm showed a purplish sky and an alien landscape of pitted rock and black vines. A rumbling of noise. And puffs of sulfur-scented gas rose up out of fissures in the dark gray rocks.

She'd never opened into this realm before. Wasn't even sure what or where it was. Except to know that it was a demon realm. A new one to her.

But not new to Betha. This was one of the many realms Betha had opened.

"Ang?" Sebastian's voice, above a riot of noise.

Angie blinked when she realized that the noise was a cacophony all around her. She hadn't noticed the sound, the shouts and screams, the…chittering.

That chittering. That sound that scraped along her nerves like nails on a chalkboard. That sound that hit at her deepest fears, struck against her darkest nightmares.

She hadn't even noticed it until Sebastian's voice.

She looked around the church then, the two portals remaining open even without her gaze. That she could keep portals open without her gaze still stunned her. Shocked her enough, it took a moment for her to really see the chaos that had erupted.

Demons. Everywhere inside the church. Churning through the air. Flying past on bat wings. Swooping down and bouncing off her protective circle. Or…no. Somehow, she'd dropped the circle. When had she done that? What was happening?

More demon screeching. A clump of monsters rushing toward her. They flew backward before getting within a few feet of her.

All around her, demons charging at them, flying around them, screaming and screeching and *chittering*.

But… How? Where did they come from?

She…she hadn't released them. Had she? None had come through the two portals she'd opened. She was certain of that. How were there so many demons here?

It was the demon plague Morty had feared. Jacob had feared. It was the very thing they thought she'd do one day. Unleash so many demons on this realm that stopping them would cost lives.

If the hunters could stop them at all.

But…she hadn't done this. This wasn't her. She hadn't unleashed the plague.

Had she?

"No." She pulled up to her full height. No. She had not done this.

A demon charged her and she slammed it with a bolt of power from her palm. An arrow of that demon magic in her web. The demon exploded. Angie tried not to think about what she'd just done.

And did it again. When another demon swooped down close to Sebastian, going for his head.

Acid scattered from that demon onto the one flying behind it and destroying a third.

She couldn't think. Had no idea what had happened or what was happening. She just acted. Another pull from the demon magic. Another demon shattered into pieces.

She released the illusion spell she'd stored, a single word, a single gesture. And the church filled with flittering, colorful lights, like demented fairies or butterflies racing around the demons. The illusion was enough to distract some of the creatures, sending them swooping around in circles or charging off in different directions.

Angie glanced at the two portals she'd opened. Fredericks stood at the foot of one, looking in, his shoulders stiff. He glanced back as if sensing Angie's gaze on him.

"Thank you," he said.

She didn't want his thanks. What the hell? Demons didn't thank her for sending them back. She couldn't ask him the obvious "why" question, though, because another demon roared and charged Aidan. Automatically, Angie threw a bolt of demon magic at the beast, turning back to look at Fredericks even as the demon exploded.

"She's coming," he said. "And she'll destroy everything." Fredericks looked back into the portal. It was the new one Angie had opened. The one onto the world with a purple sky and black vines creeping across the pitted gray rocks. "None will survive her coming. I almost didn't last time. But she had to flee that time. We won't be so lucky now. Not with two of you."

"Two of who?" Angie flung power at another demon, and took a step closer to Fredericks. "What the hell are you talking about?"

"Hell," he said, with a faint smile. "Isn't that what we demons are all about?"

Before she could ask anything else, a streak of light shot through the portal. Coming from *inside* the realm. A streak of power that slammed into Fredericks. Tossed him backward onto the church floor.

He blinked at the hole in his chest. His hand rising to the spot. His immaculate suit was charred. But there was no blood. Just a hole where the center of his body had been.

Sokolov shouted, falling to his knees beside his boss.

Fredericks blinked at him. "She's come. I was too late." He looked toward the portal. "The Apocalypse Witch has come."

Angie followed his gaze. Another bolt of white light.

And Fredericks's head exploded, spewing acid blood across Sokolov's face.

Sokolov screamed, tumbled backward. A demon swooped down and plucked Sokolov off the ground, carrying him up to the church rafters.

Angie stretched out a hand, intending on destroying the demon carrying Sokolov. But another bolt of that white light streaked across the church and slammed into both demon and man. Destroying both.

Angie gasped. Might have screamed. Her body shook with adrenaline and confusion and fear. What the hell was inside that portal? Strong enough to kill a demon like Fredericks. To *scare* a demon like Fredericks.

Whatever it was, she needed to close that portal.

She couldn't afford to let it through.

CHAPTER TWENTY-NINE

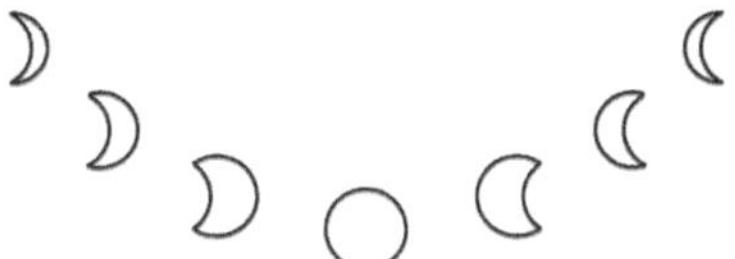

ngie felt Aidan and Sebastian move up behind her, their backs to her back. Forming a triangle in the center of the chaos still rioting through the church, knocking over and destroying the stacks of crates and boxes, threatening the very stone walls.

So many demons. How were they all here? Where had they come from?

The hoards charging toward them bounced backward as they hit up against the wills of the two hunters. And from the corner of her eye, Angie realized Sebastian had pulled out his flaming sword. She hadn't even seen that in all the mayhem.

He swung the sword, slicing through one of the chittering demons, its spiked tail splitting away and dropping to the ground. It screamed at him and then slid halfway across the floor, flung by an invisible hand that Angie was certain was the will of one of the hunters.

Her two portals were still open. Nothing had come through the new one, though. Except those powerful bolts of energy that had killed Fredericks and Sokolov.

They needed to send the demons back into those realms. Either one. Didn't matter. Both demon realms. Both good enough.

But if the thing that had killed Fredericks got through while they were sending demons into that portal…?

Even as she thought that, a demon flew into the gray rock and purple sky realm, as if tossed into the opening. It screamed as it passed through the breach. And then exploded into shards of light on the other side.

Angie hadn't seen whether or not it had been hit by one of those powerful bolts. Maybe it was the realm itself?

She didn't have time to ask. A demon charged her directly. Angie flung her hand forward, more of the demon magic pouring from her palm.

Unlike her own magic, that required time, intricate hand gestures paired with specifically worded spells, the demon magic was all brute force power, like a wizard's magic. It poured from her in streams of pure power and slammed into the approaching demon and sent it tumbling backward toward the open portals.

This demon went through the red sky, lava fields doorway, into the demon realm Angie usually opened, the one where she, Sebastian, and Carmen had been trapped. The demon didn't explode going through this time. Not from anything on that side. And not from her power.

It snarled and charged back toward the opening. Only to

get swept off the ground by something larger than it. With wings. Disappearing into the lava fields with a screech.

Angie wasn't sure whether to be relieved or not and didn't have time. Another demon charged her. Another shot of power from her hand. She didn't kill this one on accident either. Focus. Aim. Sent it flying into three more demons coming for her small group.

She hadn't trained this magic, had wanted to avoid using it. It should have felt unnatural and awkward. It should have felt *wrong*.

It didn't.

She hadn't had any control of it before, not really. She'd flung this power about like a toddler with a ball. No way to mitigate the chaos it caused. She'd killed demons with it because she hadn't known how to manage it.

Now, even without training, she started to feel how to adjust the power, how to feed just enough for a hit without killing, how to ratchet it up if she wanted to send a killing blow. She could *sense* how to do all that. Like this magic was natural to her.

Later, she knew that thought would terrify her. Demon magic *should not* come naturally to her when she wasn't a demon. Morty's warning that she was becoming like a demon now echoed in the back of her head. Touching on a fear so deep it was almost distracting.

But there were too many demons. Too much chaos. She needed to fight now. Think later.

Worry later.

So many demons. Too many demons. She wasn't even

sure what kinds of demons. No time to identify them. She just kept tossing magic at them, knocking them away. Forcing them through one portal entrance or the other.

She couldn't keep throwing them around, though. They just kept coming. The ones she managed to fling into the lava realm kept trying to crawl back into this one.

She shot power from her palm into a charging beast, this one a bat-winged being with black skin and red wings, and sent it into the new realm. It hit the portal with its wings spread open, resisting the pull. The call of a demon realm sucked it through anyway.

A screech from inside. And the demon exploded.

Fuck, she still couldn't tell if the realm was killing them or whatever had killed Fredericks was doing it. Maybe that was just the realm?

"They're gonna get out," Aidan said suddenly. "Put a circle around the church. Keep them where we can deal with them."

Angie's heart hammered. She hadn't thought…

Turning her focus inward, trusting Aidan and Sebastian to keep the beasts at bay, she focused on her witch magic. That cool blue power that flowed through her web. The feel of it as she tapped it rushed through her like a summer breeze, clearing out the stench of sulfur, filling her with that electrical surge of rightness.

She murmured the spell, formed well-practiced shapes with her fingers, mentally drew a huge circle around the entire outside of the church. The circle was big, the process took time. She could feel the brush of air from swooping demons, hear the screech as they fought the hunters. She kept her eyes half-closed, her focus on the line of blue moving around the perimeter of the building until she connected the ends.

The circle snapped into place. In her mind's eye she watched the cone of blue light flare up and over the church, felt the circle cutting them off from the outside world.

They were trapped inside the circle, inside the warehouse-church now. With a plague of demons.

But the demons wouldn't get out into the city.

The realization that she'd prevented a plague from spreading left her a little breathless. Take that Morty! she thought, before she had to refocus on the fight.

With the witch magic flowing through her, she automatically murmured a spell, instinctively formed the gestures, pulled deep at that well of power that was so much *her* there was no way to be without it.

A strike of lightning slammed into two demons charging toward Sebastian's side of their defensive triangle. Another slice of lightning hit a demon just in front of her, the light bright enough it flashed spots through her vision. Didn't matter. They were inside her circle, her world now.

More lightning hit a cluster of demons trying to come back out of the lava realm.

Angie turned her attention to that portal, to pulling lightning out of the sky inside the realm, covering the ground in front of the breach on the demon side.

"Send them through," she said, her voice deep with all the magic.

Demons screamed and three tumbled through the portal into the lava realm. Lightning dropped onto them, sending them careen farther away from the open portal.

Beside her, she saw Sebastian's sword swing. And a demon swooping down from the roof caught the sword in its chest, sending it tumbling tail over wing into the lava realm. Where a strike of lightning bounced it from view.

Angie felt the flow of power through her so strongly, it was like her body and muscles were renewed. The exhaustion that had been dragging at her earlier vanished. She only felt the wash of power. Another spell. More lightning.

A demon got too close to her and she slammed it with demon magic, sending it flying backward. Then hit it with lightning to force it through the portal opening.

She focused on getting the demons into the lava realm. But some went through the portal to the new realm. And every single one that hit that portal, that got dragged into that realm, exploded in a flash of bright white light.

Still unsure if it was the realm or something inside the realm doing that. Couldn't worry about that yet.

Except…there weren't as many demons now. The cacophony of noise still made hearing difficult. But she could hear Aidan's grunts, and Sebastian swearing, things she hadn't been able to hear just moments ago. The swarm of demonic bodies was thinner.

And she realized suddenly, there was none of the chittering anymore. Those chittering demons were gone— either banished back to the lava realm or dead. She wasn't sure. But the absence of chittering grating against her nerves released an even stronger surge of magic through her.

So strong and so powerful and so right.

She recognized that feeling. Of invincibility. Of strength. That feeling that she could do whatever she wanted. Anything at all.

That nothing and no one could stand against her.

A tempting feeling for a witch. For any witch. But in that moment, with all the power of her different magics flowing through her, Angie knew this feeling could overwhelm her quickly. Take her past a line she didn't want to cross.

She blinked hard a few times. Glanced down. Her hands were glowing a white-blue. A slight flickering of red encircled her. She was certain her eyes would be red.

As the number of demons dwindled, she worked at pulling back on all the power she'd let loose.

She let Sebastian and Aidan force the remaining demons through the portals, into the two realms. She focused on keeping them from coming back out of the lava realm with a rain of lightning. The new realm destroyed the demons as they went through, so Angie didn't worry about that one.

The sounds and screeches died away, until all she could hear were the demons inside the lava realm. The lightning slicing through the air and scattering them. She stopped dropping lightning when she felt Sebastian's brief touch. Not enough to unbalance her, but enough to get her attention.

She looked around the warehouse. The chaos of toppled boxes and splotches of burned stone and wood. Splattered streaks of things she tried not to think about.

But no more demons.

"Close the breaches," Sebastian said, his voice harsh. He was breathing hard, and sweat streaked down his cheeks. "Close the portals, Ang. We got them all."

She nodded, but it was a jerky gesture. Focusing first on the lava portal, she gave it the nudge it needed, holding the demon witch thread in one metaphysical hand as she watched the portal swirl closed. It snapped out of existence with a hiss, the break between that demon realm and the human realm sealed shut.

But when she turned her attention to the other portal, the one onto the new realm, even holding the demon witch thread of power, even giving the portal a solid "push" shut…didn't work.

The portal remained open.

And a shadow from the other side moved into view.

CHAPTER THIRTY

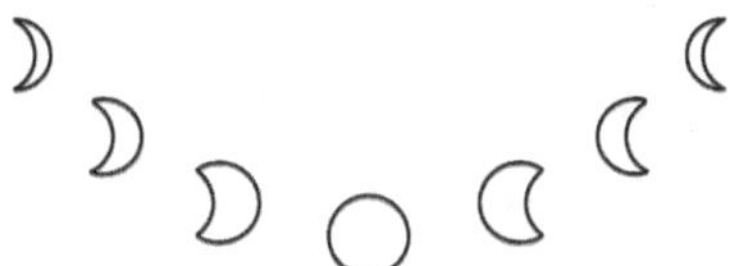

Angie, Sebastian, and Aidan all tightened together. Instead of back-to-back, as they'd been during the demon fight, they stood shoulder to shoulder. Facing the dark shadow moving out of the purple sky portal that Angie couldn't close.

"Can you see that portal?" she murmured to Sebastian.

Most of the time, people didn't see the doorways she opened or the demon realms beyond. They saw the demons once they were out into this world. And hunters saw them coming in and going back through. But they didn't *see* the breach.

But this wasn't one of her usual portals. This second one opened into a place she'd never seen before. And the fact that she couldn't now close it was terrifying.

Whatever was inside that opening, it had killed

Fredericks, Sokolov, a bunch of other demons. Every demon that went through that portal died.

Demons could kill other demons. Demons did kill other demons. But the demons capable of it were usually extremely powerful and very dangerous. And if they were powerful enough to kill a demon like Fredericks, they were not the kind of demon Angie wanted to face.

Her hands shook from the exertion of the fight. Her body trembled from all the adrenaline and lack of food and fear and guilt and everything else that had happened that day. She could barely stand up now. Her vision was blurring. Her head heavy. And the power that had just moments ago flowed through her so freely and given her a feeling of invincibility had slid back into the threads of her web and left her exhausted.

The last time she'd used the demon magic, it hadn't exhausted her. In fact, she'd felt fine after. But this time… Well, this time she'd been spent before the fight even got started. This time she'd started exhausted. And the adrenaline only carried her so far.

The church-turned-warehouse was silent now except for the creaking of all the broken boxes and dripping of fluids Angie refused to think about. The fluorescent overhead lights had all been shattered during the fight, so the only light inside the large building now came from street lights outside pouring in through the stained-glass windows at the front, painting everything in colorful reflections and shadows.

Angie was aware, in her peripheral vision, of Carmen still

slumped against the duct tape holding her to the chair. And the guilt of that didn't help her balance even a little bit.

But there was something waiting for her on the other side of that portal. She had to face that first.

"I can't see the opening," Sebastian murmured. "Or see into the realm beyond. But I can sense something there."

"A demon," Angie said.

"No," Aidan said. "Or rather…no?"

"What are you talking about?" She scowled briefly at Aidan, whose attention was focused on the breach she couldn't see.

"She's not sure if I'm actually a demon or not," a voice from the other side of the breach. A woman.

Angie blinked. That voice…

Impossible. That was centuries ago.

The shadow moved closer and stepped through the portal, into the church, looked around curiously and gave a sort of matter-of-fact nod that said she was unimpressed.

Angie was too busy trying not to fall down to wonder at that.

"Betha?" she murmured.

She felt Sebastian's sharp gaze on the side of her face, but Angie couldn't look away from the older woman.

And she was older than Angie had perceived her to be in the visions. Older than her lover Eloise had seen her. Through Eloise's eyes, Betha had been beautiful, young, and in danger. Through Angie's own eyes, without the clouding effect of looking at the other witch through other gazes, the impression was a little different.

Betha looked more like how she *felt* from the inside. Which was strange and Angie wouldn't have known how to explain that.

Except for being a little older, she looked fit, thinner than she'd been through Eloise's gaze, tall, a round face with high, harsh cheekbones. Her straight dark hair, threaded with strands of silver so pale they were white, was pulled back into a tight braid that went down her back. She was dressed in rough-made, dark trousers—she'd worn dresses in the visions—and a loose, long-sleeved shirt with many patches sewn into it. The patches were colorful against the shirt's dark brown material. She wore what looked to be leather gloves, but the leather shimmered like scales in the light pouring into the church through the stained-glass windows.

"Hello," the woman said, her eyes red, like a demon's, but her expression was gentle and friendly. "You know my name. A vision?"

Angie nodded, still not sure she could trust her own eyes. "How?" There were a lot of "how" questions in that one word.

"Long story. Which I don't have time for right now. I need to get back. But I'm glad to meet you. And we have a lot to talk about."

"Wait, what?"

"I've been waiting for someone like you," Betha said. "I'm glad you survived."

Without meaning to, Angie glanced at Carmen's slumped form.

Betha followed her gaze, and when Angie looked back at

her, she was frowning. "That's not right," Betha murmured. She removed one glove, revealing a hand that glowed with purplish red light, and flicked her fingers in a shape that *almost* looked like something Angie recognized. She even saw Betha's mouth move as if reciting a spell.

When Angie turned to see what Betha had done, the slumped form taped to the chair no longer looked like Carmen. The form looked like a demon.

"What have you done?" Angie demanded. "Why would you do that to her?"

"That's not your friend," Betha said.

"She isn't my friend." An automatic response that didn't do anything to assuage her guilt.

"That's a demon," Betha clarified. "The Khymir. Just looked like your…whatever she was to you."

Angie blinked. Felt her knees start to buckle. "What?"

Sebastian caught her before she dropped, and she focused on ensuring her psychic senses were still completely shut down so she wouldn't accidentally read him. By the time she'd finished and looked up at Betha, Betha was staring at her and Sebastian with her eyes narrowed.

"I thought she wasn't your friend," Betha said.

"I didn't want her dead."

"When the Khymir are around, you can't trust anything you see. Not here in this realm, where seeing through the guise is so difficult without practice. Anyone you're uncertain of, or even people you think you're certain of, touch them and you'll know."

"That really…really wasn't Carmen this whole time?"

She wasn't sure how to feel about that. Relief of course. But then…where was Carmen? And why had Fredericks and Sokolov killed the demon disguised as her?"

"They needed you unbalanced," Betha said as if reading Angie's mind. "With your powers now, they needed you unbalanced. It's the only way. And Othicash't wanted to ensure he'd found someone else like me, I suspect."

Angie balked at Betha using the demon's real name, but then realized, with Fredericks dead, using his real name hardly mattered. "You killed him?"

"It's what I do now. I kill demons."

"Why?"

"Why not?"

Angie wasn't sure what to say to that. So instead, she asked, "How long?"

"Depends on the realm I'm in. For me, it hasn't been that long. A lot of time has passed here, though." Betha glanced around again at the inside of the church. "I'm surprised they could function in the sacred space."

"It hasn't been a sacred space in a while, I don't think." Angie gestured to the broken crates.

"Then Othicash't just had a strange sense of humor I suppose."

"Your accent is different now." Betha spoke as if she was from this time in history, not from several centuries earlier. Her voice sounded the same as it had in the visions, as it did in her own head when Angie had been inside her perspective in the visions. But her accent was different. Her word choices different.

"I've watched the changes. We come back when we can. Though we can never stay for long." She paused as if listening, then cursed. "I'm sorry. I have to go now."

"Wait! We have…more to talk about."

"Oh yes. We do, Angela Jordan. A lot to talk about." She stepped back to the portal breach. "After you've rested and recovered from this, come find me." She looked at Sebastian, still holding Angie, and then Aidan. "You'll need them both." Her gaze flicked to the demon slumped in the chair, the demon Angie had thought was Carmen. "You'll need the real her, too." Betha's gaze drifted half closed, then she nodded sharply. "You'll need all three of them. Don't come alone. And don't leave any of them behind. You'll all die otherwise."

She stepped through the breach and Angie lurched toward her, almost without thinking. "Wait! How? How will we find you? What does that mean they'll die?"

"The gift from your mentor. Use that. Find me." She slid back into the purple sky realm and before Angie could say more, the portal whirled closed. A slight hissing sound. And then nothing.

No more breaches into demon realms.

And no real answers.

She glanced back at the demon where Carmen had been. Then pulled out of Sebastian's touch and stalked close to the slumped form. The blood under the chair looked blackish green now instead of red. There was no confusing the body in the chair for Carmen.

Still. Taking a deep breath and settling herself, Angie

opened her psychic senses and very carefully set a finger to the slumped form's shoulder.

The death and evil hit so hard she stumbled back and dropped to the ground, sucking in a rough gasp.

Sebastian was beside her instantly. "Ang?"

"I'm okay. I'm okay. That…definitely isn't Carmen."

Aidan moved closer, still standing, her gaze thoughtful. "We need to check on the others. At your workplace."

Oh shit. Angie had almost forgotten in all the chaos. "Yes. We need to hurry."

Aidan narrowed her eyes at the place where Betha had gone, but didn't comment. Just nodded.

They hurried outside, and a taxi pulled up almost instantly. Even after a fight with so many demons, when they both had to be exhausted and with very little will left, the hunters managed a quick taxi and a fast ride back into Manhattan.

Angie was grateful for them exerting the will for that. Because now that she was thinking about her friends again, the fear she'd had to suppress during the fight came roaring back.

And they couldn't get to Dana's Cauldron fast enough.

CHAPTER THIRTY-ONE

*A*ngie charged through the front door of Dana's only realizing as she did that she shouldn't have been able to get in so easily. The instant she realized the door was open and accessible, her panic shot through the roof. Sebastian was right behind her with Aidan close on their heels.

They all came to an abrupt stop on the main floor retail level when a sound from upstairs floated down to them.

Laughter.

Pleasant, non-demonic laughter.

Angie raced up the wooden stairs, leaving Sebastian and Aidan to follow her. At the second-floor landing, she turned into the café to see a group of ragged looking humans with to-go cups raised in a toast. Laura spotted her first and nearly dropped her cup in her rush to Angie's side.

"You're alive!" they both said at the same time, and then both laughed.

And Angie started to cry. She rarely cried. She rarely folded in front of other people—outside of Sebastian. But so much had happened in one fucking day, that her emotions just came spilling out.

She felt more hugs circling her, and realized it was the other Dana's employees, all getting in on the relieved hugs and tears.

She snuffled as she pulled back enough to look around. "Everyone is okay? No one hurt?"

"A few bruises," Bianca said, "but we're all good."

"The demon… Who was it?"

"Disguised as one of the customers," Jacob said, moving up to the edge of the group around Angie. His gaze darted from her, to Sebastian and Aidan hovering near the entrance to the café. "It got itself invited to the karaoke night so it could lead Sokolov to everyone."

"Sokolov and his boss are dead," Angie said bluntly.

Jacob's eyes narrowed just a little in question.

"Not me," she said. Someone else. Someone with the same powers as her. But not her.

"Shame," a new voice from beyond the group, a voice both familiar and surprising. "I was kind of hoping you'd kill that asshole Sokolov. Especially after seeing the way he set up my look-alike."

Her friends spread out enough for Angie to see Carmen sitting at one of the tables against the wall, smirking at her, looking perfectly healthy, and not dead.

Angie nodded. "You were there?"

"Stayed hidden long enough to see what they were doing, see 'me' strapped to a chair, then followed the others here. Spotted the Khymir in their midst and figured they'd need help." Her gaze flicked to Jacob. "Couldn't be sure how much help he'd be."

Jacob scowled at Carmen but didn't comment.

"What happened?" this she asked Laura because seeing Carmen alive and not dead and knowing she'd come to help the people at Dana's when she didn't need to left Angie feeling…a lot of confused emotions.

"We're gonna need more whiskey-laced tea for that story," Laura said with a chuckle.

"I have some tequila upstairs," Bianca said. "I'll get that for Angie. Girl, you look like you could use the entire bottle."

Angie started laughing. Then cried again as Bianca went to get the tequila and everyone settled at the tables around the café.

"Dana and Omar?" she asked as she scanned the group.

"They're out getting food for everyone," Laura said. "They'll be back soon. I think they mentioned sushi and Indian food. I have no idea what we'll be getting."

"Food. I could use some food." She smiled at Sebastian as he sat next to her, then collapsed against his side when he put an arm around her. She was so worn out now, she felt like she could sleep for a month. And she was so fucking relieved to see everyone, even Carmen.

Aidan settled in a seat next to Carmen, the two women

exchanging a nod, and taking whiskey-laced tea when Moon Star handed them cups. Bianca returned with the tequila. And everyone settled in to exchange stories.

There was a lot of talking over other people, the customers and employees of Dana's all having different versions of events that they'd witnessed. But the unifying element of each story was that both Carmen and Jacob had been responsible for battling the demon while the witches set a trap for banishing it.

Angie met Carmen's gaze during the story, and Carmen raised her tea cup in a little solute.

Jacob remained on the opposite side of the café from Carmen, but he relaxed at his table, with both Bianca and Moon Star making lash-fluttery eyes at him.

She'd have to warn them both not to get too interested in him. Angie still didn't trust him. But he'd helped save her friends. So she supposed she had to let go of some of her resentment. A tiny bit of it. Maybe.

She was so tired, and her emotions were in such chaos, she decided she'd better just sort those feelings out later.

After the others had finished their retelling of the events at Dana's, Angie, Aidan, and Sebastian told them some of what had happened in the church—keeping the information about Betha, and Angie killing demons, to themselves, of course.

It was during their part of the story that Angie also got answers to one of the questions she'd had, when she learned that Sebastian and Aidan had been holding off all those extra demons during the standoff in the church. That Sokolov and

Fredericks had summoned them all, kept them in weak circles, all hidden behind an illusion spell. And then freed them all right before the Carmen look-alike had been killed. The hunters had been holding off a swarm of freed demons while Angie had been losing her mind over what she'd thought was Carmen's death. And Angie had had no idea.

Apparently, the freed demons were a way to keep the hunters distracted while Fredericks escaped when she banished him.

That explained Aidan and Sebastian's strain, and the reasons they hadn't stopped Angie from killing that first demon. Aidan, at least, had also known that "Carmen" wasn't the real Carmen—which was why she hadn't stopped the demon from killing the imposter.

All those demons had remained hidden behind an illusion spell. Angie silently berated herself for not spotting the fucking thing, but she'd been so distracted. Sebastian and Aidan could feel all the demons there, though, and knew the moment they were freed.

And they held them off silently for as long as they could.

Adian suspected Fredericks had always intended on returning to a demon realm at the end of the fight, that he'd meant to break his sanctuary. Though she didn't say it out loud, Angie remembered the way Fredericks had been afraid of a mysterious "she" coming into this realm. He'd even said something about not wanting that mysterious "she" to track him. Angie thought the "she" was Betha. And she wondered if maybe Fredericks needed to break the sanctuary contract so Betha couldn't find him.

Why he felt the need to distract the hunters during his escape, she wasn't sure. And neither Sebastian or Aidan commented on that hanging question. Probably because it revealed too much about Angie's new powers. But maybe that was the point. Angie could have killed him. He'd confirmed that in his tests. Maybe he wanted to ensure all three of them were too distracted to change their minds about just banishing him.

She'd never know for sure now. And she was really too tired tonight to care.

When Dana and Omar arrived with the food, carrying bags full of sushi, Indian food, and Mexican food, they were greeted with cheers.

Angie was so depleted and hungry, she devoured three tacos, two samosas, and an entire tray of rice and carne asada before she felt a little more like herself. Sebastian stuck to her side, and ensured she got enough food, and when her eyes started to droop with her exhaustion, he let her rest her head on his shoulder.

There was more to talk about. More to figure out. But with her belly full and her friends safe, Angie figured there was time to work the rest of this out.

She caught Aidan and Carmen talking quietly as she drifted through her delightful food coma, and wondered what the two had to discuss. They seemed like they knew each other. That was definitely something Angie wanted to know more about.

Jacob found his way to Angie's side, sitting across the small, round café table, and giving Sebastian a wary glance, before meeting her gaze. He was back to wearing the tailored suits she'd first seen him in, but this one had gotten damaged during the fight because there were several big tears through the jacket and one across the thigh. His short black hair, worn loose but styled, was slicked back from his face, highlighting the dark circles under his dark eyes.

"I know it doesn't," he started slowly. "Not completely. But I hope this goes some way to showing my intentions toward you and yours are not bad. I had my reasons for doing what I did in New Mexico—"

"So you've said."

He nodded. "They were and are still valid reasons." He flicked a glance toward Carmen. "She's too undisciplined to be a hunter and always has been. But her will is…very strong." He lowered his voice. "It took the two of us to contain that demon, and it wasn't even one of the most powerful ones. Not even close to a demon like Fredericks. And even with two of us, it was close. The beast nearly escaped twice." He shook his head. "I stand by my reasoning. The hunters are not in a position to handle freed demons. Most of us, anyway. And something needs to change."

"But…?" Because she heard that at the end of his little speech even if he didn't say it aloud.

His gaze flicked to Sebastian again. "But my methods, and the methods of those who agree with me, were not productive."

"You're only saying this now because of what I can do."

"It helps," he admitted. "Things are worse than we knew, though. I only learned that in the desert. The council…

They've let things get much worse than any of us knew. We need you, Angie. Even if you're not a demon hunter properly. And we need you, too." He looked directly at Sebastian. "I'm sorry for what happened in the desert, in a lot of ways." He let out a long, deep breath. "I know you won't ever forgive me, but I'm hoping, going forward, I've proven tonight you can at least trust my intentions are to save lives."

"You want me to trust you," Sebastian said quietly, "let Angie read you."

She was leaning into Sebastian as he said that, her back against his front rather than the back of her seat. But she turned a little to look up at him in question. She was exhausted, but the food and release of tension had gone a long way toward renewing her inner strength. She still needed a good night's sleep or four. But she could manage to read enough of Jacob with a touch to know if he was sincere or hiding something.

But a hunter opening themselves up to someone else that way, allowing even a little vulnerability, and to *her*, the one they all feared… That would say a lot, even if she picked up nothing from him.

"I could will her to see what I wanted her to," Jacob said, proving the possibility of her reading him did bother him.

"You could," Sebastian said. "But I'd know. And I'd know I couldn't trust you still. Your choice. I don't have to trust you to keep doing my job and banishing demons."

Jacob nodded, and looked across the crowd toward Carmen and Aidan, still quietly talking in the corner. Then he faced Angie. "Okay. Okay."

He stretched his hand across the wooden table. A significantly smaller version than the one she used upstairs for formal readings. She wasn't wearing her usual "witch" uniform, just jeans and a t-shirt under her spring jacket—which had a hole in it too that she didn't remember getting and was annoyed by now that she had the energy to care. But being inside Dana's, surrounded by her witchy associates and friends, even the mundane pagans, doing any kind of psychic reading felt so natural, so ordinary, it was almost comforting to reach her hand out, open herself to her psychic sense, and gently touch Jacob's palm with the tips of her fingers.

She didn't allow much in. After the day she'd had, all her senses were still too raw and she didn't want to risk it. She got flashes of his fight with the Khymir, the way he'd rescued Moon Star when the demon tried to use her as a shield. The way he'd worked with Carmen to will the demon into the trap. The way he'd stood between her friends and the beast when it revealed itself.

And she picked up enough of his emotions and feelings to know…

"Letting this happen is hard for him," she said aloud. "But he is honestly only hoping to save lives. His intentions in that are trustworthy."

"But not in everything?" Sebastian asked as he stared at Jacob, who'd stared back at Sebastian during all this.

Angie shrugged, removing her hand from Jacob's. "Not in everything. But then, no one is entirely trustworthy in everything, right?" she said to Jacob.

He didn't answer, just fisted his hand and pulled it back across the table. "Will that do?" he asked Sebastian.

Sebastian continued to hold his gaze, his arm tightening around Angie. Then very quietly, he said, "We haven't found a cure. Not in the archives. There might not be one. And this could still kill her."

Jacob's nod was jerky, awkward. "Morty lied."

"Yes. But that doesn't mean Ang can stay this way forever without it hurting her. And if there's a way to prevent that, that is *my* highest priority."

Angie gripped Sebastian's hands where they were folded across her stomach.

"You understand what that means?" Sebastian said quietly. Not quite a question.

"I understand."

"So long as we understand each other, then."

Jacob nodded again, his gaze sweeping over them both. Then he stood. "I'm here if you need me," he said. "I'm on your side. If you need help, I'll be there."

Neither Sebastian nor Angie commented on that as Jacob walked away. He said a few quiet goodbyes before leaving, much to Moon Star's disappointment.

"He's sincere in his desire to save the world," Angie said quietly, as Sebastian relaxed a little at her back.

"I know." He kissed the top of her head. "But so is Carmen, in her own way."

THE PARTY BROKE UP NOT LONG AFTER THAT, WITH EVERYONE feeling safe enough to head home. Dana and Omar stayed to lock up, waving away offers of help from everyone, including the customers who'd been caught up in all this. Those customers were given lifetime friends-and-family discounts, though, and none of them turned it down.

On the sidewalk outside, Angie realized it wasn't all that late. There were still people wandering around the Village, the late-night bars and clubs were still open, music poured out of the nearby drag queen club, the tattoo shop at the basement level next to the club still had its lights on, and the delicious smells spilling out of the Tandoori fusion restaurant down the street covered the smell of traffic.

After everything that had happened that day, Angie felt like it should have been twelve days, and it definitely felt like it should be much later at night.

Carmen stopped long enough to give her an approving nod, which Angie took with the intended condescension.

She gave Carmen a speculative look, then asked, "Have you heard the term Apocalypse Witch?"

Carmen raised her brows. "Huh. Thought that was a myth. But then, demon witches are supposed to be myths too, aren't they?" She winked. "Guess we have more to talk about." But rather than say anything then, she gave them a little wave and disappeared into the crowd.

Angie really shouldn't have expected straight answers from the woman. Still, she was surprised Carmen had left like that. She'd had half expected Carmen to gloat over Angie's reaction to her death. Though, probably that was a better conversation for later. Or maybe never. Angie still wasn't sure how she felt about those moments. She didn't particularly want to talk to Carmen about them.

Aidan lingered with them until everyone else had scattered. "You two going back to the house?"

"No need now," Sebastian said. "With Fredericks and Sokolov no longer a threat."

"They still have associates out there. Might come looking for you two."

"They'll be scrambling to reorganize the business," Sebastian said. "Fighting amongst themselves for who will lead going forward. They have bigger things to worry about."

"At least for tonight," Angie said. She wanted to return to her apartment, too. The comforts of home and familiarity calling strongly as she stood just outside her place of work, her home a short walk away.

"We'll collect our stuff tomorrow," Sebastian said. "We have some things to talk about."

"Like the demon witch urging us to find her?" Aidan said. She looked at Angie. "How do you feel about that?"

"I have no idea," she answered honestly. "I'm going to need sleep. And some days to process what happened first."

"Fair enough." Aidan tipped an invisible hat at them. "I'll see you tomorrow. Afternoon sometime I assume."

She smiled as she turned and disappeared into the pedestrian traffic. Unlike the others, after only a few feet, she literally disappeared. Angie couldn't see her anymore.

"She does that just to show off, doesn't she?" Angie asked Sebastian.

He pulled her around into his arms and set his forehead to hers. "Ready to go home?"

Yes. Yes she very much was.

Angie sat on her couch, listening to Sebastian puttering around the kitchen, making tea, the afternoon sunshine warming her living room. The cozy comfort of her own home, after a good night's sleep and a lot of rest, left her feeling secure enough to pull out the amulet Esmerelda had given her in New Mexico.

The round, silver medallion fit in the palm of Angie's hand, and had a beautifully detailed etching of a butterfly on one side, and an equally detailed etching of an owl on the other. Both animals sat on tree branches, and the butterfly's wings were offset in a V-shape that revealed both the inside and outside details, all intricately carved into the half-dollar-sized disk. The silver and turquoise chain attached to the medallion hunt between Angie's fingers as she rubbed her thumb over the butterfly shape.

Esmerelda had given her the charm as a way to find Carmen in the desert. But she'd also told Angie the gift would guide her on her journey in the months ahead.

Angie wondered if Esmerelda had known someone like Betha would come into her life.

Sebastian settled on the couch next to her. He was shirtless, wearing only a loose pair of pajama bottoms, and he looked so scrumptious, she was tempted to forget about tea for a bit.

He set their respective mugs on the coffee table and then turned to her, his fingers trailing over the silver chain hanging from the medallion.

"Do you want to do this?" he asked quietly. "Do you want to find her?"

"I think I do. I still have a lot of questions. Questions I never hoped to get answers for from the source."

"It'll probably mean going into a demon realm." He spoke so gently she knew he was hedging around the truth.

"More than one," she said. "And we might have to be inside those demon realms for longer than a blink. I get it."

"You might…absorb more of the magic there." He moved his hand from the chain and slid his fingers up into her hair, toying with one of the loose curls around her shoulder. "I won't have access to my sword."

"The place is packed with demons," she added, which made him snort. "I know it would be dangerous and probably ill-advised. I know there's the possibility that this isn't what it seems. That Betha is dangerous. That her intentions are bad. I'm not even sure I can talk Carmen into coming with us. If we can even find her. Will Aidan go?"

"If we ask? Of course."

"Maybe that would be better. We still can't really trust Carmen. Even if she did help save everyone last night."

He tugged at the curl he had wrapped around his finger, a move that drew her closer. His clean, spicy soap smell surrounded her and thoughts about demon realms and

Carmen and even answers to all her questions faded to the background. She leaned into his warmth, letting the familiar feel of his solid chest and slightly rough fingertips seep into her skin.

"We won't even consider it for a few days," he said, his voice a deep, quiet murmur. "Not until you've fully recovered. Until Aidan and I fully recover."

That made sense. The two of them had exerted an obscene amount of will in that battle in the church. Even for hunters as strong as Aidan and Sebastian, they would need time to recover from that before being at their best.

And if they were going to purposefully go into demon realms, everyone needed to be at their best.

The very thought of *purposefully* going into a demon realm, walking *into* one of her most horrifying nightmares deliberately… The very idea of it left her breathless and panicky. She was trying not to think about what they'd actually be doing too closely. Because she knew if she really thought about it, she'd run screaming away from even the possibility.

She was definitely going to need time to build up to this.

Sebastian brushed his lips against her cheek, trailed a row of soft, gentle kisses down the side of her throat. She sighed and let her eyes drift shut, savoring the sensation, letting the tingles and desire building in her overwhelm the other worries. She leaned away long enough to set her medallion on the coffee table next to their cooling tea mugs, and then found her way back into his arms. Found his mouth with hers.

She pulled him back onto the couch with her, letting his heat and his kisses and his clever touch wipe her mind clean of all the worries, all the unanswered questions, and all the dangers to come.

They could worry about that later.

For now, and for the rest of the day, Angie was content to put her full focus and all her attention on the man she loved. Everyone else would just have to wait.

Thank you so much for reading DARKLING MIST WITCH! I hope you enjoyed Angie and Sebastian's latest story. And finally getting some of Sebastian's history! That was a learning moment for all of us. LOL (Okay, I had an idea, but ideas have a way of morphing and changing when they hit the page.) There's more to come with our intrepid witch and all the looming demon threats. So be sure to look out for book 5, APOCALYPSE WITCH!

In the meantime, if you aren't aware at this stage, Angie started as a secondary character in another series before I went back in time and started writing about her secretive past. The Cary Redmond series starts with the novel The Trouble with Black Cats and Demons, and throughout you get hints of Angie's past—the events playing out in the Demon Witch series—and you get to see her and Sebastian helping Cary in Book 7, The Trouble with Death and Demon Gods.

I also dropped hints in this book about another witch who collects witch history. This character has her own short novella, called *Demonic Dates*. *Demonic Dates* is out now as either a standalone eBook or as part of the Haunts and Howls Where Demons Dwell collection, available in print and eBook editions. You can also keep reading for a short excerpt from the book!

And if that's not enough reading to tide you over until the next Demon Witch book, don't miss my paranormal romance series, the Dragon Thief! This is a series that doesn't overlap my other urban fantasy/paranormal romance series, so it can be read as a standalone. If you like slow burn romance and a heist vibe, this might be this series for you. A magical thief and a dragon shifter prince? What's not to like, right? The first book in the series, Dragon Thief, is out now!

For more on my books, or to keep up with my releases and news, please consider joining my monthly reader newsletter. New subscribers get an exclusive Cary Redmond novella and an exclusive short story in my Tiger Shifters paranormal romance series (which is quite hot, so you've been warned). Subscribers also get occasional free excerpts, books, and discounts to my store.

If you prefer, you can check for updates at my website, my store, or follow my author page at BookBub or my page on FaceBook, or you can follow my author page at your favorite vendors! I do spend time on social media (probably too much lurking LOL), so you can find me most often at Instagram, Threads, and BlueSky. Also, I adore hearing from readers, so don't be shy about emailing me too!

Thanks again for reading DARKLING MIST WITCH!

~Kat

KAT SIMONS

Some houses have history...and demons.

DEMONIC DATES

First Published in
Haunts and Howls Where Demons Dwell

DEMONIC DATES

EXCERPT

CHAPTER ONE

$\mathcal{L}$exie Alexander stared at the invitation in her hand, the expensive cream card, the gold leafing, the faint fragrance of musk that emerged with the square of paper whenever she pulled it from its envelope. An envelope that had been sealed with wax and pressed with a single initial.

Then she looked up at the house. Alone on a hill, outside the borders of the nearest town, but not so far away as to make the journey to town a day long event. Surrounded by a forest of maple and oak, an earthy loam mingling with the faint musk of the invitation. The house itself was what her grandmother would have politely called…interesting.

Which was maybe an understatement.

Three stories, at least above ground. And a strange mix of Victorian peaks and porches, with a castle-like stone wing to one side and an almost New York Brownstone look to the other. A large, square of a building with all these different elements sprouting off in different directions. Everything about the arrangement looked wrong. An assault on the eyes. Like the architect had been on LSD when they'd designed the place and just tacked on whatever took their fancy.

It wasn't a pretty house either. Not even a little. Despite the lovely finial designs decorating the tops of the gables on the more Victorian parts of the roof, and the almost comically fun gargoyles spitting on the castle side, and the sweeping stairs leading up to a large oak door on the Brownstone side. None of it…went together. There was no flow or cohesion. Not even the colors worked together. A dark gray with bright purple highlights in the Victorian parts, gray stonework in the castle with no break for color, and a soft muted orange on the Brownstone walls, with some white decorative elements.

Staring at the house was disorienting. Made Lexie feel like she was falling forward even though she wasn't moving. Like if she took a step toward the house, the ground would suddenly vanish, and she'd fall on her face. Or worse, just keep falling into some kind of abyss.

The temptation to turn around, return to her car, drive back down the hill, and ignore the invitation was strong. Stronger than she'd have expected given how excited she'd been to receive the invitation in the first place.

Not every witch gets the opportunity to visit the home of one of the most notorious witches in the history of witches. The witch who'd tried to loose a hoard of demons on the fanatics who were burning witches in the seventeenth century here in the US. She'd been destroyed by her own coven in the end, because she refused to stop letting demons into this realm, and those demons weren't restricting their havoc to fanatical witch-burners.

Her name was never spoken. Not many witches even knew of her. In fact, most didn't from what Lexie had learned. Only a very few, a tiny handful over the last few centuries, kept the knowledge as a warning, a lesson from history to be avoided. Lexie had learned of the infamous witch through her own grandmother, who'd passed the knowledge down from her grandmother. Lexie was charged now with keeping that history.

The house wasn't the exact place the witch had lived of course. It had been added to over the years. But the core of it was her home. Somewhere in the middle of all that chaotic architectural junk was the place this witch had lived, learned, tested her magic, and plotted her revenge.

And because Lexie was a historical record keeper, a collector of details to record and preserve, even if the information was too dangerous to release to most, she couldn't have resisted an invitation to this particular place if she'd tried. Especially given the date.

The invitation coming from said witch's very mysterious and enigmatic ancestor was even more irresistible. There were rumors about him, some of which she'd decided had to be more myth than reality, some of which had made her… wonder. But all of it had her curious. Extremely curious.

Which, as her grandmother would say, was the trait that killed the cat.

But she wasn't a cat. She was a historian. A record keeper

for the witchy community. And this was a bit of history that, even if she couldn't share it wide, should be preserved.

Or at least that's what she'd told herself when she'd rented a car and driven up here from New York, to a house located miles outside of modern-day Salem, Massachusetts.

She'd studied the location on various map apps and had assured herself the place wasn't *that* isolated. The main road got plenty of traffic, and she could still hear that in the distance. There were some scattered farms and houses in the area, though the closest was a mile away. But really, that wasn't *that* far.

A cold autumn breeze lifted her hair off her neck, sending a chill down her spine, despite her heavy wool coat. This late in the season, almost November, and the winter cold was already creeping in, portending things to come. She didn't mind. Lexie liked all the seasons. But the breeze, in just that moment, felt like the dance of cold cold fingers along her spine.

A warning and a threat.

She huffed out an irritated breath with herself. Then she, metaphorically, pulled up her big girl pants, straightened the strap of her oversized purse on her shoulder, and marched up to what she hoped was the front door. She was here to do some research. On a historically important witch. Whose ancestor had sent her a special invitation to come to the house and do that research on this historically important date. There was nothing to fear and no reason to run.

It was just a fucking house after all.

MILES REID WATCHED AS THE WOMAN APPROACHED THE house with trepidation. He couldn't blame her. This wasn't the sort of house people approached without trepidation even if they didn't know the history of the original occupant.

And even if they did know who the original occupant had been, that part of the house was barely visible around the construction that had gone on in the following centuries. Construction designed to cover up, hide, obscure the past.

And still demons lurked in these walls.

He'd inherited the monstrosity from a cousin, who'd inherited it from another branch of the family, who'd quickly tossed it into his branch of the family at their earliest convenience. The original occupant hadn't had children, so the house had always been passed to a non-direct line from her, but it had almost become like a game of hot potato or keep away. Tossing the house quickly to the next owner so the bad stuff didn't rub off.

When Miles had inherited, it had very much felt like his cousin had said, "Tag! You're it." And run away very fast.

Now Miles was stuck with this place.

They couldn't bulldoze it—many a relative had been tempted—because the *house* resisted that. The bulldozers came out, and things went wrong. Engines broke. Tires went flat. Important bits fell off. He didn't know a lot about bulldozers—he was a journalist and not a construction worker—but two owners ago, a clever cousin did actually try to raze the place, and the stories of the disasters that befell that attempt were family legends.

Despite those legends. He was still tempted to have the place knocked. Just all of it, flattened and buried over and wiped from the world.

But first, he had to figure out what it was about the *house* that stopped all efforts to do anything but add more weird architecture around it. Why did the place insist on existing? If he could figure that out, he could figure out a way to get rid of it.

Or at the very least, make it less dangerous.

Which was why he'd sent the fancy invitation to Lexie Alexander, witch historian. He'd had to research for more than six months to find her. While a lot of Wiccans and other neo-pagans were out and open about their religion, finding a real witch who knew about the real history of his distant ancestor proved complicated. A lot of the witches he'd met and interviewed hadn't even heard of her.

There was probably a reason for that.

Her name wasn't spoken in his family. She was referred to euphemistically. And the branch of the family that had shared her last name had died off about a hundred years ago, which made it easier not to say her name. If they didn't talk about her directly within her own family, it was entirely possible those outside his family had purposefully erased her from history, too. He wasn't sure *why*, because again, no one in his family spoke about it. But whatever that original witch had done, it had been bad.

When Miles had finally discovered the existence of an

actual witch historian, a sort of record keeper for the history of witches in this country, he'd been sure he'd found the right person to help. He'd very nearly just sent off an email and invited her to the house.

And then, for some reason, he hadn't. He still wasn't entirely sure why he'd had the fancy invitation card made. Some…impulse he went with because it felt right. Maybe he thought she'd need to be intrigued or else she wouldn't knock on the door? Maybe he'd worried she'd think he was crazy if he just asked her outright? Whatever the reasoning, sending out the fancy invitation with the actual name of his ancestor in it felt…appropriate. So he'd done it.

Then felt like a fool for a week afterward. He was certain she'd think it was some kind of joke and ignore it, and he'd have to send a ridiculous email explaining why he'd sent the invitation in the first place—even though he had no idea—and she'd probably still think this was a scam of some kind. And he wouldn't even be able to blame her.

Seeing her here, walking cautiously up to the front door, was such a relief it made his chest ache. Maybe now *now* he could get some answers and find a way to divest his family of this damned house. This…curse.

He studied her as she studied the front door. She was average height, maybe a little taller, but not tall. Light brown hair—in the bright autumn sun she'd had streaks of blond and red in it—brushing her shoulders, eyes a color he couldn't see from the distance, pale skin, sharp features. Pretty. Not glamorous or head turning, but pleasant to look at. She was dressed for the cooler weather in jeans and a light wool jacket, a thin scarf wrapped around her neck. She kept looking down at the invitation in her hand and then up at the door, like she might bolt at any moment.

Miles was trying to be patient and let her ring the doorbell, or knock. If he flung the door open now, too eagerly to have her inside, she'd definitely run away. He was a little afraid his desperation for answers was going to be too obvious as it was, and he couldn't afford to scare her off. So he waited, tapping his foot, discreetly watching her from a bay window in the Victorian wing that gave a good angle on the front porch, and hoping she knocked before she spotted him. If she caught him watching her like this, he could only imagine what she'd think.

So he probably should stop watching her, he thought. But waiting for her to knock without knowing what she was doing—or if she'd turned around and left—would be worse. His nerves couldn't take it.

He needed answers. And it was entirely possible Lexie Alexander was the only person who could give him those answers.

Without her help, he'd be stuck with this house, this pit of… He hesitated to call it evil, though he frequently got that sense. But he'd seen real evil in the world before. This felt too amorphous and vague to call it evil before he figured out what *it* was. He just knew whatever *it* was, it was not good.

And he wanted away from it. He wanted out of this house, wanted the burden of it gone from his life—without having to die to achieve that. The cousin he'd inherited from had died of cancer, and he'd never seen a man so happy to die of cancer than Jim had been, when he'd informed Miles the house was about to be his. Miles really didn't want that same fate. So he'd done what he did best and researched the problem.

Lexie Alexander was his answer.

Finally, finally she put a careful finger to the doorbell button and pushed.

<hr>

Don't Miss Demonic Dates!
Out Now!

BOOKS BY KAT SIMONS

Demon Witch Series

Howling Dreadful

Moonlit Strange

1-Bone Lantern Witch

2-Spiderweb Witch

3-Storm Shadow Witch

4-Darkling Mist Witch

5-Apocalypse Witch

Urban Fantasy

The Cary Redmond Series

Cary Redmond Short Stories and Collections

Joan of Kerry Series

Friday's Curious Shop Series

Paranormal Romance

Dragon Thief Series

Seven Families: Wolf Series

Tiger Shifters Series

Destiny Cats Series

Romancing the Leopard: A Tiger Shifters-Cary Redmond Crossover Novel

ALSO BY KAT SIMONS

Contemporary Fantasy

Haunts and Howls Collections

**Tombstone Wizard * The Unshattered Sword * Going Out of Business: Everything's for Sale * Anger Management * Demonic Dates * The Museum of Small Art's Everyman * Burning Inside a Stone Circle * Bored Questless * I Just Ate a Bug * Ting Ling * Sophie Saves the World * Black Water Hawthorns * To Dance in Fallow Fields at Midnight * The Troll and the Dressmaker*

Stories from the Café

The Café Collections

Stories from the Café: Volume One

Pick Your Genre Collections

Who Steals a Dragon

Contemporary Romances

Designed for You

Poinsettias and Possibilities

Mystery and Thriller

Ross and O'Neill Adventures

Galileo's Pendulum

ABOUT THE AUTHOR

Kat Simons earned her Ph.D. in animal behavior, working with animals as diverse as dolphins and deer. She brought her experience and knowledge of biology to her paranormal romance and urban fantasy fiction, where she delights in taking nature and turning it on its ear. She writes urban fantasy, contemporary fantasy, and paranormal romance in series which combine action adventure, the otherworldly, and a frequent dose of sexy romance.

The newest book in her bestselling romantic urban fantasy series about Protector Cary Redmond, The Trouble with Shifters and Fae Courts, sees a new direction for the intrepid Protector, her sexy leopard shifter mate, and the entire crew. Kat also launched a new novella length Urban Fantasy Romance series that follows the adventures of a magical thief and the dragon shifter prince she just can't seem to shake—and really doesn't want to. The first season of the Dragon Thief series released throughout 2024. Season Two begins in 2025 with The Crown of Kingship Job.

For something a little different, Kat also publishes fantasy, science fiction, and the occasional hockey romance under the name Isabo Kelly (https://www.isabokelly.com).

After traveling the world, living in places like Hawaii, Germany, and Ireland, Kat now lives in New York City with her family and a library's worth of books.

For more on Kat and her future books

Website: https://www.katsimons.com/
Newsletter: https://bit.ly/KatSimonsNewsletter

KatSimonsBooks
https://www.katsimonsbooks.com
https://www.TheCafeatKatSimonsBooks.com

Social Media
Facebook Page: https://www.facebook.com/
KatSimonsAuthor
BookBub: https://www.bookbub.com/authors/kat-simons
Bluesky: https://bsky.app/profile/katsimons.bsky.social
Instagram: https://www.instagram.com/isabokelly/
Threads: https://www.threads.net/@isabokelly

KATSIMONSBOOKS

Mystery

Urban Fantasy

Romance

And More!

KATSIMONSBOOKS.COM

JOIN KAT'S NEWSLETTER

STAY UP-TO-DATE

On all Kat's News, Updates, and fun extras

New Subscriber Get Two Exclusive Stories Just for Signing up!

bit.ly/KatSimonsNewsletter